Death Dealers MC
Book Five

ALANA SAPPHIRE

Edited by Hot Tree Editing

Cover designed by Clarise Tan at CT Cover Creations © 2017

Cover image by Sara Eirew Photographer

Cover models – Nick Bennett and Josée Lanoue

Club logo designed by Margreet Asselbergs © 2015

Printed by CreateSpace, An Amazon.com Company

ISBN: 1977872786

ISBN-13: 978-1977872784

TABLE OF CONTENTS

Renascence (noun)
   – The revival of something that has been dormant.
   – A revival of, or renewed interest in something.
Synonym – renaissance

CHAPTER 1
Venom

"Motherfucking asshole!"

Those are the words that greet me when I walk into the pet shop. Instead of Jeff, the owner, standing behind the counter, there's a woman scowling at the screen of her phone.

"Cock-sucking bastard," she mumbles, completely unaware of my entrance.

I'm in a good mood today. I don't know why, but I feel amazing. Hopefully it stays that way and this chick doesn't ruin it with her sour mood. Her eyes are still glued to her phone, so I make my presence known.

"Hey. Jeff here?"

Startled, she jumps, drops the phone, and swears. "Fuck!"

Chuckling, I approach her as she bends at the waist to pick up the phone. Unbeknownst to her, I check out her ass before she faces me. *Not bad. Not bad at all.*

"Shit! I mean sorry. You weren't supposed to hear that." When she straightens, she catches me looking. Sad to say, she's not impressed. "Yes?" she grumbles, irritably tucking a few loose strands of blonde hair behind her ear.

Her green eyes narrow, moving over my body from head to toe. I allow her to get her fill, watching as her gaze slides over my cut and the sewn-on patches. It continues down to my silver snake belt buckle, then to the chains hanging on my hip, and finally my size twelve Doc Martens.

"I'd be more than happy to show you what's underneath, darlin'."

Her eyes flick to mine, head tilting to the side in annoyance. "How can I help you?" she snaps.

"Jeez. The customer service in here has gone to shit," I joke. "I asked you if Jeff is here."

1

She takes a deep breath, remorse creeping into her eyes before her stare drops to the floor.

"Sorry. It's not you."

"No shit."

She looks up, the exasperation slowly returning. This time, it *is* me.

"Jeff isn't here. *Can I help you?*" she repeats, emphasizing the question.

"I'm supposed to pick something up. Should be a box somewhere here with my name on it. Venom."

"You're picking up venom?" she asks, brow quirked in confused curiosity.

"No, doll." I chuckle. "Name's Venom."

"Oh." Her eyes dart back to the patch with my road name, features relaxing in understanding. "Gimme a sec."

She disappears to the back, items knocking against each other, being picked up and dropped as she searches for my box. Sighing, I lean on the counter and wait. *Where the hell is Jeff, and who is this chick?* I've never seen her before, and I know Jeff doesn't have any daughters. Knowing the old geezer, she has to be family for him to leave her here alone.

As I'm about to offer her my help, she screams bloody murder. Twice. Hopping over the counter, I hurry in the direction of her shrill voice. I find her jumping in place and flapping her hands in a panic.

"What is it? What's wrong?"

"The box!" she shrieks.

I chuckle, realizing she's found the one that's mine. Picking it up, I make my way back to the front of the store. She follows, but I swear I can still hear her teeth chattering in fear.

"You weren't supposed to open it, doll."

"I heard sounds. It's not a cage or anything else Uncle Jeff keeps the animals in, so I looked. Ugh."

I glance back just in time to see a shudder make its way through her body. *Uncle. I knew she had to be family.* Placing the box on the counter, I scale it once more, leaving her behind the register.

"What the hell are you doing with all those rats anyways?" she asks in her adorable country-girl twang.

2

"Mice."

"What?"

"They're mice, not rats."

"What's the difference?"

"Lots of differences, but let's just say rats are bigger."

"Whatever. They're still gross. What are you doing with them?"

"Snakes."

Vacant eyes blink up at me while she waits for me to continue.

"I feed them to my snakes, doll."

"You have a snake?" Her eyes widen in shock, then snap closed as she shudders again. "Eww."

I chuckle, the memory of her initial bitchiness quickly fading.

"If you like, you can come over sometime and I'll show him to you," I offer, choosing not to point out that I said *snakes*... plural.

"Is that some kind of—" Her eyes drop to my crotch, then move back to my face. "—penis joke?"

This time I laugh.

"I'm glad you find me funny," she adds, sarcasm dripping off her words.

I lean on the counter, getting close to her while bringing my face level with hers. Her breath catches, her lips slightly parting. That's when I notice how gorgeous they are—plump and naturally red.

"I actually *was* talking about my pet, but I'll show you whatever you want to see." She licks her lips, taking a step back and putting some distance between us. "Trust and believe, darlin', if I was making dick jokes, I would've said anaconda." I lean in closer. "Not snake."

She gasps, cheeks growing red. Quickly turning away, she grabs a notebook from the shelf behind her and begins flipping through the pages.

"What's your name?" I ask.

"It ain't doll, and it ain't darlin' either," she throws sass, keeping her attention on the book.

"Well, if you told me, I wouldn't need to give you nicknames."

She glances up, considering my words before replying, "Emily. Emily Pierce."

"Emily." I test her name on my tongue. *I'd like to test a whole lot more than that.* "You already know my name."

"Yeah." She continues searching the pages of the book.

"What are you looking for?"

"Uncle Jeff makes notes on who owes him what. I'm looking for you and those—" She looks to the box in contempt. "—rats."

"You won't find me in that book, pretty Emily."

The compliment throws her. Meeting my eyes, she asks, "Why?"

"Jeff and I already worked it out. Call him if you don't believe me."

"I will."

She closes the book, pulling her phone from her back pocket. As she dials and places it at her ear, it's my turn to take her in. I watch her breasts rise and fall with her breathing. I'm a breast man, so I'm thinking they have to be at least a D cup. I certainly wouldn't mind getting a mouthful of those. My gaze travels down her waist and to the flare of her hips. I imagine digging my fingers into them, sucking on her nipples as she rides me. Fuck. The woman has a body made for fucking. Lots of places to grab… to slap. That ass? Goddamn. I wouldn't mind smacking that just to watch it jiggle.

"Did you hear me?"

Snapping out of the vision, I give her my attention. "What was that?"

"You can go. Uncle Jeff said you're good."

"Okay, Em."

"Emily," she corrects me.

"Come on, Em. I thought we were friends, sharing dick jokes and all."

"I prefer Emily… *Venom*."

With a smirk, I grab my box and head for the door. I definitely haven't seen the last of pretty Emily.

Before I exit, I turn to find her watching me.

"By the way, tell Jeff you need some more training before he leaves you in charge again."

RENASCENCE
Emily

Asshole. Just what I need, another one in my life.

Venom. Such an odd name. Well, obviously, I know that's not the name his momma gave him. Still, I can't deny it fits him. There's something about him that seems slick… smooth like the way that pet snake of his slithers along a surface. With the name, the belt buckle of the coiled snake—mouth open, tongue out, fangs bared—and the actual snake, the man must have some twisted obsession with the reptile. He walked in here with his shoulder-length black hair, storm cloud-gray eyes, and an "I run the world" attitude.

I was too absorbed in the text I received earlier and didn't hear him come in. I saw him ride away on his motorcycle, though. That thing looked powerful… a little like him. It's black, sleek, and loud as hell. I'm surprised I didn't hear him pull up. He's *so* not my type, but I have to admit it was hot the way he rushed in to try and "save" me. He certainly seemed capable of doing it if I really was in trouble. Too bad he can't save me from the shit show that is my life.

When he'd leaned in, I caught a whiff of his cologne, and the smell of grapefruit and sandalwood almost made me swoon. Add in the gleam in his eye and the sexy smirk he gave me, and I lost all sense of myself for a brief moment. He may not be up my alley, but I can definitely see him there—up my alley, that is. I mean, I can see the appeal in him. I can also tell he doesn't have any problems getting women. They probably fall all over him… at his feet… in his bed. He's good-looking and has that bad boy biker image some women can't get enough of.

The dude's practically a giant next to me—way over six feet—with bulging arms covered in tattoos. His gray T-shirt stretched tight against developed pecs. I bet he has a six-pack. Maybe even an eight. I can't lie—even with clothes on, his body looked perfectly sculpted, something forged by the gods themselves. I've heard all the whispered stories from women about beards, and while I wouldn't normally go for one, his is neatly trimmed and works for him. It only adds to his handsome features. If I'm honest, I'd go a round or two with him. That surprises me

5

because it's been a long time since I've had thoughts like that. Since I've even had any kind of interest in a man.

One of the patches on his vest said "Treasurer." *Ooh, lawd, he certainly* is *a treasure!* However, guys like him aren't interested in girls like me. They want hot and easy, and those I am not. The fact that he called me pretty and did some minor flirting doesn't mean anything. He was only amused by the hysterical woman screaming at the box full of rats.

Mice.

Whatever.

A shiver runs up my spine at the thought of all those beady little eyes staring up at me from the box. Venom must have one hell of a snake back home.

I chuckle and snort at the thought. I can't believe I brought up the whole "penis joke" thing. At least I was able to make him laugh after being a bit... surly. James always told me I didn't have a sense of humor.

Jackass.

I push him out of my mind and start feeding the animals in the store. Uncle Jeff is doing me a favor by letting me stay with him for a while, so the least I can do is help out around here. He's my mom's brother, and reminds me so much of her. It's comforting. I miss her already. Daddy, too. They're the ones who suggested I come to Stony View to get my mind straight, and I'm going to try.

"Hey, baby girl," Uncle Jeff greets me when he walks in some time later.

"Hey." I kiss his cheek. "Need some help?"

I motion to the bags he's bringing in and he shakes his head.

"I'm good. How'd it go?"

"Okay. Only the one guy came in." I look away, hoping he can't see my blush and praying I sound unaffected.

"So you met Venom."

He gives me a knowing smile, making my blush deepen.

"You could've warned me about the rats, Uncle Jeff. I almost jumped out of my skin."

He chuckles, going back to his truck to get more bags.

"Why don't you take off?" he suggests when he returns. "I can manage from here."

"You sure?"

"Of course. Go explore. It's a small town, but we got a few places you can check out. The salon, Millie's diner. There's also a club not far if you wanna get out tonight."

"Yeah, at thirty-two, I think my club days are over, Uncle."

"Nonsense. You're still young. Live a little."

"I'll think about it," I reply, just to appease him.

I help him unpack all the bags, then grab my purse to see what Stony View, Georgia has to offer. I've only been here a few days, and today is the first I've left Uncle Jeff's house. I thought I'd be bored out of my mind here, but I've liked the peace and quiet. It definitely seems like a place I could live.

Starting down Main Street, I take in the buildings, trying to commit them to memory. There's an auto parts store, a bar, salon, and a bakery. The delectable scents drifting out of Sweet Treats send my tummy grumbling, but I quickly walk by. That's one place I'll be staying away from.

A few more steps and I find Millie's, the diner Uncle Jeff told me about. I step through the door, looking up at the chimes as they tinkle above it.

"Take a seat anywhere, sugar. I'll be right with you."

I follow the voice, my gaze landing on a brown-haired beauty standing behind the counter. In front of her, a man is leaning forward, obviously flirting with her from the smile that's plastered on her face. I walk to a booth, recognizing the man as I pass him—Venom. His back is to me now, and I take in the emblem on his vest. It's a grim reaper dealing the death card from a tarot deck. "Death Dealers" sits atop it in a concave semicircle with "Georgia" below in a convex one. I have no idea what any of it means, so I try not to give it another thought.

As the waitress heads my way, Venom turns, tracking her progress. When his gaze lands on me, he smiles and follows her.

"Hi there! I'm Sheila and I'll be your waitress today. Can I get you something to drink?"

"Just water, please," I tell her, taking the menu she offers.

"Coming right up."

I roll my eyes as Venom slides into the seat across from me. "Please... join me."

7

Ignoring the sarcasm in my tone, he turns up the wattage on his smile. God help me but he just became a lot more gorgeous.

"You wound me, Em." He lays his palm over his heart. "Here I was thinking we were becoming best friends."

"I don't know what gave you that impression."

"Really? Did you forget that you asked to come over and see my anaconda?"

My cheeks redden. "I did no such thing."

He chuckles, enjoying teasing me a little too much. Sheila returns with my water, and I welcome the distraction from the man's perfect teeth.

"Here you go, sugar. Watch yourself with this one." She nods to Venom. "He'll be in and out of your panties so fast, your head will spin." She giggles.

I look between the two of them, wondering exactly what I interrupted earlier. The woman definitely looks like the type he would go for—gorgeous brown eyes and hair to match, clear, tanned skin, and a curvy body I wish I had.

"Don't go telling stories, Sheila. You haven't let me into yours yet," Venom counters.

"That's because your name ain't Johnny, sugar."

"Lucky motherfucker."

Giggling again, she turns to me. "Have you had a chance to look over the menu?"

Pushing their weird exchange out of my mind, I quickly scan the menu. Everything on here probably has a million calories.

"Our special today is chicken pot pie," Sheila offers.

"Ah… I'll have the grilled chicken salad, no croutons, dressing on the side, please."

"Okay. You want something, Venom?"

"I'll have the special and a cold beer."

"You got it!" she says as she walks away.

I raise a brow at the man sitting before me. "Seriously? It's midday."

"It's five o' clock somewhere." He shrugs, the adage rolling off his tongue.

"Yeah, but not here."

"You should have one, seeing as you're not having real food. You don't strike me as a salad girl."

"You don't know what kind of girl I am," I snap.

"Whoa! Easy, darlin'. I didn't mean anything by it."

I rein in my anger because Venom doesn't deserve it. The person who does is miles away. Still, his little comment hurt.

"Sorry."

"Whatever you were looking at on your phone earlier must have really fucked with your head, huh?"

You have no idea.

"So," I try to change the subject. "You look like the kind of man who knows his way around the gym. Is there one close by?" My eyes rove over his muscular arms.

"There's one on Second Street. I can show you if you like."

"Thanks, but if you just tell me where it is, I should be able to find it on my own."

He observes me, stroking his beard between his thumb and index finger, his expression unreadable. I don't even know why he's talking to me, considering I've been a bitch to him all day.

Sheila returns with our food, and as we eat, he begins throwing out questions.

"How come I've never seen you before? I've been doing business with Jeff for years."

I shrug. "He's always come to visit us, I guess. This is my first time here."

"Where are you from?"

"Atlanta."

"You staying or just visiting?"

"Just visiting… for now."

"Cool."

I look from his plate to mine, wishing I could eat like him. However, I need to stick to my diet; one wrong thing and I blow up like a balloon.

"You want some?" he asks with a grin, offering a healthy bite on his fork.

"No, thanks."

9

I stab some lettuce with my fork, cursing my slow metabolism and people like Venom and Sheila who could probably eat whatever they want.

"What's the Death Dealers?" I ask.

"It's the MC I belong to."

"MC?"

"Motorcycle club."

"So what, you guys ride together, talk about bikes and stuff?"

He chuckles, shaking his head. "Something like that. It's much more, though. We have elected officers, meetings every month, pay dues, stuff like that."

"And you're the treasurer?" I point to the patch on his vest with my fork.

"That's right. I handle all the money."

"Okay. And you all wear those leather vests?"

"It's called a cut, and yeah, we all wear them."

"Sounds interesting. Can women join?"

"Not our club, but there are female MCs all over."

"Oh."

Without missing a beat, he asks, "You wanna get outta here, Em?"

The fork falls from my fingers. "Wh... what?"

"I said...." He leans forward, lowering his voice, his deep register sending tingles shooting through my body. "Do you want to get out of here?"

"But... why?"

"Why do you think?"

"I don't understand. Other things aside, I've been bitchy to you since the moment we met."

"Maybe I like bitchy. Besides, you're obviously angry about something, and angry sex is *the best*."

"You want to have sex... with *me*?"

"Why did you say it like that?" His brows knit in concern.

"Like what?"

"Like you think I'd never even consider it."

"Because that's exactly what I think."

He looks down at my plate, then back to me, eyes boring into mine. His penetrating gaze is too much for me, so I avoid it.

10

"Is it because she turned you down?" I indicate Sheila with a slight jerk of my head.

"You're a beautiful woman, Emily. Fucking sexy as hell. I'm pretty sure most men would give up their left nut to fuck you."

I stare at my plate, pushing the contents around with the fork. I don't know why he's saying these things to me, but I wish I could believe them. I wish they were true.

But he's wrong.

So wrong.

I feel the shift in him, the change. Him pulling away. I keep my gaze averted, oblivious as to why I care. *I just met the man; so what if he thinks... whatever it is he thinks about me? It* shouldn't *matter.*

But it does.

While keeping my eyes down, I'm still able to see him toss his napkin on the table before sliding out of the booth.

"When you leave here, continue down Main Street. Take the first left onto Second Street and the gym is the third building on the right."

I finally meet his gaze, unable to read anything in his passive expression.

"See you around, Emily."

After making a stop at the counter, he leaves the diner without a backward glance. I push the remaining portion of my salad away, no longer hungry. Venom may not know it, but I did him a favor. Having sex with me would be awful, angry or not.

"Can I get you anything else?" Sheila asks as she bounces up to the table.

"Just the check, please."

"No need to worry about that." She winks, confusing the hell out of me. "Venom took care of it. My tip, too," she adds, compounding my confusion.

"He did?"

"Yep. Told you, in and out." She giggles, clearing the table and walking away.

Yeah. Not my *panties.* Even if I believed he wanted to have sex with me, it would take more than paying for my lunch to make it

11

happen. I have to admit, though, it was a nice thing to do, considering the shitty day I've been having.

Since my day is looking up, I try to keep the momentum going by heading straight to the gym. The sign on the building says "SHED." The letters seem to be stripping, but a closer look reveals that's actually the design... the letters are shedding. That's pretty cool.

The cute guy behind the front desk gives me a bright smile, his teeth shining like a whitening commercial. "Hi there!" He steps from behind the desk, voice injected with more pep than a high school cheerleader. Okay, maybe I'm exaggerating. He is pretty upbeat, though. By the size of him, he must have adrenaline to spare. I'm talking *swole*. "Welcome to Shed. I'm Kurt. How are you doing today?"

"Good. Nice to meet you, Kurt. I'm Emily."

I take his outstretched hand, glancing at his bicep and how it's straining against the sleeve of his red polo shirt.

"What can I do for you today, Emily?"

"Well, I'm in town visiting and was wondering if I need a membership. I'm not sure how long I'll be here."

"You're in luck!" he announces, grabbing a brochure from the desk and handing it to me. "We have a special going on right now. You can get the first month free, access to all our equipment and classes, and fifty percent off at our juice bar."

"Wow. That sounds amazing. What's the catch?" I raise a curious brow.

"No catch. Most people end up getting memberships before their month is up. I'll make an exception for you since you're a guest in our little town."

I blush, averting my eyes when his gaze goes from business to something quite the opposite. What is it with the men in this town? Two in one day is certainly a record for me.

"Would you like a tour?" Kurt asks.

"Sure."

I let him lead the way, watching his khaki-clad ass as he walks ahead of me. He points out a juice bar and the showers before showing me the main area, which is *huge*. It contains every machine you could possibly think of. On one side, there are

12

treadmills, stationary bikes, ellipticals, steppers, rowers, and a bunch of others. The opposite side is devoted to weight training. The walls are mirrored and there are water coolers scattered around the room. Next, we move on to several studios.

"We have aerobics classes on Mondays, Wednesdays, and Fridays, and yoga on the weekends. For the more adventurous ladies," his brows lift, lips curling up in a smirk, "we have pole dancing classes on Tuesdays and Thursdays."

Okay then. That's my cue to go.

"Thanks, Kurt. Everything looks great. I'll probably come in tomorrow. What time do you close?" I start making my way back to the exit.

"Awesome. We're open until ten every night."

"Okay."

He reaches over his desk, snagging some forms and handing them to me. "Look these over, take your time and fill them out, and then you can turn them in tomorrow."

"Thanks again. See you tomorrow."

"Looking forward to it, Emily."

I walk out, retracing my steps to the pet shop. Thumbing through the brochure, I wonder how this small town has such a well-equipped gym. It could rival anything in the city. And pole dancing? Sheesh. That's one class I will *not* be participating in. I'll just do what I usually do—keep my head down, get my workout done, and get the hell out of there.

CHAPTER 2
Venom

"'Sup, brother?" I toss a chin lift in Razor's direction, dropping down next to him on the couch.

"Not a damn thing. Kinda quiet around here."

I nod, watching a few Hellhounds—our club girls—clean up the clubhouse bar. This place was my home for so long. It still is in some ways, even though I have my own house now. My family is here, from my brothers to the girls who take care of us. These men may not be my blood, but I'd bleed for any one of them, the same way they would for me. I never had that growing up, being the only child of parents who had time for everything but me. Now I have a house full of men who would do anything to help me.

Die for me.

Kill for me.

And fuck if I wouldn't do the same for them. "Death before disloyalty." We'll all uphold the club motto until the motherfucking grim reaper himself claims us all in a fiery hell. Men who live the way we do? There's no other way we can go. The deaths of two of my brothers proved it. They didn't go silently in the night. No, they were painfully ripped from this life, leaving the rest of us wondering when our time will come. I'm lucky I've made it all the way to thirty-five.

I glance toward the DJ booth and the picture of our most recent fallen brother. Like Razor said, it's been quiet around here, but not in a good way.

Growing up, I never thought I'd be a member of a motorcycle club, let alone an officer in one. What I've found with this group of people gives me the courage to face my fate head on. Because of them, I've lived a full life.

"Hey, fuckers." Crow walks up, taking the empty spot next to Razor, scratching the scar zigzagging down his cheek.

"Hey, asshole," I reply, making Razor chuckle.

We're joined by Tek, who, as usual, produces his laptop and starts tapping away at the keys. The way his tongue is worrying his snake bite piercings, I'd say he's in hacking mode. The fucker does that shit for fun, hacking sites just to prove he can. Makes sense, I guess—practice makes perfect. Based on some of the places he's gotten into, I'm surprised the FBI, CIA, NSA and every other organization haven't busted down our doors yet.

"How was that chick last night?" Razor asks, nudging my leg to get my attention.

"Shit." I'd already forgotten about the girl I took to my room last night. One of the Hounds brought her around. She was pretty enough, but that was the extent of her pleasing qualities.

"That bad?" Crow chuckles. Tek glances up from his screen, waiting for my answer.

"That shit was like the big bad wolf huffed and puffed through it. Bitch had no walls. I had to fuck her mouth to get off."

"You sure her being big was the issue?" Razor laughs and the others join in.

"Fuck y'all. You've seen my monster. Ain't nothin' little about me, so just imagine what her pussy was like. Shit."

"Maybe you should follow in the steps of the prez and VP," Tek suggests, returning his attention to his screen.

"An old lady? Fuck no. I'm not built for that shit."

My old lady's father is dead, and her mother hasn't been born yet. You know what that means? She doesn't and will never exist.

"You know who you sound like right now?" Razor asks.

Sighing, I shake my head as I remember my prez's pre–old lady days. "Gage."

"Exactly. He fought that shit so hard, but we all knew he was a goner the moment he met Raven."

"Yeah, but look at everything they went through."

"Ask him and I'm pretty sure he'll tell you it was all worth it," Tek chimes in without looking up.

"Maybe."

As Melody, one of the newer Hounds, passes by, I snag her wrist and tug her down onto my lap. She giggles, admonishing me, but at the same time grinding her ass on my dick. I'm about to bury my face between the blonde's tits when my phone rings, interrupting me.

"Yo, Prez," I answer, squeezing Melody's ass as she kisses my neck. "What's up?"

"A party," he answers.

"What are we celebrating?"

"Got big news. I'll be there in a few hours, but get the girls and the prospect on it, yeah?"

"You got it." I smack Melody's ass, getting her to slide to the couch while I hop to my feet. I catch her little whine of disappointment but ignore it as I head to the chapel. "Party tonight, boys!" I shout. After grabbing some money from the safe and recording the withdrawal, I make my way back to the bar. Chopper, our ex-president and Gage's father, walks in with Mikey, his daughter's four-year-old son.

"Hey, Chopper. Prez says there's a party tonight."

"Hear that, little man?" He turns to Mikey. "Looks like you get to help me on the grill today."

"Burgers! Cool!" He pumps his little fists in the air.

The kid is cute, looks just like his daddy. Too bad Eddie died before his son was born.

Eddie. Another casualty of the lifestyle.

"What's the occasion?" Chopper asks. "Not that I mind. Gives me an excuse to be on the grill before the weather makes it impossible."

"No idea. He just told me to get the ball rolling."

He chuckles. "That's my son for ya. Let me know if you need anything."

"Thanks, Chopper."

I recruit Tyler, our prospect, and two of the Hounds, Trixie and Melody, sending them on a store run. I have no idea what we're celebrating, but Trixie and the prospect know the drill. We haven't had a party in a while, and since we've turned the DJ area into a showcase, I head back into town to get some equipment. I grab some Bluetooth speakers, then stop by my house to pick up my iPod. These will have to do for now. I'll talk to Gage about a better setup later.

By the time I have everything connected and music playing low, Tyler and company return, stocking the bar and laying out snacks.

RENASCENCE

Gage walks in with his VP, Einstein, their old ladies in tow. As much as that life's not for me, I'm happy for them. Raven and Ellen are gorgeous. More than that, they're good women and they love their men. I couldn't ask for better for my brothers.

I watch as Mikey runs to Einstein and the man lifts him into his arms. His mother says something to him that has his eyes going wide.

"Yay!" he shouts, loud enough to catch everyone's attention. "I'm gonna be a big brother!"

Well, shit. First Gage, now Einstein. This place will be crawling with little tykes soon.

"Yeah, you heard right. We got a bun in the oven," Einstein announces to the room.

Everyone cheers, including me. Before the noise can die down, Gage leads Raven, Ellen, and Einstein to the front of the room. He instantly commands everyone's attention without even uttering a word. We listen expectantly, waiting for his announcement as he raises his beer for a toast.

"I know it's been a little depressing around here, but today we have reasons to celebrate," he says before turning to Einstein and Ellen. "My sister and VP are expecting a little one." That gets more cheers. "And we found out my baby doll is having twins."

"Holy shit!" I exclaim. "Y'all some fertile mother—" I remember the kid in the room and quickly stop myself. "—people."

"Yeah, well… life is short," Gage says, facing the now empty DJ booth. "So we're going to live it to the fullest." He tips his beer bottle, splashing some of the liquid on the floor for our fallen brother. "In memory of our brother, Graham 'Alla' McKnight. Rest in peace, bro. You're truly riding free now. See you on the other side."

"Hear, hear!" we all shout, then scatter when it's evident this portion of the evening is over. I take a stool on the far side of the bar, away from everyone. I watch Gage, his hand resting protectively on Raven's stomach as he talks to her. Shifting my attention to Einstein, I notice him hustling Ellen in my direction.

They're happy. After all that happened to both their old ladies, they've moved on, starting families. I couldn't do it. That's why I have snakes. Well, one of the reasons.

17

Thinking about my snakes has my mind drifting back to Emily in the pet shop today. The look on her face when she found the mice was priceless. I don't even realize it put a smile on my face until Einstein stops in front of me.

"What are you grinning at?" he asks.

"Nothing. Just thinking about something that happened today."

"Bullshit. That smile involves a woman. Who is she?"

I chuckle, scratching my chin for distraction. "It's not like that, bro."

"Yeah, we'll see."

His sarcasm amuses me, leaving me grinning at his retreating back. I can't say I'm not attracted to the sexy blonde, but that's as far as it goes. I'd fuck her in a heartbeat, but I'm not looking to make anyone my old lady.

Not now, not ever.

Emily

I'm wiping the sweat from the back of my neck when a familiar voice sends a tingle up my spine.

"Emily."

That. Voice. It's deep and smoky, lighting up my nerve endings.

I legit think if the right words were whispered in my ear, I would come with zero physical contact.

That's exactly why I need to stay away from him.

Slowly, I turn to face the owner of the voice. "Venom," I acknowledge him.

He's wearing his vest like the day I met him, but this time he's in all black, and just as hot as I remember.

"Good workout?"

Workout. Damn it. There he stands, looking good enough to eat, and here I am looking like shit. Probably smell like it, too.

"Yeah." I take a self-conscious step back. "The equipment here is awesome." I motion toward the treadmill I vacated. "Getting on?"

"I was heading out actually. You need a ride home?"

"No, thanks. I have Uncle Jeff's truck."

"Cool. I'll walk you out."

"No need. I have to shower first anyway."

"I'll wait."

"Really, you don't need to—"

"Emily," he cuts me off, tone stern. "I'll wait."

"Fine." I roll my eyes, giving him a wide berth as I pass him on my way to the showers. If he wants to sit there and wait, that's his problem.

Usually there's no one here at this time of night; it's why I choose to come near closing. I like my solitude. For the last week, I've mostly had the gym all to myself and I've loved it. Now *he* shows up. I figured I'd run into him sometime, whether here or the pet store... or anywhere, really. It's a small town, after all.

A part of me longed to see him, if only for him to look at me like he wants to rip my clothes off. A man hasn't looked at me like that in a long time and well, I liked the way he did it. The other part of me hoped I'd imagined it, prayed I'd daydreamed the entire scenario. Nothing good can come of it.

After a quick shower and change, I find Venom waiting for me by the front desk. He's talking to Kurt, a conversation that ends the moment they become aware of my presence.

"Ready?" Venom asks.

"Yeah."

"Let's go."

He places his hand at the small of my back, and even through my clothes, his heat warms my skin.

"See you tomorrow, Emily." Kurt waves.

"Bye, Kurt."

Venom pushes the glass door open, allowing me to exit ahead of him.

"So, you sticking around?" he asks.

"I like it here," I reply with a shrug. "It could probably become home, but I haven't made any decisions yet."

"I know Jeff would love having you around. He's usually an ornery motherfucker, but that's changed since you've been here."

"Uncle Jeff loves me," I say in my best spoiled brat voice, smiling at the man next to me.

Venom chuckles. "Can't argue with that."

We enter the parking lot, and I'm a little disappointed to see the truck come into view. As much as I know I should stay away from him, I like being in his presence. I open the door of the old truck, but as I turn to thank Venom, the look in his eyes stops me.

"What's your deal?" he asks, brows furrowed in confusion.

"What do you mean?" I lean on the truck, waiting for his answer.

He takes a step closer, caging me in with his arms. My breath gets caught in my throat, heart beating so fast, and so loudly, he can probably hear it.

"You want me. I know you do. The question is why are you fighting it?"

"Why do *you* want *me*?"

His eyes slowly slide down my body before meeting mine again. I can't stop the shiver that gaze induces.

"Don't tell me you're that clueless, Emily."

Yeah, right, 'cause I'm so hot. Not. "I just met you. I don't jump into bed with men I don't know."

"Okay." He drops his arms, shoving his hands into his pockets. "What do you need to know?"

"Excuse me?"

"I'm single, no kids, and I'm clean. What else?"

"You think throwing out a few pieces of random information is going to get me to sleep with you?" I ask, completely taken aback.

"Not random, completely relevant. Besides, who's talkin' about sleeping, darlin'?"

"I... you... what?"

My sputtering turns his smirk into a grin. He's infuriating but gorgeous in a disarming way. It's the only reason I'm still standing here. There's something about him, something I can sense but not recognize, underneath all the conceit and swagger. It makes me want to dig deeper, to find what he's hiding... to unearth his secrets.

"Emily." I snap out of my haze, meeting his stare. "That look you're giving me? It's getting my dick hard."

My mouth falls open in shock. "Wh...what?"

He takes a step forward, standing so close his chest is rubbing against my breasts. My lids flutter closed, nipples aching from the

20

contact. His scent. It's some kind of woodsy, manly cologne with a hint of leather. *Christ, he smells delicious.*

"This little innocent thing you got going... I can't tell if it's an act. Is it, Emily?" A firm hand grips my hip, pulling me forward. As his hardness presses into my thigh, I realize he wasn't kidding. "Are you just a cocktease?"

I shake my head, eyes still closed. There's no way I can look at him now. *He thinks I'm a cocktease. I'm not* any *kind of tease.*

"Open your eyes."

Ugh! Why does this man want to wreck me?

"Look at me, Emily."

I slowly open my eyes, gasping at his proximity. If I licked my lips, my tongue would probably touch his lips, too. It's a struggle to stop myself from doing just that.

"I want to fuck you... in every position I know. Hell, I'll probably make up a few just for you. I want you under me, on top of me, on your hands and knees. I want your naked body in my bed. I want to spread your thighs and sink my dick so deep inside you, you won't question what I want ever again."

Jesus.

Buddha.

Shiva.

Zeus.

Holy Mother of God.

My knees weaken. I have to press my palms into the side of the truck to keep myself upright when he pulls away.

"Do you understand?" I think I nod, because he continues, "Glad we cleared that up."

He motions for me to get in the truck. I climb in, my entire body trembling. The door closing startles me, and I look over to see him walking to his bike. With shaking fingers, I start the truck and slowly make my way out of the parking lot. One question is playing on a loop in my head: What the fuck just happened?

Venom wants me.

The gray-eyed, bearded, tattooed god of a man wants *me* in his bed. He wants to do all sorts of things to my body and... I want him to. *God,* I want him to. I *want* him to do all the things he wants. How can I feel like this when I just met him? I know absolutely nothing about him!

Other than he's single, has no kids, and no STDs.

Well, at least that's what he says. What I do know is that I haven't felt like this in a long time. I know that, when I was practically in his arms, I didn't want to move. I know he charged into the back of the pet shop like a superhero to save me from a box of mice. It could have been anything, but he didn't care. A man who'd known me for only a few seconds was willing to put himself in danger for me. I wish I'd met someone like him a long time ago.

I glance in the rearview mirror, and there he is behind me. Every turn I make, he follows. I think nothing of it until I turn onto Uncle Jeff's street. *What the hell is he doing? Does he think he's going to do all those things to me tonight? I didn't agree to anything earlier, did I? Shit.*

When I pull into the driveway, he stops at the curb, though he doesn't shut the bike off or make any attempt to dismount. I watch him as I hop down and lock up the truck. Still no movement. I make my way toward the porch, tossing the occasional look over my shoulder. With the front door open, I turn to face him.

That's when it hits me. He only wanted to make sure I got home okay. That's... sweet.

He gives me a two-fingered salute, and I return a small wave. The minute I close the door, I hear his bike thundering back the way we came.

Staying away from that man just became a hell of a lot harder.

CHAPTER 3
Venom

My workout tonight has been very strategic.

Every machine I've used has been perfectly positioned to ensure I've been in Emily's direct line of vision for the last thirty minutes. This isn't even my regular time, but since Kurt told me it's hers, here I am. This is what my life has become—basically stalking.

It's working, though. She hasn't taken her eyes off me. I've pretended to ignore her, but I've never been more aware of anyone or anything in my life. Having her body pressed against me last night had me running every possible scenario through my mind of what I could do to it. To her. I got zero sleep.

I'd love nothing more than to walk over and rip her ridiculously large T-shirt off and see exactly what she's hiding under there. Give her a real workout.

I grab some weights, taking them to a bench directly in front of her. I can almost hear the gulp as she swallows. Her step falters and she grabs the bars on the treadmill, trying to play it off. I know I'm a little conceited, but I've worked hard to get my body where it is; I'm entitled to a big ego.

After my third curl, she reaches for her water. I finally meet her stare, smirking as her eyes widen. *I'm tired of this game.* I drop the weights, making my way toward her. She removes her earbuds, watching expectantly.

"Hi, Em."

"He—" She clears her throat. "Hello."

"You almost done?"

She glances down at the treadmill's display, then nods.

"Cool. I'm gonna grab a shower and wait for you out front."

I walk away, not giving her the opportunity to brush me off. She's a "good girl." I know that now. She isn't playing games or being a tease; it's just the way she is. I'm not looking to corrupt her, nor do I want her to save me from anything. I don't need to be saved. What I need is soft, wet, tight, and hidden between her thick thighs. Emily is probably used to men wooing her with flowers and candy, not telling her how many positions they want to fuck her in. There's no way in Hell she'll get that from me, but if she wants to know more about me before I can get my dick inside her, I'll play along. I want her that much. A few nights—days, too—of her in my bed should satisfy my craving.

I don't know what it is about her that's calling to me. It definitely isn't the innocent thing; I like my women with experience—ones who give as good as they get. Then again, the quiet ones sometimes turn out to be the biggest freaks. *Fuck, I can't wait to get my hands on her.*

After my shower, I grab us some drinks and wait for her at the juice bar. Surprisingly, she shows up not much later. The leggings and oversized T-shirt are gone, replaced by jeans and a tee. Her hair is wet and up in a ponytail. The woman isn't even trying to be sexy and still the situation in my jeans is getting uncomfortable.

"Hi." She approaches nervously, rubbing her palms on her thighs.

"Hey." I hand her one of the cups. "This is for you."

She takes a sip, her lips wrapping around the straw in a way that makes me wish she were doing it to my dick. Fuck, I'm gone. As much as I'm a horny motherfucker, I can't remember a woman ever having this strong of an effect on me.

Dropping her bag on the floor, she takes the stool next to me, brows knitted.

"Mmm… this tastes like… chocolate milk." She takes another sip. "With a hint of banana?"

"Very good." I nod, smiling at her confusion.

"That seems a bit counterproductive after a workout."

"It's low fat, with the banana for additional carbs. It helps to replenish muscle tissue and reduces recovery time."

"If you say so. I mean, who am I to argue with someone who looks like you?"

"I do say so. And now that I've seen the way you suck on that straw, I'll make sure I'm waiting here with one for you every night."

"What do you mean?"

I place my hand on her knee, leaning closer. She gasps but doesn't move. "Think about it, darlin'."

Her cheeks turn red, but then she throws her head back, laughing. "Okay, this time it's not me. That was *definitely* a penis joke."

I join her, liking the sound of her laughter more than anything else. In the short time I've known her, she's always seemed so weighed down. Now, for the first time, she looks unburdened.

And *I* did that.

"You're a sharp one, Miss Emily."

"What can I say? My parents didn't pay for college for nothin'."

"Money well spent." I shift in discomfort, attempting to change the subject. "Why were you avoiding me all night?"

"I wasn't. The conditions weren't exactly conducive to conversation."

"Not even to say hi?"

Her gaze drops to the counter. "You didn't either. I figured you didn't want to talk to me."

"I thought I made myself clear last night. Is there something you need clarification on?"

"I just... I can't. I can't do that with you."

"Why?"

"You don't want me, Venom. Trust me." She slides off the stool, grabbing her bag before walking away from me. "Thanks for the drink."

I follow, catching up to her outside. "Why?" I repeat.

"Just drop it, okay?"

"Are you afraid to say you're too good for me?" My nostrils flare, teeth clenching.

She stops in her tracks, turning to me with eyes wide in horror. "What?"

"You heard me. You think I'm biker trash, or whatever it is your kind calls mine nowadays."

"That is *so* far from the truth. In fact, *you're* the one who's probably too good for me."

"What the fuck is that supposed to mean?"

"Look, it's not a condescending, social hierarchy type thing. What you want? I'm severely lacking in the skills department. You'd be better off with your hand."

Emily spins on her heels, leaving me to watch her retreating back with a confused frown. *Skills? What, she thinks she can't satisfy me? That's the biggest load of bullshit I've ever heard out of a woman's mouth.*

"Emily!" I call out, jogging to get to her side. "Are you fucking with me right now?" I grip her elbow, forcing her to look at me. "Usually it's the woman worried about the man not pleasing her."

"Yeah, well… I doubt you have that problem."

"Shit. You're fucked up in the head, aren't you?" I look her up and down, seriously contemplating if it's even worth trying to fuck her anymore. I don't do crazy bitches. I don't do whiny bitches either, and Emily's self-deprecating behavior is beginning to turn me off.

"Why, thank you." Her voice breaks as she tugs out of my hold, hurrying toward her uncle's truck.

Fuck me. Sometimes I don't know how to keep my fucking mouth shut. "Emily, wait!"

She pauses by the truck but doesn't turn around. I make my way to her, taking a deep breath as I lean on the vehicle.

"Look, I'm sorry. This whole situation's just been a little weird for me. This is not how it usually goes down when I try to get with a woman."

"No." She shakes her head. "You're right. I *am* fucked up in the head, and you need to stay far away from me."

She still can't look at me, keeping her eyes glued to the ground. Her entire demeanor screams "damaged," and she's right, I should stay away from her. *So why am I still standing here?*

"I was wrong, Emily. I don't think you're fucked up."

"You don't?" Her eyes meet mine, hope in her tone.

"No. I believe someone fucked with your head and is taking up valuable real estate in there. You need to evict them."

"That's easy for you to say."

With a sigh, I take her hand in mine while extending the other for her to give me the key. "Come on. I'll take you home."

"But… what about your bike?"

"I'll get someone to pick me up."

"There's no need—"

"Emily, get in the truck, please," I cut her off, my voice calm and controlled.

She drops the key in my palm, climbing in and sliding across to the passenger side. When I'm seated next to her, I text Jeff's address to the prospect and tell him to pick me up.

"Thank you," Emily whispers next to me.

"No problem, darlin'."

The drive to Jeff's is quiet. I don't know what to say because I don't know what the hell I'm doing. I should have gone my way and allowed her to go hers. Instead, here I am, taking her home with the intention of doubling back to get my bike. I've put in way too much work already. I'm better off going back to the clubhouse and picking one of the Hounds, but for once, easy pussy has no appeal for me. Well, not right this moment.

I'll try another approach with Emily. If this doesn't work, then I'll call it quits. She's probably leaving soon anyway.

I pull into the driveway and we both sit quietly, staring up at the porch. When I can't take the silence anymore, I clear my throat.

"I'm sorry for the way I've been behaving. You're obviously not used to guys like me, and I shouldn't have said the things I've said."

"Thank you, but that's who you are. You shouldn't change for anyone."

"I want you, Emily, but the fact of the matter is you won't be around forever. You need to tell me if I'm wasting my time here."

"It's not you," she insists. "It's me. It's *all* me. I do need to get my mind right, and I don't want to drag you or anyone else into my mess. Can we... can we be friends?"

"Yeah." I let out a mirthless chuckle, watching the prospect pull up to the sidewalk in one of the club's Chargers. "Sure, Emily."

I can't believe it. Me, Venom, fucking friend-zoned.

Emily

Friend.

Friend?

I could kick myself for even thinking, let alone suggesting it. I can't be Venom's *friend*. How can I even be around him knowing that, in no uncertain terms, he wants me in his bed? Knowing that's exactly where I want to be, how am I supposed to be friendly?

And him. He may have agreed to my silly request, but he doesn't like it; it's evident in his behavior. He hasn't been hostile, only a little indifferent. Over the last week, we've barely talked, even though I've seen him every day. He came into the pet shop once for a refill on mice, and he's seen me home from the gym every night. I always find him waiting for me by the juice bar, cup in hand. "Thank you" and "no problem, darlin'" have probably been the extent of our conversations. Every day I watch him work out, track the droplets of sweat as they trickle down his face and arms, lick my lips when the bulge and ripple of his muscles make them dry. Then at the end, I get to smell him, freshly showered and sense-tinglingly awesome.

God, I want him.

Why can't I be less complicated and give in to what my body wants? Stupid brain always wants to be in charge. For once, I wish I could be someone else... someone normal.

Sighing, I finish my shower, get dressed, and prepare to face Venom. He's right where he always is, but tonight Kurt is with him. My text alert sounds from my phone, and I pull it out of my pocket. My mood goes sour the moment I see who the message is from.

James: Have an answer for me?

Emily: The answer is and always will be NO.

James: We'll see.

"You okay?" Venom asks, brows creased.

"Yeah. No worries," I brush off his concern. It's not like he can do anything about the situation.

"Sit." He motions to the stool next to him. Kurt steps back as I take my seat. "You head on home," Venom tells him. "I'll do the rest."

"Thanks. See you guys tomorrow," he says.

"Bye, Kurt," I reply.

I have no idea what they're talking about, but Kurt nods and walks away. My brain is still addled by thoughts of James the asshole, so I drown out the two men and suck on the straw sticking out of my cup.

"What's going on with you?" Venom's voice drags me back to the moment.

"Huh?"

"Something on that phone is fucking with you again. What's wrong?"

"Nothing. It's personal."

"Anything I can do to help?"

"No, but thanks."

"Hey, what are friends for, right?" He shrugs.

"Yeah... friends." I roll my eyes internally at the word.

"So... have you decided when you're going back to Atlanta?"

"I think I might stick around for a while. Stony View is growing on me." *So is a certain bearded hunk.*

"What about work? Don't you have a job to get back to?"

"No. Uncle Jeff is friends with the principal of the high school, and he said he may be able to get me in part time or as a sub when school starts back up."

"You're a teacher?"

"I used to be. This should give me some room to breathe while I figure things out."

"What are you trying to figure out?" His gray eyes meet mine, searching for an answer I don't want to give.

I break our gaze, looking down at my cup. "Life. It hasn't really turned out the way I hoped."

"What were you hoping for?"

"I don't know. Something different, I guess. I love to bake and always thought I'd be running my own catering business by now."

"So why aren't you?"

"Again, life. It got in the way."

"Emily, look at me."

I face him, unable to turn away from his eyes this time. They hold me captive, making me their willing prisoner.

ALANA SAPPHIRE

"Life's too short to not do what makes you happy. If that's what you want, you should go for it."

Yeah, like it's that easy. I can't just start a business. Besides, baking is why I now have to live in the gym. I'm a stress eater, and with everything I've gone through over the years, chocolate cake became my best friend. So did red velvet. Hell, anything with sugar. Once I passed the two-hundred-pound mark and my doctor said I was borderline diabetic, I decided I had to change my habits. I gave up baking and did my best to steer clear of anything that could be labeled "dessert."

"What about you? Are you doing what makes you happy?"

"Fuck yeah. Don't I look it?" His lips curl up in a smile, exposing his impossibly white teeth.

"What's that? Feeding rats to your snake?"

"A part of it." He chuckles.

"Tell me about it."

"What, the snake?" he asks, smirking and leaving the unasked portion of the question in the air.

Nope. The anaconda. Tell me about that. "Of course, the snake!" I giggle, gently smacking his arm. Shit. That arm? Hard. That's all I can say. I feel like I hit a wall.

"Do you really wanna hear about it?"

"I wanna hear about you. What do you do?"

"Well, the MC owns a few businesses. We're all equal partners in those."

"What businesses?" I take another sip of my drink, eager to hear more about the man sitting next to me.

"Patch, the auto parts store, and the Pretty Kitty, a strip club outside of town."

"Strip club?" I raise a brow. "You guys must love that."

"We're men." He lifts a shoulder. "What's not to love about naked women dancing?"

"What about guys?"

"What?" he asks, confused.

"What about male dancers? I'm sure women enjoy naked men dancing." I waggle my brows, then run my gaze over his body, hoping he can take a joke.

30

"Fuck no. And don't get any ideas." He points at me. "Unless *you* want to give *me* a little show."

I almost choke on my drink. "Um, no."

"We do have pole dancing classes here, you know," he adds with a smirk.

"Oh shit!" I look at the time on my phone, now realizing we've been sitting here for a while. The place should have closed thirty minutes ago. And... Kurt left. "It just occurred to me... *you* told Kurt to go home. Who's going to lock up?"

"I am." He drops a bunch of keys on the counter.

"You have keys? Why do you have keys? Do you know the owner or something?"

"Or something."

"Wait... it's you, isn't it? This is your gym?"

"It is." He nods, watching me with a keen eye, assessing my reaction. "Kurt manages it for me."

I don't know why I didn't realize it sooner. All the hushed conversations I've seen him having with members of staff, especially Kurt. The way he would disappear into the back sometimes, how helpful he is to the members. I'm such a dumbass. Oh, God... I really *am* a dumbass!

"There's no promotion, is there?" I ask, voice accusatory.

"Promotion?"

"When I tried to sign up, Kurt said there was some kind of promotion going on for a free month of membership."

"That's what he told you?" Venom chuckles, not at all bothered by my now defensive mood.

"Yes. What was this, some other ploy to get me in your bed?" I hop to my feet, no longer able to sit quietly.

His jaw clenches. "I don't need ploys to fuck a woman, darlin'," he spits out, his voice quite... well, venomous.

I reach into my bag, snagging my credit card and slapping it on the counter. He's clenching his teeth so hard, I can practically hear them gnashing against each other.

"I don't want your money."

"Fine." I pick up my bag and my card, leaving him sitting at the juice bar. "I'll just have Kurt charge it tomorrow."

ALANA SAPPHIRE

I'm fuming all the way to the truck, cursing myself under my breath. Since when have I had the luck to get anything for free? When the fuck did I become so gullible? Shit. I toss my bag in the front seat, but before I can climb in, someone grabs me from behind. I'm pulled against a hard body, my startled scream muffled when a hand clamps over my mouth.

Fuck.

CHAPTER 4
Venom

"It's me, Emily," I assure her as she struggles against me. "I'm going to move my hand, just calm down."

It's a good thing Kurt had already shut everything down; I wouldn't have caught up to her if I had to do more than lock the front doors. The moment I release her, she spins to face me, fists flying everywhere.

"You asshole! You scared the shit out of me!" she screams.

I grab her hands, forcing her against the truck and stilling her movements with my body. She freezes. Her ragged breathing no longer indicates anger but something else entirely.

This woman is killing me.

Why did she think I could ever be friends with her? There's nothing friendly about the thoughts that run through my mind whenever I see her. Whenever I *don't* see her. Being around her every day doesn't make it any better. I swear I have the worst case of blue balls since I left high school. I've even avoided the Hounds because I know I can't substitute one woman for another. I need the one whose body is crushed to mine right now.

"I'm sorry. I didn't mean to scare you."

"Well, you did."

"Look." I ease off, giving us both some room. "I promise you, it was no ploy. If it was, I would've told you it was my gym, made you feel obligated, or impressed, or whatever you think it was supposed to do. Think about it."

She chews on her lip and I can see it on her face that she knows I'm right. She just won't admit it so easily.

"You were having a shitty day. I wanted to do something nice for you."

"You paid for my lunch that day, too. Why?"

"Same reason. I wasn't expecting you to fuck me because I paid for your salad, Emily." I take a deep breath, running my fingers through my hair.

"Venom." She expels a breath through her mouth, shaking her head. "I'm sorry. I just... I told you. I told you to stay away from me."

"I don't know how, darlin'. I want you too much." She lets out another breath, a shiver running through her. I step closer, taking her chin and tilting her face up toward mine. "Stop fighting, Emily."

"I can't. It's the only thing I know," she whispers, tears shimmering in her eyes.

Fuck.

Pulling her into my arms, I hold her until her rigid body relaxes, and then I keep holding her. Her hands slide around my waist, face pressing into my chest.

What are you hiding, Emily? What's going on in that pretty little head of yours?

"I should go." She sniffs. "Uncle Jeff will be wondering where I am."

"Okay, darlin'. Let's go."

I see her home like every other night, this time wondering how I'm going to get through to her. I should be running for the hills. Women like Emily never want the same thing I do—no strings attached. But I can't run. Not when staying means I could help her.

Unlike the other nights, I park and walk with her to the door. She mumbles her thanks while pushing the key into the lock.

"Emily, wait."

She pauses, an expectant look in her eyes as she watches me. Even with a tinge of sadness, they're still gorgeous. I've never seen eyes as green as hers. The things I've imagined about those eyes... staring up as she kneels before me, open wide when I sink into her for the first time, gazing at me fully sated.

Now I would give anything for them not to seem so lifeless.

"Here." I hand her my phone. "Put your number in." She doesn't argue, punching in her name and number, then handing my cell back to me. "I'll call you tomorrow."

"Okay."

I want to tug her into my arms and kiss away everything weighing her down, but I restrain myself. That's not me. It's bordering on emotional territory; way out of bounds for me. I need to find out who's fucking with her. I eliminate that problem, she opens up.

She opens up to me.

Hopefully her thighs first.

Shit. I head to the clubhouse, knowing I won't be able to sleep yet. I'm bound to find something there to keep me occupied.

Sure as hell, Razor, Tek, Booker, and Charger are seated on the couch, observing what seems to be a game of strip pool between two of the girls. Melody's tits jiggle, nipples sliding on the table as she makes a shot. Her ball rolls into the corner pocket, leading Trixie to remove the last of her clothes—her panties. The redhead makes a show of it, wiggling her ass in the guys' direction.

Shaking my head, I make my way to the bar. Marisol hands me a beer, her glossy, bubble gum–pink lips curling up in a smile.

"Hi, Venom."

"Hey, Marisol. Your girls are enjoying themselves, I see."

We're down to three Hounds now. There used to be more, but after weeding out a few bad apples, and most of the guys having old ladies, we decided to get all new girls. We got one of each, too: a blonde, a redhead, and a brunette. These three seem to be fitting in well. As long as they do their jobs—taking care of the men in and out of the bedroom—they might last a while. Raven keeps them in check, too, making sure they show respect to all the old ladies. She's fierce, that one. They don't want to cross her.

"What do you say? You and me next?" Marisol asks.

She's my favorite of the three, and I've taken her to my room more times than I can count, but tonight, the dark-haired beauty isn't doing it for me.

Cursing under my breath, I shake my head. "Not tonight, sugar lips."

This is all Emily's fault.

Fuck.

I leave the bar, taking a chair and joining my brothers. "What's up, perverts?"

"Look who's talking!" Razor chuckles. "Birds of a feather, motherfucker."

"Yeah, yeah." I take a sip of my beer, watching the pool game with disinterest.

35

"What the fuck's wrong with you?"

"Yeah," Tek chimes in. "Figured you'd have dragged Marisol back to your room already."

"Just not feeling it tonight."

"Oh, shit. Don't tell me you found a woman, too?"

Gage and Einstein walk in right in time to hear the question. I throw a death glare at Razor.

"Who's got a woman?" Gage asks.

The prez and VP stand before our little group, gazes sliding over our faces. Einstein smirks at me.

Fuck.

"I bet it's Venom," he says, his grin telling me he's getting back at me for a little stunt I pulled a while back with his old lady and her kid. He's the only one who didn't find it funny.

"Who is it? Anyone we know?" Gage asks, pulling up a chair.

"There's no woman."

"Bullshit," Charger says. "He's been sulking around here for days, and he just passed up Marisol."

Einstein laughs, while Gage tries his damnedest not to as he asks, "The brunette? Isn't she your favorite?"

"What are you two doing here, anyway?" I try to change the subject. "Your old ladies give you your balls back for the night?"

The men on the couch snicker, but Gage and Einstein aren't bothered.

"Hey, my balls have never been happier," Gage says, quickly turning to Einstein and pointing a finger in warning. "Not a word about my sister and your balls."

"Yeah, yeah. I know."

The prez pushes to his feet, tapping Einstein's shoulder. "We came to check on things but," he glances over his shoulder at the girls, "I see you have everything under control. We're gonna head out."

"Cool." I stand also, deciding to turn in. "See you tomorrow, fellas."

As I pass the pool table, Trixie bends over for a shot and I playfully smack her ass. She giggles but I don't stop or look back, discouraging further interaction.

Locking the door behind me, I undress and climb into bed. I know my brothers mean well, but if you give them an inch, they'll go *ten miles*. If I even mention Emily, they'll start designing my tat. It's a Dealer tradition—you claim a woman, you ink her on your back. It could be her name or a symbol, anything that represents her. I don't know Emily well enough to tell if she's wifey material, but it doesn't matter. That's not what I'm looking for.

I grab my phone to set the alarm, and before I can stop it, my thumb is scrolling to Emily's name, tapping it to send the call. I wasn't expecting her to answer, but her voice comes through the speaker after the third ring.

"Hello?" she answers in a curious voice.

"Did I wake you?"

"Venom? Um... no. I was in bed, but I was reading."

"What book?" *What book? What. Book? Really, that's the best you can do?*

"You wouldn't be interested," she replies with a soft laugh. "It's a romance novel."

Now we're talking. "Were you at the good part?"

"The good part? You mean where the hero declares his undying love for the heroine and they live happily ever after?"

"I mean the part where she finally stops playing hard to get and lets the dude fuck her."

She goes silent, and I wonder if I've gone too far. I'm about to apologize when she speaks up.

"I'm only a few chapters in. They haven't known each other long enough to do that."

"I see. How long is she making him wait?" I ask, continuing our little game.

"I can't tell. Right now he seems nice, but she's afraid of trusting him. She doesn't want to get hurt."

"Because she's been hurt before?"

There's another pause, and then she says, "There's some allusion to it, but nothing's been revealed yet."

Just as I thought. Some asshole hurt her, so she's built a wall around herself. Sometimes I don't understand my own gender.

37

What's so hard about treating a woman right? If you know you can't settle down, why promise exclusivity?

"Okay, Em. You let me know how it goes. I'll see you tomorrow."

"Bye."

Looks like I'm going to have my hands full with Emily.

I'm not giving up on her.

Emily

Venom's not at the gym today.

However, he did text to let me know he had things to take care of and that Kurt would follow me home. A part of me is bummed that I won't see him; our little routine has grown on me and I realize I've looked forward to it every day. Another part of me is worried that after our phone conversation last night, he's finally decided I'm not worth the effort after all.

That he's given up on me.

What am I even thinking? I've been chasing him away since the day we met. He *shouldn't* be giving me the time of day. He needs to focus on someone who can give him what he wants, and that definitely is *not* me.

"Ready?" Kurt asks, interrupting my thoughts.

"Yeah."

He takes my bag, letting me precede him out of the building. I wait, eyes darting up and down the street, as he locks the doors. As a woman, that's something I'd normally do when I'm travelling alone—look for dangers lurking about. Tonight, it feels weird. I realize I haven't done that on the nights Venom was with me. It's even weirder that I feel so safe with him, subconsciously knowing he would and could protect me. Kurt's a nice guy and all, but he doesn't give me that kind of assurance.

Taking brisk steps, I set the pace to the parking lot. I want to get home and curl back up with my book.

"So, you and the boss getting along okay?"

"The boss? Oh, you mean Venom? I guess." I shrug. "He seems like a nice guy."

He chuckles. "Nice?"

I glance over at him with curiosity. "What, he isn't nice?"

"He's a good guy. Just never heard a woman describe him as 'nice.'"

"Wait." I stop, turning to face him. "What do you think's going on between me and him?"

"I'm sorry. I didn't mean to offend you. I figured…." He cocks his head to the side, raising a brow. "So you two aren't seeing each other?"

"No, we're not," I reply, resuming our walk.

"I see."

At the truck, I take my bag from him and toss it on the seat. "You don't have to follow me, you know. I'm fine. I have no idea why Venom insists on doing it."

"It's no worries. I don't live far from your uncle."

I'd ask how he knows about my uncle, but it's a small town. It could also be that Venom told him. "Okay." I nod, climbing into the truck.

I drive at a different pace tonight also. Every other night, I check my rearview mirror for Venom following on his bike, just to get a glimpse of him. It's not the same looking back and seeing Kurt's SUV.

When I pull into our driveway, I hop out, giving him a quick wave. Unexpectedly and without invitation, he catches up to me and accompanies me to the door.

"Thanks, Kurt. I appreciate you doing this." I insert the key in the door, hoping he'll take the hint. For some reason it appears he believes he has a chance with me since I'm not with Venom. Why he would even want one, I don't know.

"Listen, Emily." He touches my elbow to stop me. "I was wondering—if you're not busy, that is—if you'd like to have dinner some time."

He's giving me a smile that probably melts a lot of panties, but it does nothing for me. He's an attractive man, but I guess he's not my type. *Not my type? Since when is a good-looking, nice, gainfully employed man not my type? Sheesh.*

"Kurt, look—"

"Let me stop you. If you don't want to, it's cool. I understand."

"It has nothing to do with you. You seem like a good guy."

"But I'm not Venom."

"That's not it either." *Well, that's part of it, but I can't tell him that.* "I'm trying to be by myself right now. Besides, I don't even know how long I'm going to be around."

"I see," he says, nodding. I know he's not buying it, but he doesn't seem bitter. "No worries. I'll see you tomorrow?"

"Sure. Thanks for understanding."

"Good night, Emily."

"Good night, Kurt."

Uncle Jeff is watching TV when I walk in. Usually he's not still up when I come home, but he seems wide awake tonight.

I drop my bag by his favorite chair and kiss his cheek. "Hey, Uncle Jeff. How come you're still up?"

"Hey, baby girl. I was just doing some work. Trying to settle my mind before I hit the sack."

"Oh, okay. Don't stay up too late. I'm gonna head in."

"I won't. Good night, sweetheart."

"Good night."

I grab my gym bag and head to my room, tossing the contents in the hamper before undressing. I didn't get a chance to wash my hair at the gym, so I need to get it done or I won't be able to sleep.

When I get out of the shower, I blow-dry my hair, grab the first nightgown my fingers touch, and crawl into bed with my book. Last night I stopped at what Venom calls "the good part." I snuggle up, getting ready to read about all the fabulous sex with the abnormally "gifted" man. If only real life was the same.

In the middle of the scene, my phone rings. Sighing in annoyance, I grab it from the nightstand. When I see the name flashing on the screen, my heart skips a beat.

Venom.

Taking a deep breath, I answer in the calmest voice I can muster. "Hey."

"Hey, darlin'. Kurt told me he dropped you off."

"Yeah. Thanks, but you didn't need to set that up."

"I know I don't *need* to. Doesn't mean I shouldn't. I feel better knowing you're home safe."

"Oh." *Oh. My safety is important to him. But… why?* "Well, you'll be happy to know that Kurt did a good job."

"He behave?"

"Of course. I mean, he kinda asked me out—"

"He did what?" Venom practically growls around the words.

"Um… what I mean is," I stammer, my brain working overtime to find a way to diffuse the anger in his voice. *It's not like he owns me. He has no right to be upset.* "He asked if you and I were together and I told him the truth, that we're not. Anyway, I said no."

He takes a deep breath, no doubt getting his emotions in check.

"You in bed?" he asks in a calmer voice.

"Yeah. Just reading my book."

"Any action yet?"

"Actually, that's where I am now." I lick my lips, anticipating what he'll say next.

"Read it to me."

"What?"

"Read it to me," he repeats, his voice husky and firm.

"Are you serious?"

"I'm waiting."

I reach for my tablet, picking up where I left off. *I can't believe I'm doing this. Why am I doing this? Shit.*

"Reese slides inside me, stretching me like no one else has. God…." My voice falters.

"Keep going."

"God, he's huge. But he feels so good. 'Reese,' I moan, wrapping my legs around his waist. He begins to move, each stroke an assault on my senses. I…." I pause, heat rising in my body. It's not the words in the book, per se, it's reading them aloud to *him*. "I contract my muscles around him, making him groan, muttering curses under his breath."

"Did he eat her pussy?" Venom asks.

"Um… no."

"Then your book needs a new hero. If I had you in my bed, that's one of the first things I'd do."

My clit pulses. "Venom…."

"Any man can fuck a woman. Eating pussy properly is an art. Done right, a woman can come in a second, while she can ride a dick for hours and all she'll be is sore and frustrated. Unless it's *my* dick, of course."

I know the last part was to lighten the mood, but it doesn't stop me from pressing my thighs together. I want to ask if he's mastered the art, but that would come dangerously close to flirting, and extend a conversation I don't want to continue.

"You shouldn't do that." My voice is soft and lacking in conviction.

"What?"

"I'm just… not comfortable with you talking like that."

"It's not supposed to make you comfortable, Emily. My only aim is to make your pussy wet."

"See what I mean? You can't say things like that." I reach up to loosen my collar, only to find I don't have one. *Jeez. What is this man doing to me?*

"Of course I can. I just did."

"Yes, well, friends don't talk to each other like that."

There's a pause before he replies, "Friends. Right. I'm gonna let you get back to your pussy-ass hero. Later, Emily."

Disappointment rattles my body. I don't want him to hang up, but I'm not exactly offering engaging conversation, am I? I want to keep talking to him, only with a change of topic.

"Sure. Later."

I return my phone to its place on the nightstand and try to get back into my book. It's simply not the same after what just happened in real life. I put it aside and end up tossing and turning for God knows how long. My mind is frazzled. Venom has me fucked up and I have no clue how to deal with it. He's so ingrained in my thoughts, I think I hear his bike pull up. Don't ask me how I even know how to differentiate the sound of his bike from any other.

I fluff my pillow, change positions for the umpteenth time, and try to fall asleep. My ears perk up when Uncle Jeff's voice floats into my room.

Who the hell is he talking to?

42

CHAPTER 5
Venom

"Come on in, son," Jeff greets me, stepping aside so I can enter.

"Thanks, Jeff."

Our business could have easily waited until morning, but I need something to keep me occupied tonight. Numbers. They've kept me calm since I was a kid. Over the years, I've found other things that help, but nothing like those numbers. I love the structure, the set rules, the logic, the reliability. Numbers are constant. They don't change because you want them to. That's why I'm here at Jeff's door, close to midnight.

Maybe I was hoping to see Emily, too.

Fuck, while she was reading to me, all I could imagine was sinking into her. When she told me about Kurt hitting on her, I visualized putting my fist through his teeth, but Emily was right. She's not mine. If she wanted to go out with him, that's her prerogative. Hell, he'd probably be better for her. He can offer all the things I can't. Maybe I'll tell him to try again once I'm done with her.

Jeff leads me to the dining room, offering me a seat. I drop down into one of the chairs, listening for a sign that Emily's around. The Christmas decorations are a new addition for Jeff, and certainly Emily's doing.

"Let me get those papers for you."

"I'll wait here," I tell him.

"Uncle Jeff? Did you say something?"

Emily's curious voice precedes her walking into the room. The moment she does, my dick twitches.

Fuck. Me.

She's wearing one of those silky nighties, the tops of her breasts peeking out of the V neckline. It's clinging to her body, outlining her curves to perfection. If her uncle wasn't here, I'd throw her down on the table and fuck her until neither of us could walk.

Her eyes land on me and she gasps, immediately trying to cover herself with her hands.

43

"Sorry! I didn't know you had company."

She starts to back away, but Jeff waves her forward. "Come in, Emily. You can keep Venom occupied while I find what he needs."

What I need is standing at the door, staring at me like a deer caught in the headlights. Jeff leaves the room, not giving her a chance to say no. She takes a deep breath, pulling up the bodice of the nightie as she takes the chair across from me.

"Hi, Em."

"Hello."

I can't help it. My gaze falls back to her breasts. It only makes her increase her efforts to hide them.

"Why do you always do that? I was enjoying the view."

"Why do *you* always do that?" she counters.

"What? Compliment you?"

"Try to flatter me."

"That's not what I'm doing." I lean forward, placing my arms on the table, lacing my fingers together. "I want you. Why shouldn't I tell you how beautiful you are? How sexy? How much I want to feel your pussy wrapped around my dick?"

Flustered, she seems to be searching for a comeback, but Jeff interrupts us when he re-enters the room.

"Here you go, son." He drops the envelope on the table. "Let me know if you need anything else." He nods, his way of concluding our business. "Emily can see you out."

Once he's gone again, Emily jerks her head at the envelope. "What's that?"

"Receipts and invoices from the pet store."

"What are you doing with those?" Her brows knit in confusion.

"In return for doing the books and taxes, Jeff supplies me with unlimited mice."

"The books?" Her brows crease even more.

"What, you think the dirty biker isn't capable of doing a little double entry?"

"No!" Horrified, she shakes her head, the movements frantic. "Of course not. Just surprised at the arrangement, is all."

"Uh-huh."

I sit back in my chair, observing her. *Fuck, I think I really would give my left nut to fuck her. Maybe both.*

She stands, shaky fingers tugging on the straps of the nightie once more.

"Well, I think it's time I got to bed."

"Is that an invitation?"

A blush colors her cheeks as she averts her eyes. "No. I meant now that you're done with Uncle Jeff, you'll be leaving."

"I'm done with Jeff, but not with you."

I rise, stalking toward her. She licks those juicy lips, eyes darting around the room as she puts distance between us. Hell, she's practically moonwalking away from me. I'm through with this game. I need to see if there really is something between us. She's not getting away this time.

"Stop running, Emily."

She halts, her chest rapidly rising and falling as her eyes meet mine. Behind the fear, there's an invitation in those gorgeous greens. I know she's not afraid of me; she's afraid of what we'll both know the minute my lips touch hers—that she wants me, too.

Grabbing her wrist, I pull her to me, sliding my free hand into her hair. I tug on it, raising her face to mine. Before she can object, I press my lips to hers. Instead of protesting like I thought she would, she moans, relaxing against me. She opens for me, granting me entry to her sweet mouth. I instantly slide my tongue in, eager to taste. And she lets me. I explore every inch I can reach, marveled that a woman could taste this good. My hand tightens in her peach-scented hair, holding her head in place while I plunder. My other hand moves instinctively to her ass, squeezing the cheek and pressing my hard dick into her stomach. She whimpers, hands coming to rest on my hips. I suck on her lips, nipping at them with my teeth before finally breaking away.

Her lids flutter open, glazed-over eyes staring up at me, swollen lips parted. Her body shivers.

"Ooh, lawd," she whispers.

Fuck. I need more, but not here.

"As much as I love this little outfit of yours, I want you to get changed. We're getting out of here."

"Venom, I—"

I silence her with another kiss, her body lax against me as the opposition drains from it.

"Change, Emily. I promise we won't do anything you don't want to do. I'll wait for you outside."

Releasing her, I grab the envelope from the table and walk to my bike. After dropping the package in the saddlebag, I lean against it, watching Jeff's front door and hoping Emily comes walking out any minute. I'm about to go check on her when she surfaces. She's changed into a pink dress, light sweater, and sandals, looking feminine, conservative, but still sexy as hell. I adjust my aching dick as she gets closer. Once she's in front of me, she gives me a sheepish smile, looking between her dress and the bike.

"Guess I didn't think this through."

"You'll be fine, just watch out for the pipes."

Taking off my jacket, I drape it over her shoulders and watch as she sticks her arms in. The temperature has begun to drop, and although it isn't cold, the wind can be pretty harsh when riding at night.

"Thanks. I *really* didn't think this through."

I watch her standing there in my jacket, and I'm glad she didn't. Taking her chin between my fingers, I place a gentle kiss on her lips before throwing my leg over the bike. I show her where to put her feet, then tell her to hop on. She follows my instructions, climbing on but keeping her distance.

"Closer, Em." She slides down the saddle, her thighs hugging my hips. I grab her hands, wrapping them around my waist. "Unless you want to fall off."

Her arms tighten, her body pressing against my back. I crank up the bike, twisting the throttle when we move off. *God, she feels good behind me*.

I had no plans when I left her place, but I somehow end up at mine. I help her off, then retrieve the envelope Jeff gave me.

"Is this your house?" she asks.

"Yeah," I reply, trying to see it from her point of view.

It's pretty isolated, no other houses around for a few miles. That's why I bought it. It was in pretty bad shape, but I got it at a steal and fixed it up. There are three bedrooms, two baths, kitchen, and living room. It's only one story, but I made it so I could add more if I wanted to.

"It's nice."

"Thanks."

Inside, I flip on the lights before heading to the kitchen. Emily follows quietly behind.

"You want something to drink? Eat?"

"Just some water, please," she replies, rubbing her hands together.

"You cold? Want some coffee?"

"Water's fine."

I grab a bottle for her and a beer for me from the fridge. She leans on the counter, taking a sip when I hand the water to her, then leaving it on the surface behind her.

"Oh." She removes my jacket, handing it to me with a smile. "Thanks for that. I probably would've frozen to death without it."

I hang it on the back of one of the dining chairs, moving toward her. I need to taste those lips again. Sliding my hand to the back of her neck, I grip it as I lean in.

"Venom, wait."

"What is it, baby?" I ask, nipping at her lips.

"I need to tell you something… something you should know." Her words come out shaky, breathless.

I pull back, giving her my full attention. She's chewing on her bottom lip, eyes not meeting mine.

"What?" I hurry her along.

"I'm…."

"You're what?"

"I'm married."

Emily

Venom's eyes narrow, his hand leaving my neck. He takes a step back, shock overtaking his features.

"What the fuck, Emily? You don't think you should've told me that before?" he demands.

"It's not like that. We're separated... getting a divorce. That's if James ever signs the papers."

He takes a deep breath in, expelling it through his mouth in relief. His relief turns to scrutiny, and I can almost see the wheels turning in his head.

"He the reason you think I'm trying to flatter you?"

"Part of it. He was a shitty husband. Always made me feel like I was never good enough for him."

"Babe." Venom steps closer. "He's the one who's not good enough for you."

"Thanks." I drop my gaze.

"How long were you married?"

"Ten years."

"And how long you been separated?"

"Six months. Although it seems like longer. We stopped being a married couple long before that." I chuckle, but only to keep myself from breaking down. "When he started getting sex elsewhere, I was actually relieved. He even blamed me for his cheating, saying I was no good in bed. He hadn't touched me for over two years before I found out he got one of his women pregnant. That was the last straw. I moved back in with my parents and served him divorce papers."

Venom's hand returns to my neck, his thumb brushing my skin in comfort. It gives me the strength to continue. "He keeps sending them back without his signature, though."

"Maybe he's realized what he's losing."

"Hardly." I fold my arms across my chest, tears pricking my eyes. "You know what he called me? Miss Piggy. Said I disgusted him and he wouldn't touch me if I was the last woman on Earth."

"Motherfucker," he growls, pulling me into his arms. "He's a cocksucker who deserves to swallow a bullet for spewing that bullshit to you."

RENASCENCE

I wrap my arms around Venom, breathing in his scent. It's calming yet arousing at the same time. He's so strong and confident, not needing to put others down in order to feel better about himself. So different from James.

"He wants money."

"Money?" He pulls back, brows furrowed as he stares down at me in confusion.

"I'm not rich or anything like that," I clarify. "A couple years ago, I found out James had been hiding more than his cheating from me. We split the bills. He had the bigger ones, mortgage and electric, and I had food and the other utilities. He was behind, and we were facing foreclosure on the house. I sold my car, worked *two* full-time jobs to get us out of the hole. After school, I worked as a waitress to supplement my income."

"Fuck, Em…." Venom shakes his head.

Taking a deep breath, I continue. "I kept both jobs, but started putting money away in a separate account. When I left, some mail came for me at the house, and that's how he found out. I don't think he knows how much is in the account, but he probably thinks it's a lot. It really isn't. The day we met, the reason I was such a bitch to you? I got a message from him saying he won't sign the divorce papers until I pay him. It really pissed me off."

Venom pulls me back into his arms, gently rubbing circles on my back. He kisses the top of my head, his lips slowly moving down the side of my face and toward my lips.

"You're beautiful, Emily. Trust and believe me when I say that."

I relax, letting him claim my mouth like he did earlier. I've never been kissed like this.

Passionate.

Hungry.

Moaning, I slide my hands around his neck and up into his hair. As his tongue dominates my mouth, a hand squeezes my breast. He grunts, pressing his erection into my stomach. I let him kiss me within an inch of my life, massaging my breast and pinching the nipple through my dress. It was never like this with anyone else. The sensations running through my body are so new to me, I want to prolong them for as long as possible. Before Venom loses what little interest he seems to have in me. There's a danger in him, in

49

his touch, his kiss. It's in his blood, pumping in his veins. I know I'll be its victim eventually, but my pleasure now is worth the pain later.

My body shivers as the hand on my breast glides down my side, slipping under my dress and into my panties. A long groan of approval leaves my throat when his fingers swipe over my lips.

"Fuck," he mumbles against my mouth. "You're wet already. I want to taste you, Emily."

My body goes rigid.

He pulls back, regarding me cautiously. "What?"

"I've never... that is, no one's ever...."

"Don't tell me that asshole never ate your pussy."

"No." I shake my head, uncomfortable not only with the conversation, but the reason why James wouldn't... engage in that activity.

"Why the hell not?" Venom demands an answer.

"He said...." I avert my gaze but he grabs my chin, forcing me to look at him. "He didn't like the smell." I rush the words out, trying to make it quick and painless.

Venom swears, grumbling about James being a worthless piece of shit. I won't disagree there.

"Why the fuck were you with him so long?"

I shrug. I've asked myself that question so many times, but never found a satisfactory answer.

Venom falls to his knees before me, pressing his face between my thighs before I can stop him.

"What are you doing?" I ask in a panic.

He pushes my dress up, dragging his nose from the crotch of my panties to where they cover my mound. My knees tremble, embarrassment forgotten as more beautiful sensations travel through my body. My lids flutter closed, head falling back with a moan.

"That smell? It tells me you're aroused. Even if I hadn't touched you, it would've told me that if I ripped these fucking panties off, I'd find you wet. For *me*. You smell like fucking Heaven, and I bet you taste even better."

His fingers hook into the leg of my underwear, moving it aside.

"Venom, don't."

RENASCENCE

My plea is weak at best, my resolve slowly weakening when our gazes lock. Here is a man, kneeling at my feet, eyes begging me to allow him to perform an act my own husband wouldn't. He promised me we wouldn't do anything I'm not comfortable with, so he's waiting for my permission. As self-conscious as I am, I desperately want him to do it.

I nod, my fear turning into something quite different when his tongue slides between my lips. My legs quiver, goose bumps popping up on my skin.

"Oh, God...."

I've definitely never experienced anything like this before, and not just the pleasure from his tongue. I feel *wanted.*

"Look at me, Emily."

I didn't even realize my eyes had closed again. They fly open, and I watch as Venom buries his lips in my sex. Our eyes meet, the look in his making it impossible for me to break our stare. I couldn't even if I wanted to. For years I thought there was something wrong with me. Now, after a few minutes and even fewer words, this man makes me feel like the dessert section of an all-you-can-eat buffet. It's in his eyes, the way he's staring up at me like there's nowhere else in the world he'd rather be, like he can't get enough of me... of my... *taste.*

"Venom...."

At the sound of his name, he growls, ripping my panties off and spreading my thighs to his liking.

"You're going to come on my tongue, Emily. I'm going to make you come so hard, you'll forget every word that motherfucker ever said to you." My body shudders, leaving no doubt in my mind that he could achieve that feat. "I'm going to make you come so many times, it will completely wipe him from your memory."

"Please...."

I don't know what I'm begging for. Maybe it's for him to keep talking, or for him to lick me again. Maybe I need him to make good on his promise.

To make me forget.

"You want my tongue, Emily?" he asks, punctuating his words with a lick to my clit.

My breaths come hard and heavy.

"Yes."

"Tell me. Tell me you want me to fuck you with my tongue. That you want to come on my lips."

"Fuck me with your tongue, Venom," I tell him, more confidence than I've ever felt in my life surging through me. "I want to come on your lips."

With a grunt, he sucks my clit into his mouth. I cry out, grabbing a handful of his hair. His tongue swirls, the combined actions making it hard for me to stay upright. Venom's fingers dig into the backs of my thighs as he positively devours me. I won't last much longer. When he pulls away, I groan my disappointment. His fingers spread my lips, baring my clit to his gaze. I watch him lick his lips, eyeing me like he can't wait to dive back in.

"Fucking prettiest pussy I've ever seen."

My knees quiver. Muscles clench.

"Get rid of this, Emily." He tugs on the hair on my mound. "I plan on spending a lot of time down here, and I don't want anything in my way."

Jesus.

He licks at my clit with the tip of his tongue, then glides it from my entrance up, with a long, leisurely stroke. His beard tickles my inner thighs.

"Fuck, you taste good."

That does it. The moment he touches my clit again, my climax barrels through me like a boulder down a mountain. I cry out, pulling his hair.

"Venom!"

He continues to lap at my juices, making my orgasm more intense. I've never come so hard in my damn life. *Yep...* definitely *mastered the art.*

When my knees threaten to give out, he picks me up, and I have the vague sense of being carried. That couldn't be. Even with all his muscles, I'm way too heavy for Venom to walk around with me.

Finally down from my high, I find myself in his bed. *What the hell?* Shocked, I look to Venom, but all words escape me when he slides off his cut, revealing a gun strapped to his shoulder. He loses it, reaching behind him to drag his T-shirt over his head, tossing it aside. All of a sudden, I'm not concerned with how I got here, or his gun. My only focus is the naked chest mere inches from me.

Perfection.

That's what he is. All the hours in the gym have certainly paid off for him. The man is huge, from his pecs to his arms. The ripples in his stomach look like a goddamn ice tray, leading down to the V at his hips. Tattoos cover his skin, and I make a mental note to study them the first chance I get. The silver barbells in his nipples glisten at me, calling to my tongue. His jeans are next to go, revealing muscular thighs encased in tight, sexy-as-sin boxer briefs. He certainly hasn't missed a leg day. His dick is hard, snaking up toward his stomach. I swallow hard at the promise of the size of his bulge. I guess I'll finally find out if size *does* matter.

"Take off your dress, Emily. I want to see you."

I hesitate, not wanting to taint the amazingness we just shared. Surely when he sees me naked, he won't want to continue. I close my eyes, feeling the bed dip beneath his weight.

"Can you… turn off the light?" I ask, unsure if he even heard the timid words I whispered.

"Emily… babe.…" He grabs my chin and I open my eyes to find his gray ones boring into me. "I can tell you all day how gorgeous you are, but you won't believe me. So I'm going to show you."

"How?"

I allow him to slip off my sweater, then pull my dress up and off, all while my eyes are closed. I won't be able to manage the disappointment in his when he finally sees my body. My bra follows, its removal making my too-big breasts fall to the side, parting as the Red Sea did for Moses and his rod. They weren't pert enough for James, and he never let me forget it. Venom sucks in a breath, a groan coming from deep in his throat.

Well, that sounded… not disappointed.

"Fuck, Emily." He settles between my legs, his rock-hard erection connecting with my pussy. I gasp, shocked that *I* did that to him. "You're fucking gorgeous. See what you do to me?"

Our eyes finally meet, and he grinds his hardness against my clenching core. My hips rise up to meet him stroke for stroke.

"I'm not going to fuck you tonight. Tonight… it's all about you."

A finger replaces his crotch, and he slowly slides it inside me. I moan, wrapping my arms around his shoulders and digging my nails in, unable to think about what his words mean.

"So fucking tight," he mumbles, more to himself than me.

No one has ever spoken to me the way Venom does. He's crude and crass... and my body is eating it all up. Every filthy word goes straight to my clit, making it pulse with need. As if he knows, he shifts his attention there. His fingers move in a circular motion, intent on wringing another life-altering orgasm from me. I whimper, pulling his face into my neck. His lips latch on to a spot there, sucking as his tongue moves in lazy circles. The man is a sex god. I haven't even seen his dick yet, but I'm on the verge of coming twice within mere minutes.

"Come for me, Emily. I want to feel your body shaking under me."

"Yes...."

He moves faster, fingers pressing into my sensitive flesh. My muscles contract, and I sink my teeth into my bottom lip to keep from screaming. Venom begins to rock, his chest rubbing against my aching nipples. It's exactly what I needed to push me over the edge. I scream, convulsions ripping through me as I crush his body to mine.

He grunts, actions slowing before he slides to the bed next to me. His fingers remain in my pussy, trailing featherlight touches up and down. I shudder, a moan passing my lips as I settle in against him.

"How do you feel?" he asks.

"*Amazing*. Those were my first non-self-induced orgasms, ever." I giggle before realizing what I admitted to him.

"Don't worry, darlin'. There are many more to come."

His arm curls around my waist, pulling my back against his front. Sighing in contentment, I allow sleep to take me.

***

"Mmm...."

I don't know what's going on, but something feels incredibly good. I open my eyes and realize there are fingers pinching my nipple. Venom. He's still nestled behind me, his erection digging into my ass. *God, he's so hard and I haven't even touched him.* Of course, James always blamed me when he couldn't get it up.

A twist of my nipple sends all thoughts fleeing from my mind. I turn onto my back with another moan. He doesn't hesitate, his mouth replacing his fingers.

"Your tits are amazing," he mumbles.

I grasp a handful of his hair, hips rising off the bed when his hand glides down my stomach. By the time his fingers brush over my lips, I'm soaking wet.

"Fuck," he groans, sliding a digit inside me. "You're killing me, Emily. I want inside you so fucking bad."

Me, too! "Yes, Venom. Please…."

"Patience."

My muscles clench, squeezing his fingers when he adds another. I spread my thighs, giving him more room. A grunt of—I can't believe it—satisfaction leaves his lips. His teeth graze my nipple, biting into it when I whimper. The fingers inside me start to move slowly, picking up pace as I grind on them in wanton abandon. I don't know what he's doing to me, but I like it. I *love* it. I want more.

"Venom…."

"Love the way you say my name. You'll be screaming it soon."

Oh, God. My hand tightens in his hair, keeping him at my breast. He fucks me with his fingers, hooking them and pressing on my top wall. With each thrust, he pushes them as far as he can, his thumb connecting with my clit on every in motion. His beard is rough against my skin as his mouth works my nipple, sucking, licking, biting. It throbs, but there is no pain. Just pleasure.

Just him.

Just *us*.

"Come, Emily. Come for me."

It can't be possible, but it's happening. The quickening sensation zips through me, my pussy clamping down on his fingers.

"Emily…."

My name on his lips is my undoing. "Venom!"

My body shudders, back arching, eyes squeezed shut. I feel empty when his fingers leave me, sliding between my lips, over my clit, and up my stomach. He turns off the lamp by his bed, pulling me against him once more.

"Sleep, babe."

CHAPTER 6
Emily

My body twists in a languid stretch before I even open my eyes. That's the best night's sleep I've had since… I don't remember when. Three orgasms will do that to a woman. Three orgasms from a man—a very hot, dirty-talking biker kind of man. Damn. I can't help the smile that spreads across my lips.

"Wanna share what's put that look on your face?"

Startled, I turn my head in the direction of the voice. Venom is watching me from the bathroom doorway, arms crossed on his massive chest. His boxer-only state makes my mouth dry. I lick my parched lips, eyes widening at his tented underwear. His hair is wet, and the scent of his body wash wafts over to me. The smirk he's sporting tells me he knows exactly why I'm smiling.

"Had a good night's sleep, that's all," I answer.

"That's all, huh?"

"Yup."

His lids lower, fingers curling around his crotch to adjust it. That's when I notice I'm only covered from the waist down, and my breasts are on display. I tug the blanket up, avoiding his gaze. Before I know what's happening, he stalks over, yanking the blanket completely away from my body. My hands instinctively fly to my breasts, shielding them. He perches on the edge of the bed, his stare intense. However, he doesn't try to move my hands.

"Tell me one thing you love about yourself."

"What?"

"Just one thing, Em. Tell me."

Still not meeting his eyes, I think about how to answer. Racking my brain, I can't come up with a single thing. I've been focused on my faults for so long, I don't even know if I have anything to be proud of.

"It's okay, darlin'. Not many people know how to answer."

"If I can't think of any, then I must not have any good qualities, right?"

ALANA SAPPHIRE

"You're beautiful, smart, and funny. That's three right there, and I can give you a ton more. You never need to be ashamed or hide from me, Emily. I fucking love your body. Every fucking inch of you. I know it's going to take more than a few days to undo the damage that fucker did to you, but I'll get you to own your sexiness if it's the last fucking thing I do. Trust and believe that."

My breathing accelerates as I watch him rise to his feet. Even being next to him, he strikes an imposing figure. Standing over me the way he is now? He's like a god surveying his creation from above. It's apt, because that's exactly what he intends to do—mold me into what he wants me to be. What he thinks I should be. What he believes I am deep down inside.

"Shower and meet me in the kitchen," he orders before walking away.

I don't know why, but I wait until he leaves the room before I climb out of the bed and head to the bathroom.

This room is heavenly! I think the word is quite an appropriate description, because everything is in gold and white. The tub is huge, able to fit two people easily. There are jet streams on the sides, which means it doubles as a Jacuzzi. I'd love a bath, but Venom is waiting for me. I spot closet doors, opening them to find neatly stacked towels, washcloths, and tissue. Grabbing a towel and washcloth, I shower and wash my hair, then stand before the huge mirror. Surprisingly, there are hair products neatly organized on his sink. I didn't expect that from my big bad biker.

The moment the thought is formed, I shake it out of my head. *What was that?* My *biker? There's no way that man* could *ever or* will *ever be mine.*

I eye his toothbrush with longing, wishing I had mine. Settling for the mouthwash, I gargle until I feel acceptable. I think my panties are useless and still on the kitchen floor, so I slip into my dress, run his comb through my hair, then set out to find him. The scent of pancakes lingers in the air, making my stomach growl in anger.

Venom smiles as I approach, setting a plate with a stack on the table, then motioning for me to sit. They look so good. There's nothing more I'd rather do than dig into them, but I can't.

58

"Um… toast and coffee would've been fine. I don't really eat breakfast."

"It's the most important meal of the day, darlin'. Besides, you'll need your energy for what I have planned for you."

He winks, turning back to the stove. My muscles clench.

"Really, I'm not hung—"

"Eat, Emily." He stops the lie before I can say it, his voice gruff and commanding.

He turns off the stove, adding another plate to the table before going to the fridge and returning with butter, syrup, and orange juice. After pouring us two glasses of the OJ, he drops a dollop of butter on my pancakes, then drowns them in syrup. Taking the chair opposite me, he glares at me until I pick up the fork and take a bite.

Holy shit. I don't remember pancakes being this good! Then again, it's been a while since I indulged in anything sweet. On my third bite, he finally starts eating.

"This is really good," I tell him.

"Thanks. I'll make you more tomorrow."

"Tomorrow?" My eyes snap to his.

"I told you last night was yours, babe. Tonight? All mine."

This muscle clenching is going to become a normal occurrence if I keep spending time with this man. The way he's looking at me alone is threatening to make me come. Shit. I swallow hard.

"What… What are you going to do?"

One corner of his lips curls up. "Everything."

My heart skips a beat. I turn back to my pancakes, wondering what "everything" entails. Before I know it, my plate is empty. I finish my orange juice, then watch as he clears the table.

"Thanks, Venom. I haven't had anyone but my mom cook for me since I left my parents' house. I forgot how much I like it."

He does that grumbling thing again, and I can't make out what he's saying. Reaching for my hand, he pulls me to my feet and into his arms. My breathing picks up, rivaled only by my rapid heartbeat. His fingers slide to the back of my neck, holding me in place as his lips descend to mine.

"What did he do to you?" he whispers, but I think it's more for him than me.

What did he do? He broke me. The worst part is, I let him do it.

Venom's lips crash into mine, relegating James to a distant memory. One hand lifts my dress for the other to disappear beneath it. When his fingers find my bare pussy, he moans.

"Fuck me. You're going to drive me crazy, Emily."

He lifts me into his arms like I weigh nothing at all, rushing us back to the bedroom. My dress ends up on the floor once more, Venom kneeling over my naked body. I fight the urge to hide, not because I don't want to, but because I want him to keep looking at me the way he is right now, like he can't believe I'm real.

"Touch your pussy. Show me how you make yourself come."

He wants me to do what?

I watch in awe as he pushes his boxers down to release his dick. He wraps a fist around the hardened length, stroking it while staring down at me. Fascination overtakes me, not just at the size of him but that he's jerking off. To a vision of *me*. Our eyes meet, his gray irises smoldering with heat.

"Now, Emily."

Tentatively, I reach down between my legs. I keep my eyes on his, because seeing how much he wants me is the only thing stopping me from shutting down and running away. When I spread my thighs, he moves closer, kneeling between them. I swipe a finger across my clit, gasping at the sensation.

"Play with your nipples."

My free hand palms a breast, and then I pinch the nipple between my thumb and the side of my index finger. Venom groans his appreciation. Feeling bolder, I work my clit with two fingers, sliding them inside me when his hand moves faster. I can tell how hard he's clenching his dick, stroking from root to tip. I imagine it's him inside me as I grind on my fingers while still kneading my breast. In and out, my fingers move, the evidence of my arousal dripping down my knuckles. As good as it feels, I think my visual stimuli are more pleasurable than anything I could do to myself. Venom's actions, his grunts, groans, and moans, the way he bites into his bottom lip as he watches me fuck myself—they're enough to send me speeding toward my orgasm.

Withdrawing my fingers from my soaked pussy, I circle my clit.

"Venom," I moan, feeling that sensation quickly approaching.

"Fuck, Emily. You're going to make me come so fucking hard."

He moves faster, his hand stroking at a dizzying speed. I can't hold on any longer. My muscles clench tightly, announcing the point of no return. As my body convulses, I cry out, eyes snapping shut at the force of my orgasm. Warm liquid bounces off my fingers, and I open my eyes to see Venom shooting cum toward my pussy.

"Fuck!" he growls, throwing his head back in ecstasy.

His hand slows down, his gaze returning to where he shot his load. I have no idea what ghost is possessing me right now, but I stroke myself, spreading his cum over my lips. He groans, eyes not leaving my fingers as I bring them up to my mouth, sucking our liquids from them. I've never done anything like this before, but I'm glad I did. The look on his face is reward enough.

"You're so fucking hot."

His words send a shiver down my spine. I've been called cute, pretty, and various other things, but never hot. I don't know why, but coming from him, I *want* to believe it.

Climbing off the bed, he tucks his dick back in his boxers and heads to the bathroom. It's not until he returns with a wet washcloth and begins to clean me up that I notice I didn't cover myself. I didn't even think about it.

"I'm gonna take you home, babe. Got something I need to take care of."

"Okay."

He tosses the washcloth in a nearby basket, then pulls on jeans, a T-shirt, and his cut. Grabbing socks, he jerks his head at me.

"I'll wait for you outside."

I pull on my dress, briefly lamenting the loss of my panties. I can't hop on Venom's bike with no underwear, so I search his drawers, borrowing a pair of stretchy boxer briefs. After running my fingers through my hair and grabbing my sweater, I meet him in the living room.

"Ready?" he asks.

"Yeah, but... have you, um...." I look away, embarrassment flushing my cheeks.

"What?"

"My panties. Have you seen them?"

"Maybe."

The mischievous tone of his voice makes me glance up at him. Sure enough, he's perched on the back of the couch, smirking at me.

"What's it going to take for you to tell me where?"

"A kiss."

Well, that doesn't sound too bad. I approach him with caution, gasping when he grabs my hand and tugs me between his legs.

"Maybe a suck on your nipple… or a taste of your pussy. I can't decide."

"You can't be serious!" My eyes widen in shock.

"Okay, tell you what. I'll settle for the kiss. The rest you can give me later."

Without giving me a chance to either agree or object, he tangles his hand in my hair and pulls my lips to his. What little fight I had drains from my body and I melt against him in zero point one second flat. His beard tickles, but the pleasure from his tongue against mine elicits a moan, not a giggle. His free hand massages my breast, pinching the nipple through my dress. In the recesses of my mind, the thought occurs to me that he's taking more than a kiss, but I can't find the wherewithal to care. I press my hips against him, searching for the hardness I crave. That's when he breaks away.

"Fuck, babe. You always this responsive?"

"Um…." My brain is still fuzzy from his kiss, and no words are coming to me.

"Don't answer that. If we don't leave now, I'm going to bend you over this couch and shove my dick so deep inside you, you'll feel me for a month."

I step back, jaws slack in horror, and yes, excitement. *Hell* yes.

With space between our bodies, my brain begins to function, so I try to change the subject.

"I hope you don't mind, but I borrowed a pair of your underwear."

"You're wearing my boxers, babe?" He raises a brow, a smile tugging at his lips.

"Yes" is my bashful answer.

"Let me see."

I quickly lift my dress, then drop it, moving past him.

"Fuck, woman. You're going to have me hard for the entire day thinking about you in my clothes. I don't know how I'm going to get through the ride to your place."

"Well." I turn to face him, intending to do something I haven't done in a really long time. "Hurry back from your errands so we can continue what we started."

His smile turns into a grin, liking what he heard.

There, I did it.

I flirted.

Venom

I pull up to Jeff's place, shutting off the bike and kicking down the stand. I wish he lived farther, so I could keep riding with Emily pressed to my back, her arms wrapped tightly around me.

She feels amazing.

Last night? I've never done anything like that for any woman before, but I know she needed it. She needs to know that I want her, that she's desirable. I know there's still some distance to go before she's comfortable with herself, but for the first time since I met her, there's hope. She's coming around slowly but surely.

As I walk her to the door, I take her hand in mine, giving her fingers a squeeze. She smiles over at me, a sight that could brighten the darkest night.

"I need you to do something for me, darlin'," I tell her.

"What?"

"I need those divorce papers, and for you to tell me where I can find your asshole ex."

Her eyes widen in surprise. "What are you going to do?"

"I'm going to make him sign them."

Surprise turns to fright.

"Venom, please. I know you mean well, but like you said, he's an asshole. I don't want to make things worse."

"They won't be, because he'll sign them and be the fuck out of your life."

"You're not going to hurt him, are you?"

"Do you want me to?"

"No, and not because he doesn't deserve it, but because he'd use it to make my life a living hell."

"If you don't want me to, I won't," I promise. I might not do what I really want to, but there's no way I'm leaving there without at least a few punches.

Emily gives me a skeptical gaze before disappearing into the house and returning with an A4 envelope. There's also a note with two addresses—work and home.

"Thanks, babe. I'll see you later."

Pulling her underwear from my pocket, I hand it to her with a grin. She snatches it, bunching it into a ball in her fist.

"Could you be any less discreet?" she hisses, eyes darting around, looking for witnesses.

Chuckling, I drop a kiss on her lips, then head back to my bike and over to the clubhouse. Backup isn't needed, but maybe having a few of my brothers with me would send the fucker a louder message.

The first one I encounter is Razor. Towering over my 6'4", he's a huge motherfucker who'd strike fear into any sane person. He's also my closest friend and the club's sergeant at arms, so he'd be perfect for this little excursion.

"Hey, Razor. Wanna go scare the shit out of a dumbass motherfucker?"

"Fuck yeah." He jumps to his feet, ready to go without an explanation.

"Where we going?" Crow asks, walking into the bar.

"Let's roll."

We run into Gage on our way out. "Where are you fuckers going?" he asks.

"Got something to handle, thought the guys might want to have some fun."

"Fuck." He shakes his head, then jerks it at Crow. "It's *that* serious?"

Crow is our cleanup guy. Let's just say he makes sure there are no literal skeletons in our closet.

"Nah. We good."

"Okay. Let's keep it that way. I could use some fucking peace and quiet around here."

"No problem, Prez."

We ride out, my brothers at my back, my mind focused on our destination. I can't wait to see who this asshole is. How in the world could he have a woman like Emily, only to mistreat and abuse her the way he did? She may never tell me all the things she endured, but the way she talks, walks, behaves... I know the hurt runs deep.

Twisting the throttle, the bike shoots forward. By the end of the day, I'll erase the fucker from her life. Physically at least. One way or the other.

After a two-hour ride, we pull up to the first address on the note. It's a garage with at least three guys, their heads buried under the hoods of various cars. We park alongside each other and I remove the envelope from my saddlebag, along with the small black pouch that I hid there while Emily was getting dressed. As we walk in, I stick the pouch in the back pocket of my jeans.

"What can I do for you boys?" the man closest to us asks.

"Looking for James."

"He's back there." He nods in the general direction. "Working on an Avenger."

I jerk my head at Razor, a signal for him to clear the place out. While he handles that, Crow and I make our way toward the target.

"You James?" I ask.

The man looks up from the engine, tugging a rag from his pocket and wiping his hands as he faces us.

"Yeah. Who wants to know?" His gaze flicks between me and Crow.

I observe him, trying to figure out what Emily ever saw in him. I figured he'd at least be good-looking since his personality is shit. He's okay, I guess, but his eyes are too close together, and his beard is scraggly like he can't grow a proper one. *Pussy*.

"I'm a friend of Emily's."

"Is that so?" He smirks. "What does that bitch want now?"

My fingers flex, wanting to knock his teeth down his throat. Instead, I smack his chest with the envelope. He instinctively raises his hand, holding it there.

ALANA SAPPHIRE

"You're gonna sign this and then we'll be on our way."

He pulls out the stack of papers, letting it slide back down when he sees what they are.

"I ain't signing shit until I get what's due to me," he sneers.

Razor joins us, nodding to confirm he's handled his end of things. That means the other men are gone, and they never saw us. James's eyes widen at the sight of the big man. I step closer to the fucker, bringing his attention back to me.

"Yeah, she told me you think you have some claim to what's *hers*. I don't know the whole story, but from what I've heard, you should be fucking happy the only thing she's doing is divorcing your filthy ass."

"Me? Filthy? She's the one slumming it with a bunch of dirty bikers."

I figured he wasn't too smart, but now I see he's a stupid motherfucker. I'm two seconds away from ending him.

"I know I broke her heart, but she's really stooped low. Then again, Emily has always been a frigid bitch—"

I plant my fist in his stomach, cutting off the rest of whatever he was going to say. He doubles over, grabbing where the punch landed.

"Call her a bitch again," I dare him. He finally begins to show some fear, eyes scanning the garage for help. "No one around to help you, Jimmy. Sign the fucking papers so I can get outta here."

"I'm not signing shit. You won't get away with this."

Pulling my riding gloves down, I motion to Razor and Crow, then reach for the pouch in my pocket. They grab James's arms, restraining him. His eyes follow the zipper on the pouch as I open it, going wide when two hypodermic needles are revealed.

"What's that?" he asks in a panic, trying to free himself.

"This—" I slowly remove the first needle. "—is the venom from an Inland Taipan." He begins to struggle, but the guys have him locked down. "Not the most dangerous snake in the world, but certainly the most venomous. It's said that the venom from one bite is enough to kill a hundred humans."

Razor whistles, impressed.

"Hear that?" Crow asks. "One bite, a hundred motherfuckers dead."

RENASCENCE

They both laugh, the taunting making James turn green. "You can't... you can't do this." He swallows hard, eyes glued to the needle.

"Sign the papers." I close the hood of the car he was working on, dropping the papers and the pen on top of it.

"My lawyer's gonna hear about this!"

"Answer's still no?" I ask, raising a brow. Without hesitation, I stick the needle in his neck. He cries out, thrashing from side to side. "The hyaluronidase enzyme in this venom increases the rate of absorption." I remove the other needle from my pouch and wave it at James. "Sign the papers and I'll give you the antivenom. Don't, and it makes no difference. You're out of Emily's life." I only gave him a microscopic dose, but it's enough to do some damage.

"Who the hell are you guys?" he demands.

"You're wasting time, Jimmy," I singsong. He has about fifteen minutes before symptoms start showing, but I don't intend to wait that long. I need to hurry this up. "You got about five minutes. It's gonna start off simple: sweating, headache, vomiting, blurred vision. Then"—I rub my palms together, a maniacal grin in place—"respiratory arrest. That means you stop breathing, by the way. The rest of your body follows, shutting down. You wanna die, Jimmy?"

He eyes the papers, and I dangle the needle once more.

"Fine! I'll sign the stupid papers!"

I nod to the guys and they release him. He scrambles toward the car, feverishly signing everywhere he should.

"There. Now just give me the antivenom. Please!"

I inspect the document, making sure everything is okay, then turn to James once more. "This is it, you understand? Don't call her, don't text, don't even think about her. I hear you're harassing her again, I'll bring more than a needle on my next visit. Got me?"

"Yes, yes!" He nods impatiently. "I can already feel it. Come on!"

"You don't breathe a word of this to anyone—cops, lawyers, your momma."

"Yes, yes," he repeats, hurrying me along.

67

I jam the needle into his arm, watching him slide to the floor in relief. I pack up my pouch, gather the documents, then leave the asshole behind.

"Hope I don't see you around, Jimmy."

In the parking lot, Razor turns to me. "Wanna tell us who Emily is?"

"She the one got your nuts in a vise?" Crow asks.

"Let's just go." I ignore their questions, only one thing on my mind—getting back to Emily.

I only need to make one stop first.

CHAPTER 7
Venom

I resist the urge to ride straight to Emily's, heading home instead for a shower since I've been on the road all day. However, I do call her the moment I get in.

"Hi," she answers, her voice low and sultry.

"Hey, darlin'."

"How'd it go?"

"We'll talk about it later. I'm coming to get you in about thirty minutes. That good?"

"Yeah. I'll be ready."

"Cool. See you in a bit."

Before my shower, I head to my room in the back to check on my babies. It's locked, constructed to keep them in. It would be a shame for them to get out, and then I get killed by my own pets or some shit. Well, not all of them are my pets. Some of them are for occasions like today, when I need to hurt. Or when I need to kill.

I'm no saint. The first man I killed is so far in my rearview mirror, I can't even see him. I've had to end lives for my country and my club. Most of the guys in the MC think of themselves as basically good guys who have to do bad shit occasionally. Me? The Army trained me, but I like the taste of blood. I thrived in the war. Maybe I was working off all the angst and anger from my childhood and teenage years, but I loved it. I have no regrets about the lives I've taken for the MC because there's a reason for those deaths. They died so I could live. So my brothers, my *family* could live.

I inspect the glass terrariums in the room, making sure everything's okay. I once told Raven I had twelve snakes and that's why my road name is Venom. If she saw this room, she'd freak. There are actually twenty, and I was given that name because it's my preferred method of killing.

Doom, the first snake I ever got, slithers to the front of the terrarium when I approach. I open it, carefully lifting him out. He's a ball python, and I've had him since he was a snakelet.

"Hey, boy. What you been up to?"

He curls around my arm, forked tongue darting out. I slide my fingers over his skin, loving the silky smooth feeling. I'm always at home in this room, and tonight's no different. How ironic is it that one of the places I feel safest is a room filled with snakes?

Chuckling, I make another sweep of the room.

Snakes get a bad rap. Even in the Bible, they're depicted as evil—the serpent who got Adam and Eve kicked out of the Garden. They're not dangerous, just driven by instinct. They're what humans would be like if we didn't let emotions cloud our judgement. Hell, their brains aren't even developed enough for emotions; they simply don't have the cerebral capacity. Sometimes I wish humans didn't either because feelings only get in the way. They live by their own rules. While they tolerate captivity and handling, they can't be trained. They bend to no will but their own. Just like me.

Contrary to popular belief, they're not cold-blooded. They can regulate their body temperature to suit their environment. Adaptability. Another thing I strive for. If I can't adapt, I get the fuck out; shed the situation or location like a snake sheds the outer layer of scales when he's outgrown it.

Just like I did my old life.

Standing in front of the display case in the corner, I admire my gun collection. This room is for *all* my snakes, including the Colt Python, Anaconda, Diamondback, and King Cobra. I'd love to carry around that Python with the eight-inch barrel, but my Beretta 92 FS is more discreet.

One final glance around, and then I place Doom back in his terrarium. After locking up, I hop in the shower, more than ready to see Emily. I wash my hair, putting it in a ponytail before getting a few good spritzes of cologne. After all, every woman likes a man who smells good. I pull on jeans and a T-shirt, strapping on my Beretta before covering it with my cut. Hurrying to my bike, I crank it up and make my way to Jeff's house.

I only have to wait a few seconds after knocking before Emily comes to the door. This time, she's dressed for the back of my bike—jeans, boots, a plain white tee, and a leather jacket. She bites into her bottom lip, blushing as her head falls forward. Her hair is in a loose ponytail at the nape of her neck, she's not wearing a stitch of makeup, and yet she's the most beautiful thing I've ever set eyes on.

Fuck.

Without a word, I take her hand and tug her close. The aroma of fresh peaches tickles my nostrils. When her face tips up toward mine, I waste no time in claiming her lips. Emily moans, immediately opening for me. Her arms curl around my neck, body leaning in to mine. I slide my hands around her waist and under her clothes, pressing my palms to the bare skin of her back. She shivers, a soft whimper coming from her.

Fuck, I can't wait to be inside her.

Hear her scream my name.

Tonight. That's definitely fucking happening tonight.

"Hi." She smiles up at me when I finally come up for air.

"Babe." It's all I can say, lightheaded from all the blood rushing to my dick. My voice is little more than a grumble, low and gruff.

Her green eyes widen, twinkling up at me like she's discovering a new wonder. After being with a dickhead like her ex, a man who shows her how much he wants her is probably alien to her. I allow her to lock up, then take her hand, leading her to my bike.

"Did you eat already?"

"Yeah."

"Did you *eat*, Em?"

"I had a Caesar salad," she replies as I strap on her helmet.

Shaking my head, I place her purse in my saddlebag, then hop on and wait until she climbs on behind me. With her arms securely around my waist, I head into town. She's more relaxed than she was last night, or even this morning, melting into me. I've had women on the back of my bike before, but none of them have incited the kinds of feelings Emily does. She feels *right*.

I pull up to Millie's, helping her off and removing her helmet.

"Are you getting something? I'll wait for you here," she says, a nervous lilt to her voice.

I place my hand at the small of her back and nudge her forward, opening the door to the diner so she can enter. Her gaze is skeptical, watching my every move after I point her to a booth and slide in opposite her.

71

"I told you, I already ate."

"Yeah, right."

Scoffing, she begins to slide out of her seat.

"Sit your ass right there or I swear I'll bend you over this table and tan it until you *can't* sit."

Her eyes widen, fear and horror staring back at me. She quickly scoots out of the booth, rushing for the door.

"Fuck."

When I catch up to her, I grab her elbow.

"Don't touch me!" she shrieks.

I block her path, forcing her to look at me. "What's wrong?"

"What's wrong? I endured a lot of things being with James, but he never put his hands on me. I'm not going to go from one type of abuse to another!"

"You think I'd hurt you?" I demand.

"You just said—"

"I said I was going to spank you."

"I'm not a naughty child you need to discipline. I'm a grown woman."

"I know, babe. A lot of women like that shit. Well, when *I* do it."

"You mean...?" The anger slowly drains from her, curiosity replacing it.

I step forward, trapping her against the wall of the building.

"I *mean* when I do it, you'll be begging for more."

Her head moves from side to side, her brain unable to reconcile what's happening to her body. She thinks she shouldn't want it, but she does. She wants everything I have to give her.

"Emily." I take her chin between my fingers, lifting her face to mine. "Trust and believe, I'd never hurt you, physically or otherwise. If I ever do, know it's not intentional."

"How can I trust you? I barely know you."

"You will." I stroke her cheek with my thumb. "Just give it time."

"Okay, but... no more talks of spankings."

"You got it, darlin'." *For now.*

We head back into the diner, quietly climbing into our booth.

"Hey, you two!" Sheila bounces over, grinning and winking at me.

72

RENASCENCE

"Hey, Sheila. Two burgers with fries. A raspberry lemonade for her, and a beer for me."

Emily waits until the waitress disappears before narrowing her eyes at me.

"Emily." I take her hand. "I told you this morning, I like you just the way you are. To me, your body is fucking perfection. However, being happy with yourself is more important than what people think of you. If you think you need to lose weight to be happy… if it's something you want to do for you, and not to please some asshole who didn't know what he had, then I'll help you."

"You will?"

"Of course. I'll come up with a meal plan and workout regimen for you that won't involve you starving yourself."

"I'm not starving myself. I eat." Her eyes drop to the table. "I just need to lose twenty pounds. That's it."

"That's it, huh? What are you, five seven, five eight?"

"Five eight."

"About one-fifty?" She cringes, trying to pull her hand from mine. "I need info if I'm going to help you, Em."

"One-sixty," she answers quietly.

I quickly do the math, her BMI telling me what I already know. "You know you're at a normal weight for someone your height, right?"

Her brows crease, nose crinkling in deep thought.

"I'm going to need some basic health info, and if you want to go ahead, I'll talk to one of the trainers at the gym and work something out for you."

She finally meets my stare, her fingers tightening around mine. "Thank you."

"No need, babe. I want you to be happy." Tears shimmer in her eyes, but she quickly wipes them away when Sheila shows up with our food. "You can thank me by cleaning your plate."

She eyes the juicy burger, licking her lips.

"Enjoy, sugar," Sheila throws over her shoulder as she walks away.

"I don't know…." Emily shakes her head, looking between me and her plate.

"Eat, Em. We'll talk more tomorrow."

73

Hesitantly, she picks it up and takes a bite. Her appreciative moan warms my body. I dig into mine, the taste just a little better as I watch her enjoy her meal. She doesn't speak, and I don't bother her. I finish, relishing in my view as I drink my beer. It's such a simple thing, yet it seems to be pumping life into her. She's been depriving herself for too long, and not only with food. Emily deserves everything that's good in this world, and I'll see to it that she gets it, or die trying.

After wiping her fingers with a napkin, she reaches for her drink, flashing me a dazzling smile.

"That was awesome! I don't think I remember burgers being this good."

"I'm glad. I need you full for the night I have planned for you."

She almost chokes on her lemonade.

"You mean with the... everything and... s-stuff?" she stutters.

"*Every... thing.*" I lean forward, grasping her knee under the table. She gasps, licking her lips. "Luckily you had a good night's sleep. You won't be getting any tonight."

"Jesus."

"No, darlin'. Even he can't save you from what's coming."

Her knee trembles in my hold. I wave down Sheila, motioning for her to bring the check. Once it's taken care of, I lead Emily out of the diner.

"I feel weird."

I halt outside the doors, turning to face her. "What's wrong?"

"Are we... on a date?"

"Why do you feel weird?" I ask, avoiding the question.

"Because it's been a long time since I've been on one. James and I were friends since high school and kinda transitioned to a relationship. He never really did the wine-and-dine thing."

I take both her hands in mine, my thumbs making circles in her palms. She lets out a shaky breath, pride surging through me at how much I affect her. "Is that what you want?"

"I don't know. I mean... I guess every woman does, but it's not like I'm going to force you into doing something you don't want to. I don't even know what's happening between us."

"Stop thinking about it, Em. Just enjoy whatever *this* is."

"Okay." She takes a deep breath, smiling up at me.

RENASCENCE

With one last squeeze of her fingers, we continue up the street and into Sweet Treats.

"Venom...."

She stops at the door, eyes darting around like a criminal surrounded by cops. I step behind her, gently pushing her forward. The girl behind the counter approaches with a seductive smile, attention centered on me.

"Hi, Venom." She bats her lashes. "What can I get you?"

Usually, I'd be all over her. It's a small town, and the pickings are slim when it comes to women. It's hard finding one I haven't fucked yet, and this chick falls in that category. However, there's only one pussy on my mind tonight. I look to Emily, who seems to be eyeing the cannoli to her right.

"I'll take four of those." I point to them, paying after she hands me the box with the pastries.

"Enjoy!"

"Thanks."

I take Emily's hand, leading her out of the shop and back to my bike. While I stow the pastries, she gets her helmet strapped on. I climb on and offer her my hand. She takes it, fitting behind me and plastering her body to my back. The way her soft curves align with my hard edges is giving me a stiff dick. Twisting the throttle prompts her to tighten her arms around my waist, and I take off toward my place. I can't wait to get her alone.

It's the longest motherfucking ride of my life.

What is it about Emily that gets my blood pumping? It's like I'm a goddamn teenager when I'm around her, only able to think about one thing—getting inside her. God, I hope tonight lives up to my expectations.

Back at the house, I try my best not to drag her straight to my bedroom. There are things we need to discuss first. I take her jacket, placing it and my cut on the back of the couch. Her eyes fly to my gun, so I remove the holster, laying it aside.

"Don't worry about that. It's for protection."

"From anything specific?"

"It's better to have it and not need it than need it and not have it, darlin'."

"That's true. It's a dangerous world."

"It is."

"Speaking of danger, I just realized I haven't seen your snake. Not that I want to, but where is it?" she asks, looking around the living room.

"I keep him locked up." Again, I don't correct her. There's no way I can tell her the real number because she would probably run far and fast. "Can't afford to have him escape."

"Good. Wouldn't want him strangling me in my sleep."

"Don't worry. You're safe."

"Am I?" Her voice is soft as she turns to face me. I know we're not talking about snakes anymore.

I stroke her cheek but otherwise keep some distance between us. "You are. I'm not James, Emily."

"I know. How'd it go today?" She raises both brows, twisting her hands.

I grab the envelope from the table, handing it to her. She slowly removes the papers, eyes going wide.

"He signed it?"

"Of course he did."

"Oh, Venom!" Two steps and she throws herself into my arms. "Thank you! God, I can't believe I'm finally going to be free!"

"You're welcome, darlin'."

"I'll call my lawyer first thing in the morning."

She pulls back, practically bouncing in place. Other than the look on her face each time I made her come, this is the happiest I've seen her.

"How did you do it?"

"Just made him see reason. He shouldn't be bothering you anymore."

"Made him see reason? That's not the James I know. What did you really do, Venom?" Her joy disappears and she raises a concerned brow.

"Okay, fine. I brought a couple of my brothers with me. I guess three huge bikers are a lot more persuasive than you. He's fine, I promise."

"Good. You have brothers? How many? If they all look like you, I can understand the fear you must have struck in him."

76

"I'm an only child." I shift in discomfort. My "family" is a bit of a sore spot for me. "My brothers are the men in my MC."

"Oh." She looks down at the papers again, her smile returning. "Oh, my God, you...." She shakes her head in disbelief. "Thank you."

"No worries."

"No. Not anymore."

As she stares at me with grateful eyes, I feel the need to give her more. Of what, I'm not quite sure. "I have something else I want to show you." With brows drawn together, I lead her to the bedroom I converted into an office. I also keep this one locked, so I open it, motioning for her to enter. Curiosity takes her to the wall with my certifications. First, she looks over my accounting degrees.

"Liam Alexander Hughes... that's you?" She glances back at me, clearly surprised.

"Yeah."

"I like it. I think 'Venom' suits you better, though." She winks.

"Me, too."

She moves on to my licenses, clearly impressed as she eyes the certificates. Finally, she approaches me, taking both my hands in hers.

"Why are you showing me this?"

I shrug. "Guess I wanted to show you that I know what I'm doing with your uncle's records."

"Thank you, but I know my uncle. I knew you had to be good for him to trust you."

I breathe an internal sigh of relief. I don't even know why I brought her in here, or why it makes me feel better now that she's privy to my education.

"Come on." I jerk my head toward the door and we head back to the living room. "Sit, Emily."

"What's up?" she asks as she perches on the couch.

"There are some things we need to talk about before we go any further."

"Okay." Her fingers tap a nervous beat on her knee.

Taking a deep breath, I turn so I'm facing her. "First of all, this is about me, not you. Got it?"

"Yeah...."

"You're probably not ready for anything serious anyways, but you need to know I'm not looking for that. At all. I've wanted you since the moment I saw you and you know that… but I don't do relationships."

"I understand… and you're right. I'm not looking for that either." Relief floods my body. "I just have one request."

"What's that?"

"While we're doing… whatever it is we're doing… there can't be anyone else."

Normally, this is where I'd tell a woman "thanks, but no thanks," and we part ways, but I understand where Emily's coming from. She's been cheated on, and even though she's not my woman, me fucking around would stir up old hurts. *Fuck James.*

"I can do that, darlin'."

"Good."

"So we're agreed on those terms?"

"Yeah. No wine and dine, no feelings. Just sex… with each other." She cracks a smile.

"You should also know that I love to have sex… a lot. And by a lot, I mean frequency."

Her eyes drop to her hands, folded in her lap. "Doesn't sound like a problem to me."

Fuck, I want to throw her over my shoulder right now, but there's more I need to get out.

"Since we'll be spending all our time in the bedroom—" I pause for dramatic effect, smirking at her sudden intake of breath. "—you need to know… in there? I'm in control."

"Oh. Okay." She blushes. "I kinda need to defer to you anyways. I'm not really experienced. Well, not like you."

"Darlin'." I squeeze her fingers. "I don't think you understand. I mean you do what I say, when I say, how I say."

Her eyes widen. "You mean… like that BDSM stuff?"

She seems so innocent, I can't help but laugh. Confused at my reaction, she watches until I calm down.

"Not entirely. There are some aspects of the lifestyle I enjoy, but you don't need to call me 'Sir' or 'Master' or anything like that. I don't want to control *you*, just your pleasure. Everything I'll do to you is for mutual gratification. If you don't like something, all you have to do is say so and I'll stop."

"Okay." She squirms a little in her seat, the action indicating she's getting excited.

Fuck. Yes. With how responsive she is? I can't wait to get my hands on her.

"I would like you to have an open mind, though, Emily. Some things I want to do to you may make you uncomfortable."

"Like what?"

"Things no one has ever done to you."

She snorts. "That's a mighty long list, buddy."

"Is that so?" I move closer to her, her words giving me an idea. Her breathing picks up, lids lowering, tongue sliding over her bottom lip.

"Yes." The word is nothing but a breathy whisper.

"I need you to make that list for me."

"Huh?" Her eyes meet mine, a secret thrill lurking behind the confusion.

"Make me a list, darlin'. I want you to write down everything you've ever wanted to do, or wanted done to you sexually, and we'll work on that list one item at a time."

"Are you serious?"

"Emily." I slide my palm to the back of her neck, pulling her face close to mine. "I'm going to make all your fantasies come true."

CHAPTER 8
Emily

Ho-ly shit.

This just keeps getting better. Or does it? I mean, I barely know him. How am I supposed to share my most intimate fantasies with him?

Because if anyone can make each one a reality, it's him.

"All—" I clear my throat to get rid of the squeak. "All of them?"

"Every single one, darlin'."

My gaze drops to his lips and I lick mine. I've been thinking about them all day, about how they felt on my skin last night, what they'll do to me tonight. What he *promised* to do. My mind's been going crazy with all the possibilities. Now that I'm one step closer to being free of James, a major weight has been lifted from my shoulders. And it's all because of him. Venom. I can't believe I've been depriving myself of him all this time.

"Want to start tonight?" he asks.

"Well, after what happened *last* night, we can definitely cross one thing off the list."

"Trust me, Emily, I can do much better than last night."

My gulp is audible as he leans in. He doesn't waste time, diving into a hard and demanding kiss. His mustache and beard drag against my skin, the soft hairs caressing in a blissful motion. Arms around my waist, he pulls me to him, making me straddle his lap. I return his kiss, palms to his cheeks, hips grinding on his growing erection. A groan sounds from deep in his throat, fingertips digging into my skin. Our tongues meet, sliding against each other in a wild and erotic dance. It reminds me what his tongue is capable of, and I moan at the thought of experiencing it again.

He powers to his feet, lips not leaving mine as he carries me to his bedroom. When my back hits the mattress, I slide my arms around his shoulders, palms pressing down to keep him close. God, he smells incredible. Like sex. Good sex... no, *great* sex. The kind I've never had before and for damn sure will have tonight. Venom is fully erect now, his hardness rubbing against my pulsating pussy.

Clothes. They need to go.

I tug at his shirt, and he finally breaks our kiss so I can remove it. When I reach for his jeans, he stops me, grabbing my wrists and pinning them above my head.

"You first, Emily."

My boots and socks are first to go. Next is my top, tossed somewhere in the corner. He gently trails his fingers down my neck, between my breasts, and down my stomach before yanking at the waistband of my jeans to undo the button. I gasp as it's dragged over my thighs and down my legs before being thrown in the corner opposite my shirt. Left in my bra and panties, I stare up at him, chest heaving.

"Stay there."

He leaves me lying diagonally on the bed, hands still above my head. The longer he's gone, the more aroused I become. All I can think about is what's going to happen when he returns. Jesus. It's been so long since I've had a man inside me.

I press my thighs together at the memory of Venom's dick.

I may not be able to walk tomorrow.

He returns with the box from Sweet Treats, removing a cannolo and placing the rest on the nightstand.

"Open up, Emily."

I do as I'm told because one, he's the boss in here, and two, those things look fucking delicious. He places it at my lips and I take a bite, closing my eyes and moaning. I was right.

Before I can swallow, my bra is pushed up, exposing my breasts to him. He flips the pastry over, spreading the ricotta filling over my nipples. My back arches, a garbled cry coming from me when he leans forward and licks it away.

"Tastes so much better like this," he says, offering me another bite.

This time he waits for me to finish before sucking the filling away from my other nipple. His lips move south, kissing my stomach, dipping his tongue into my navel. The brush of his beard adds another level to the sensations. I writhe beneath him, impatient for more. Standing over me, he dips his finger in the

81

sweet cream, placing it at my lips. I take the offering, swirling my tongue around his finger as my eyes meet his.

"Good girl. I'll let you put that mouth to use soon."

Yes, please.

He lets me have the last piece of the pastry, hooking his fingers into the waistband of my panties. Raising my hips, I allow him to remove them. Instead of adding it to one of the corners of his room, he shoves it in his pocket.

"Fuck, Emily."

For the first time tonight, I get the urge to hide. I reach down to cover myself but he restrains my hands once more, gripping and keeping them above my head. His free hand slides over my mound, then slowly down to glide over my now slippery lips.

"You shaved for me?"

"Well... you... you asked me to."

"Fuck," he murmurs, then immediately drags the elastic band out of his hair, falls to his knees, and buries his lips in my pussy.

"Venom!"

If I thought his beard against my stomach was something... holy hell. As his tongue swirls, his head follows its movements, the hair on his face prickling my clit, lips, mound, and inner thighs. I reach down, realizing why he freed his hair when I grab a handful. He sucks my clit into his mouth, both hands sliding up my stomach to palm my breasts. I moan and groan and whimper, hips rising off the bed. He pinches my nipples, twisting them in a way that should hurt but only amplifies my pleasure. While one hand continues to torment my nipple, the other joins his tongue in its assault on my pussy. Two fingers slip inside me, moving in and out while he licks at my clit. Those fingers curl, dragging against my top wall.

"Oh God!"

He moans, tongue flicking faster. The hand on my breast alternates between massaging my flesh and pinching my nipple. I grip the sheets above my head, back arching and pushing my breast into his palm. My breathing stops when he sucks on my clit. Resting on my elbows, I watch him. Our eyes meet, his stare unwavering. The hand on my breast moves to my face, fingers on my cheek, thumb in my mouth. I suck on it, wishing it was his dick instead. He must be reading my mind because he groans, actions becoming more vigorous. I won't be able to hold on much longer. I can't. My muscles clench, body tenses.

"That's it. Come for me, Emily."

I scream, body convulsing as I come. He wasn't lying. I didn't think it possible, but he outdid his performance from last night. When I open my eyes, he's removing his jeans.

His turn.

I watch him undress, admiring his physique. His arms and chest are covered in tattoos, the ink only adding to his appeal. I want to run my tongue over every inch of skin. As he reaches into the drawer on the nightstand, I sit up, trailing a finger around the metal running through his nipple.

"You like?" he asks.

I slide my gaze from head to toe. *Definitely.* "I do."

"I need you naked, Emily," he says with a smirk.

I remove my bra, licking my lips as he rolls on a condom. Climbing in next to me, he leans against the headboard and extends a hand. I take it, moving to sit astride him. His eyes lock on to my breasts. This time there's no desire to hide.

"I've wanted you like this since the day we met."

My breath catches.

Grabbing my ass, he guides me until I'm sliding down his hard dick. I grip his shoulders, moaning as I take every inch. *Christ. Yup, definitely won't be walking tomorrow.* I rise up, adjusting my position before slowly sinking down. Fully seated, I take a moment to get my bearings before I begin to move.

"Fuck, Emily. You feel amazing." Leaning forward, he pulls a nipple into his mouth. "Fucking amazing." His fingers dig into my hips as he moves to my other breast. "So fucking tight."

"Or you're just huge."

His knowing smirk assures me he's heard that countless times. However, as big as he is, he's the one who feels amazing. I slide my fingers into his hair, getting lost in the moment. Moving faster, I glide back and forth, gripping him with my muscles. He groans, hands moving back down to grab my ass in order to control my actions. Up and down I go, concluding that size definitely matters. The stretch, the depth... I'll never be a "motion of the ocean" girl again.

83

"Venom… oh, God… yes!"

"You like my dick, Emily?"

"Yes. Fuck yes!"

"Then ride it, Emily. Ride my fucking dick until you come all over it."

That's it.

My mouth falls open, nails dig into his shoulders, movements out of control as my orgasm approaches. Venom grabs the back of my neck, pulling me in for a feverish kiss. I tear my lips from his, gaze centered on his face as he grips my hips once more. His eyes are glued to where our hips meet, teeth sunk into his bottom lip, watching as he thrusts up into me. His hands move to my upper arms, pulling me forward and holding me immobilized as he positively devours my nipple. Lick, suck, release, repeat. All while he's driving up into me.

"Venom!"

My body stills and then shudders, the tremors intensifying with each additional thrust. He grunts, a long groan following as he jerks beneath me. I fall on his chest, utterly spent and out of breath.

"Fuck," he mumbles.

"I second that."

He chuckles, gently smacking my ass so I'll move. I hate the emptiness I feel when he slips out of me. I could have stayed like that for the rest of the night.

On his way to the bathroom, he grabs his boxers. *Aw, man. Please don't cover up that perfection!* His tight ass disappears, returning hidden beneath his underwear. I run to pee and clean up before joining him in bed once more.

"You know, I don't normally do the sleepover thing," he says in a low voice.

"Oh." I sit up, crushed as I begin looking for my clothes.

He grabs my hand, tugging me back into his arms.

"Normally. But if you think having you once was enough for tonight, you have another think coming, Miss Pierce."

"I do?"

"Just give me a few minutes."

***

Venom wasn't joking about not getting enough. It seems like when I finally doze off, a gentle touch pulls me from blissful sleep. My body has never been this... *utilized* in my entire life. Groaning, I force my eyes open to find him between my legs, kissing his way up my thighs.

"Venom...."

From the sound of my voice, I can't tell if I'm begging for more or for a reprieve. The pad of his thumb connects with my clit, and from the way it glides across the slick surface, I deduce it's more.

Definitely more.

I whimper when a finger pushes past my entrance. He freezes.

"Fuck, Emily. Please tell me you're not sore."

"More" is all I can get out, rocking my hips to get him to go deeper. The drawer on the nightstand rattles, and then comes the unmistakable crinkle of a condom wrapper. Without warning, he flips me onto my stomach, positioning me on my hands and knees. I cry out when he sinks inside me, not used to this position.

"Spread your legs wider, Emily. Put your face to the bed."

I follow his instructions and find it's much better. While I adjust, his hands work the flesh of my ass, massaging it. I moan, pushing back into him. A slap to one cheek surprises me, sending me forward before slamming backward. He hisses, smacking the other cheek. Grabbing my hips, he begins to move, pounding into me. The sound of skin slapping against skin fills the room, slowly being drowned out by my moaning and his labored breathing. He pulls out of me, and I whimper at the loss. Dragging me to the edge of the bed, he positions one foot on the floor, the other knee on the mattress. The bed is high enough that when he's inside me once more, I realize I'm perfectly aligned with his dick. I cry out, gripping the sheets when he begins to move again. A hand coils in my hair, tugging my head back. Another smack to my ass has me biting my lip, ashamed to ask for more. He's reading my body like a book. I don't need to say a word because he knows exactly what I need.

God, he was right. Why does it feel so good?

"You like it," he declares, as if daring me to admit I do.

"Yes. Yes, I like it!"

Slowing his movements, he leans forward, kissing along my spine as he grinds against me, sweat dripping from his skin to mine. The shiver that runs the length of my body makes me tremble beneath him. I match his movements, hips in sync with his. His hold on my hair tightens, pulling my head back so his free hand can wrap around my neck.

"Trust me, Emily."

"I do." *Like I'd say anything else right now.* I'm pretty sure if he asks me to sign over my soul, I'll ask where the pen is. That's how good this man is fucking me.

"Good girl," he growls in my ear.

The two words, the throaty way he said them, turn me into a molten mess. His grip on my neck gets tighter, another of those things that should hurt but doesn't. He sure knows how to ride the line between pleasure and pain. He squeezes and releases in intervals, never losing the rhythm of our hips. Releasing my neck and hair, he grabs my ass, dragging his fingers up my flesh. Mine curl into the sheets, needing to hang on to something for fear I'll float away on bliss. Venom's palms connect with my cheeks simultaneously, his pelvis slamming against me with each thrust.

"Venom!"

He grunts and is gone again, this time turning me over onto my back. My thighs are spread wide to accommodate him as he slides inside me once more. Leaning in, he sucks a nipple into his mouth, massaging the other breast.

"You fit me perfectly, Emily. Do you feel that?"

I moan at his words, my muscles clenching around him.

"Your pussy was designed for my dick."

"Oh, God…."

He grasps both breasts, pushing them together.

"Your tits were made for me to suck on."

I fist my hand in his hair as his mouth showers attention on my nipples. *Why does he say these things? Why does he want me as much as he seems to? Why—?*

"You're perfect, Emily."

Me? Perfect?

He begins to grind against me, circling his hips with every push in. I wrap my legs around his hips, my hand keeping his lips at my breast. Pleasure courses through my body, and not just from his actions. His words touched something deep inside me. Something buried under years of feeling unwanted and unattractive. Something Venom has now set free.

Desire.

"Venom, I'm coming!"

He moves faster, pounding into me as he grips my breasts for traction. My body explodes, shattering into a million pieces, which Venom puts back together when he climaxes, shouting my name. He collapses on top of me, slowly kissing his way up my neck.

"Holy fucking hell, woman. Where did you get this pussy from?"

I giggle, sleep already threatening to pull me under. "I don't know... God?"

Standing upright, he pulls out of me, sliding four fingers up and down my pussy before slipping two inside me.

"Shit. I'm not a religious man, but you just might make me a believer."

His fingers leave me, but before he walks away, he lifts me into his arms, laying my head on the pillow. I'm way too hot and sweaty for the blanket so I kick it away, and then I'm out like a light before my next breath.

***

The smell of coffee serves as my wake-up call. Stretching, I reach for my phone and check the time: 10:18 a.m. Damn. I've never slept this late before. Then again, Venom has me doing a lot of things I've never done.

Dragging my sore ass out of bed, I get my toothbrush and the extra pair of panties I stuck in my bag last night. Yes. Yes, I came prepared this time. After the night I had, I desperately need a shower before I even think of facing Venom. The tub is wet, so I know he's been up for a while. After a good scrub, washing my hair and brushing my teeth, I feel somewhat ready to face the day. My clothes are nowhere to be found, so I borrow another item of clothing—a T-shirt—before I gingerly head to the kitchen. He's standing at the stove, wearing nothing but a pair of gray sweatpants. My mouth begins to water, and it's not because of the pancakes he's making. No siree. The man has a body built for sin.

"Good morning," he says without looking my way.

"Good morning. What have you done with my clothes?"

"They're—" He glances in my direction, then does a double take. "Fuck."

His eyes roam over my body, the hunger I see in them definitely not for pancakes. Turning off the burners, he strides toward me with purpose, wrapping an arm around my waist and pulling me against him.

"You look good in my clothes, darlin'."

His lips possess mine the way I'm becoming accustomed to, leaving no doubt as to who's in charge. His tongue slips between my parted lips, free hand reaching under the shirt. He groans when his fingers connect with my underwear.

"Where the fuck did you get this?" he growls in irritation.

"Um…." I find a spot on his chest and focus on it. "I brought it with me last night."

Falling to his knees, he pulls it down my legs. I step out of it, watching him tuck the garment into his pocket.

"Sit. Breakfast is almost ready," he says, as if he didn't just steal my panties.

I take a chair, licking my lips as I watch him walk back to the stove. His muscles ripple and flex, reminding me of every deliriously awesome second of last night. I didn't even know my body was capable of so many orgasms in such a short period of time. I've never achieved more than two in my solo sessions. Damn it.

I take in the tattoo running down his right arm, a snake coiled around the length, the tail wrapped around his wrist. Its head rests on his upper arm, fangs bared, the word "Doom" above it. My muscles clench when he turns to face me and I see the outline of his dick snaking down his thigh. I swallow hard, my eyes glued to his crotch as he approaches with a stack of pancakes. Today it's joined by eggs, bacon, and toast.

"Eat up, babe."

I snap out of my haze, turning my attention to breakfast. This time I don't argue. I'm *starving*. I guess he was right about needing a full stomach to handle a night with him. He pours me a glass of juice, dropping down in a chair next to me.

"You're not eating?"

"I've been up for a while, so I already had breakfast. I'm looking to eat something else."

"What?" I turn to him with a mouthful of food.

His eyes find mine, holding my stare as he licks his lips.

"You."

I swallow. Hard. I hadn't even finished chewing.

"M-me?" I stutter through a cough.

"I'm dying for another taste, darlin'." His hand glides up my leg, my wanton thighs parting to give him access to what he seeks. I close my eyes, moaning as his finger slides between my lips. When he gets to my entrance, I flinch.

"Sore?" he asks, stroking my inner thigh.

"A little."

"I figured. My tongue will just have to suffice for now."

A shiver runs down my spine.

He leans in, nipping my earlobe before whispering, "But not until you eat every last bite."

And I do. I clean my plate like a good girl, practically bouncing in my seat as he does the dishes, waiting for my treat. When he begins to stalk back to me, I jump to my feet, ready to sprint to the bedroom. However, he grabs my waist, lifting me and planting my ass on the table.

"Wait... what—?"

He pushes my thighs apart, licking his lips as he lowers his head.

"Time for my kind of breakfast."

CHAPTER 9
Venom

I ride into the clubhouse in a fucking fantastic mood. Being with Emily last night surpassed anything I ever imagined. The woman is sexual crack. Her body is perfection, and I could get lost in it for days with no wish to be found or make my way out. Just thinking about the way she submits to me gets me hard. Fucking hell. I can't wait to see her tonight.

We have church today, so the guys are gathered in the bar, hanging out before we head into the chapel. I make a beeline for the couch where most of them are gathered.

"What's up, my *brothas*?" I throw out to everyone, dropping down on the couch.

"What the fuck are you so happy about?" Motor asks, his shaggy hair shaking with the movement of his head.

"I bet I know," Razor says to my left, winking.

"Me, too," Crow chimes in.

"It seems Miss Emily showed her gratitude for them papers, huh?" Razor nudges my arm.

Einstein stares at me with that goddamn "I told you so" smirk. I can't even find the energy to care. They can tease me all they want; nothing can get me down today.

Reaching into the inner pocket of my cut, I pull out a cigar and lighter, lighting up without a word.

"Who's Emily?" Gage asks.

"The reason we rode to Atlanta yesterday to shake down some asshole," Razor answers.

My prez's brows draw together as he scrutinizes me. "Shit. You got the look, brother."

Blowing a puff of smoke in the air, I ask, "What look?"

"The 'I got some good pussy' look. Welcome to the club, motherfucker!"

They all laugh while I sit back savoring my cigar, the sound drawing everyone else close. "Good pussy" is an understatement. Emily has that diamond-coated, voodoo pussy that would make a lesser man lose his mind. I don't know what the fuck is wrong with James, but his loss is my gain.

And I hit the motherfucking jackpot.

"Come on, man. What was it like?" Razor asks.

I take another puff of my cigar, making them wait. The men who are seated lean forward, impatient for my answer.

"Look, all I'm going to say is that I exploded like a fucking block of C4."

Laughter booms around the room, punctuated by the odd word of encouragement. I meet Einstein's eyes, daring him to say something. Using his middle finger to push his black-rimmed glasses up his nose, he accepts the challenge.

"When are we going to meet her?"

"You're not."

"Why the fuck not?" Gage asks.

"It's not that kind of deal."

"Fuck that shit. Bring her to the Christmas party. The girls will love having another woman around."

"She's not my woman. I bring her around here and your old ladies"—I motion to Gage and Einstein—"will put ideas in her head. We're good."

"What kind of ideas?" Einstein raises a brow.

"Are you kidding me?" I give my full attention to the prez. "You're married, and your woman is pregnant with *twins*. And you." I point to Einstein. "Your woman is knocked up, too, and I'm pretty sure you bought the ring already. Like I said, we're good."

"What? You afraid monogamy will rub off on you?"

The men chuckle at Gage's question.

"Fuck yeah. Keep that shit to yourselves, far away from me and Emily."

"Whatever. We'll see, Mr. C4," he says, rising to his feet. "Let's get church over with so I can get home to my *wife*. My pregnant wife who I have monogamous sex with every day."

I shake my head, following my laughing brothers into the chapel. There's no way I'll hear the end of this anytime soon. Too bad I don't care.

91

I take my chair, scanning the room. Gage sits at the head of the table, Einstein to his left, Razor to his right and my left. Rico, our road captain, is to my right, and Tek, our secretary, to his. Chopper sits at the opposite end, across from his son. Crow, Motor, Charger, and Booker occupy the other side of the table.

"Okay, fuckers." Gage taps the table. "Let's get this show on the road. Tek, anything outstanding?"

"No, boss. Just a reminder that dues will be collected today."

"Got it. Everyone see Venom before you leave." After words of agreement, he continues. "He'll also have quarterly dividends from the Kitty and Patch, along with the payout from the Snakes. Merry Christmas, motherfuckers."

The men break out into cheers and hoots, beating the table. It will be a merry Christmas, indeed. The Pretty Kitty is our top legit business, and it's done very well this year, especially this quarter. Patch is the only auto parts store around for miles, so it does okay, too. However, most of our money is made under the table, providing security for contraband. No matter what it is—guns, drugs, even people—we'll get it where it needs to go safely. The Black Snakes are a MC from Mississippi, who partner with our Jacksonville charter to run pain meds. Gage brokered a deal after a run-in with them last year, and we get a kickback as part of their penalty.

Every man at this table earns outside of the club. Gage insists on it. Even without club earnings, we're all good. For instance, Gage owns a couple other businesses, Einstein is a doctor, and Razor owns a gun store and shooting range. I have the gym and my accounting. With tax season coming up, I'll be pretty busy.

"Okay, okay." Prez raises both hands, trying to quiet the men down. "I have something I want to put on the table." Everyone gives him their undivided attention, some sitting forward. "We don't have to vote on it tonight, but give it some thought." Leaning back in his chair, he takes a deep breath. "I'm thinking we should give up the protection runs."

His statement is met with mumbles of unease. The men love the money that comes from those runs. The thing is, Gage is the brains behind them. If he wants out, then that's basically the end of it. He's the reason the clients come to us.

RENASCENCE

"How you plannin' on filling that gap, son?" Chopper asks.

"I want to invest in another business. A legit one."

"Like what?"

"I don't know yet. I got my wife, plus two kids on the way, Pop. I need to find something that won't keep me away for days on end and put my life in danger."

"I hear you," Einstein agrees.

"Nothing we do will bring in the kind of money the runs do, but it will be safer, and will keep us off police radar... keep us out of trouble."

"You hanging up the robe and scythe?" Razor asks.

Gage earned the road name "Reaper." He isn't like me, though; he may be skilled at killing, but he doesn't enjoy it. Now that he has his family, I can see why he would want to take us legit.

"I'd love to, brother, but it's a club decision. I'll go with the vote."

"Shit, man." I shake my head. "Don't put that on us. Like we'd vote money over family."

Every man at the table agrees with me, and this is why I would kill and die for each one. We may be criminals, but we know what's important.

"Okay, it's on the table. We give up the protection runs. Second?"

"I second," Einstein backs up Gage.

It ends up being a unanimous vote, as I expected.

"Thank you," Prez says, looking around the table. "I promise I'll figure this shit out."

"We know, boss." Tek gives him a chin lift, grinning as he adds, "That's why you're the boss."

"About that...."

Prez takes another deep breath, glancing at Einstein, who gives him a nod of encouragement. Those two are thick as thieves, so it makes sense they've already discussed the matter. A hush falls over the table, everyone hoping he's not about to say what we think he's going to say. This club probably wouldn't function without him. Einstein doesn't want the chair, and neither does anyone else.

"Back in September when Krueger showed up at my wedding party? He and I had a little chat."

Shit. Krueger is our national president. My ears perk up, anxious to hear what's next.

"He told me he's retiring next year."

"Shit," Chopper mumbles. He's usually quiet in our meetings, and now he's spoken twice already. "He's tapping you to take over, isn't he?"

"He said he likes what I've done with our charter, mentioned he'd endorse me in the election."

"With his endorsement, it means the position is yours," Einstein says what everyone is thinking.

"You don't just say 'thanks, but no thanks' to Krueger." Chopper gives his son a solemn stare.

"I know. Hence the dilemma."

Dilemma indeed. A man like Krueger wouldn't understand Gage's need to put his family first. He's MC through and through, putting the club above everything else.

"You thought about it?" Razor asks.

"Some. On one hand, I could do some good for the entire organization. On the other, it puts me in more danger and gives me less time with my family. You can all guess which way I'm leaning."

"Which means we also need to find another candidate for Krueger to back," Einstein says.

"You're just a regular shit stirrer tonight, aren't you?" I chuckle. "Don't worry, Prez. We got your back."

"Thanks, brother. I appreciate it."

To lighten the mood, I head to the safe and start distributing payouts. It works, the men's attention now on their envelopes.

"Anybody got anything to put to the table?" Prez asks.

When everyone replies with a no, he adjourns the meeting. I move to the door, collecting dues as the men mill out of the chapel. I record it all, stash it in the safe, then join my brothers in the bar. The Hounds have arrived and are busy serving up drinks and snacks with the prospect. He's young, but he seems to be fitting in so far. If he sticks with it, he might make a good Dealer.

"Hey, Venom."

I turn to find Marisol smiling up at me. She hands me a beer, threading her fingers through mine and tugging me toward the couch. I allow her to sit in my lap the way she's done a hundred times, but tonight it feels weird.

Wrong.

I'm single so it shouldn't matter, but for some reason it does.

"I miss you," she whispers in my ear, pushing her tits in my face. "Want me to come to your room tonight?"

"Sorry, dollface. I got plans."

"Oh."

The disappointment is evident in her voice. These women may be Hounds, but they're more than available pussy. I don't want her to feel shitty.

"Some other time."

"Okay."

She shuffles off my lap, heading back to the bar. The clubhouse door bangs against the wall and Millie comes bursting in, a flash of red hair, leather pants, and low-cut top. The woman has to be in her fifties but acts half her age. I'm not ashamed to admit I hit that. I'm not the only Dealer either. She owns the diner in town, and is Nita's best friend, so she's a club friend. She's been hanging out with Chopper lately, and it looks like Gage and Ellen may be getting a stepmom soon. That would make Nita happy. She's Chopper's sister, and practically raised his kids after their mother died.

My phone vibrates in my pocket, and I pull it out to find a text from Emily.

Emily: Don't think I can make it to the gym tonight.

Venom: You ok?

Emily: Too sore, Mr. Huge Dick.

Even though I'm concerned, I type out my reply with a grin.

Venom: Take a warm bath with Epsom salts. Baking soda if you don't have any.

Emily: Well, look who's versed in remedies for vaginal soreness.

Venom: Why do you think I took your panties this morning? If you're wearing any, lose 'em. Wear some sweat pants. Use coconut oil too if you have that.

95

Emily: Ok, Doctor.
Venom: Good. I'll pick you up around 9.
Emily: See earlier text.
Venom: Just be ready.
Emily: Fine. See you then.

"Is that your future old lady?" a grinning Razor taunts as he joins me.

"Fuck off."

"Don't fight it, brother. I figured you might stick out this single life with me, but another one bites the dust."

Tek chuckles without looking up from his screen.

"What the fuck is funny, goth boy? When's the last time you even got laid?"

"Don't worry about me. I have no issues in that department."

"Cybersex doesn't count."

"Go ahead, make fun of me. We'll see how funny it is next time you need my help."

The boy's a fucking genius when it comes to that computer shit. I don't know what we'd do without him. Sometimes I think he doesn't even sleep, always trying to hack into something.

"Maybe it's time I helped you. The Hounds not doing it for you? What kind of women do you like?"

"I don't need you to set me up, Venom."

"Okay, man. You change your mind, just let me know."

"I won't."

Without another word, he picks up his laptop and marches off toward the rooms. Did I hit a nerve? I'm a bit of a troublemaker around here and I mess with these guys all the time, including Tek. No one's been offended so far. We're not exactly a sensitive bunch.

"Why don't you leave the kid alone?" Razor asks. "You're the expert now because you got an old lady?"

"She's *not* my old lady."

"You seeing her tonight?"

"Yeah. So?"

"When was the last time you spent two consecutive nights with a woman? Other than a Hound?"

"We have an agreement. That's it."

96

"If you say so." He chuckles.

"Fuck it, I'm outta here. Gonna head to the gym."

"Say hi to Emily for me."

Yeah. And fuck you.

Emily

I hate to admit it, but he was right.

The bath and the coconut oil helped tremendously. I'm currently lounging in front of the TV in my most comfortable sweats, minus my underwear. Uncle Jeff joins me, reclining in his favorite chair.

"Going out tonight, sweetheart?"

"In a bit. Why, do you need me?"

"No, no. I'm glad you're getting out. How are things going with Venom?"

I clear my throat, sitting upright at his question. What am I supposed to tell him? That I made a sex-only deal with one of his customers?

"Okay. Nothing serious."

"I see. I suppose you're not ready to jump into another relationship."

"Nope."

"I think someone like Venom is what you need right now. Something to get your mind off that idiot you married." He grunts his disapproval of my ex.

"Well, thanks to Venom, I won't be married to him much longer."

"Those boys have always been quite resourceful. I'm just glad you'll finally be rid of him. Don't know what you saw in him in the first place."

"Yeah. Honestly, I don't even remember what it was. Guess it's buried under all the shit I've had to put up with over the years."

"You're a gem, Emily. You deserve the best. Remember that when the next one comes along."

"Uncle Jeff...."

Hopping out of my seat, I hurry the couple steps to him and throw my arms around him. He can be a hard-ass sometimes, but

I've never known him as anything but a loving uncle. One who says the sweetest things when I need to hear them. He seemed to be as happy as I was this morning when I showed him the signed divorce papers. In fact, so were my parents when I told them.

"Careful now." He chuckles, stroking my arm.

"Thank you."

"Just speaking the truth, sweetheart."

"Love you, Uncle Jeff."

"Love you, too. Now, don't you have to get ready for your date?"

Date. I almost snicker. What Venom and I are doing is nothing close to dating. I kiss his cheek, then head to my room. As I shower, I think about "the list." I've been thinking about it all day. I mean, what do I put on it? After the last two nights, I'd be perfectly happy if he continued doing his thing. My only fantasy these last couple of years was to be rid of James, and now I am.

And Venom made that happen.

He's already fulfilled my number one fantasy, he just doesn't know it. Maybe I should put some crazy stuff on it to see how he'll react—like a foursome with two of his biker friends. I giggle at the thought. Then again, he might be into that type of thing. Maybe I shouldn't poke the beast.

I'll just let the beast poke me.

I laugh at my own joke as I dry off. I can't tell the last time I felt this happy, this... *free*. It's as if I'm floating on a cloud, everything that was toxic gone from my life. *Venom, my antivenom. Who'd have thought he'd be the one to release me?*

Eager to see him, I apply more coconut oil to my lady bits and pull on a fresh pair of leggings with a long-sleeved shirt. The nights are getting chilly and the cold hits even harder on the back of Venom's bike. After securing my hair in a ponytail, I grab a pair of socks and my sneakers, then head back to the living room.

"That's what you're wearing on your date?" Uncle Jeff asks, brows drawing together in disappointment.

"It's not a date. We're just gonna hang out."

"You should wear something pretty, do up your hair and makeup."

"Uncle, he saw me at my sweaty and stinky worst at the gym and didn't care. I don't think leggings and sneakers are going to be a deal breaker." I chuckle, sniff-checking my pits to mess with him. "I even used deodorant."

"Emily." He cocks his head to the side, giving me that fatherly scowl.

The doorbell rings and I toss Uncle Jeff a grin. "Too late to change now. See you later!"

I snatch up my purse and jacket, trotting to the door. A bearded smile is waiting for me when I throw the door open. I can't get over how gorgeous he is. Tonight, there's a gray hoodie under his cut, with the same grim reaper printed on the front. His hair is down and it's wet. That and the scents rolling off him tell me he's freshly showered and wearing another cologne that smells like it was made for him. Or better yet, by him, like his body manufactures it and it's being secreted from his pores.

"Hey, darlin'. You ready?"

"Yeah." He helps me into my jacket, then leads me to a shiny black Jeep Wrangler. "Where's the bike?"

"Figured you'd be more comfortable in this. Warmer, too."

"Thanks. Does it feel weird, not being on the bike?"

"It does. Cages aren't my thing, but at least with this I can lose the top and the doors."

"Cages?"

"Cars."

"Oh."

He gives me a hand up, and as I sink into the warm leather seat, he climbs in next to me. When he starts it up, country music floats from the speakers.

"Didn't figure you for a country fan."

"Don't let the leather fool you, Em. At heart, I'm just a good ol' country boy."

"Yeah. If you say so." I roll my eyes, returning his smile.

"I do. How was your day, darlin'?"

"Good. I was pretty much a couch potato today. Not much movement." He chuckles, and I turn in my seat to smack him. "I'm glad that amuses you."

"Don't get me wrong, Em. I feel bad that you're experiencing all this pain and discomfort, but it's also fucking amazing that it's because of me."

"Yeah? Why is that?"

"Because every time you moved, you thought of me."

He's right, of course. Everything I feel is a reminder that he was inside me last night. "Yeah, well, I hope you're not looking for a repeat tonight."

"Trust and believe, Emily. I know a million ways to make you come without even touching your pussy."

That very traitorous body part jumps. I shift in my seat, crossing my legs. Maybe I should put some real thought into that list.

"What about my list?" I ask, hating how timid my voice sounds.

"Is it ready?"

"I haven't written it down."

"You don't need to. I don't want you to give me the entire thing. We'll work through it one at a time. It's up to you how fast or slow we move."

"Oh. Okay."

Back at his place, he turns on the TV, a basketball game playing as we climb into his huge bed. Surprisingly, he extends his arm, letting me lay my head on his chest. This doesn't seem like anything that would be covered in our agreement, but I'm not complaining. In fact, I wish we could do this every night.

"How do you feel?"

"Fine. Good."

I know what he's really asking. I may still be suffering from the effects of last night, but something tells me if he touched me, I'd be more than willing.

"Hungry?"

"No. Why are you always trying to feed me?"

"Why shouldn't I? I'm the one fucking you now. I need to make sure you're fed and hydrated."

"I see."

"Emily, this is about more than just sex. As long as you're with me, you can be damn sure you'll be taken care of. Whatever you need, I got you."

My throat locks up. After all our years of marriage, I never once heard James utter those words. He was all about what I was bringing to the table.

RENASCENCE

"I don't need you to take care of me," I whisper the lie. This is not about money. What I need is a man who can recognize and appreciate an independent woman, yet still make her feel like a princess. A man who will be her strength when she can't find hers. A man who recommends coconut oil for a vagina he's made sore; a man who holds that woman in his arms and makes sure she's eaten.

"I know, but *I* need to. Making sure you're okay and that you have everything you need is my duty. Even something as small as knowing you've eaten. I'm going to spoil you, Emily. Get used to it."

"I'm fine," I tell him, fighting the urge to swoon. "Uncle Jeff made steaks because he thought I was sick. I'm quite full."

"Good. Now come here."

Without him telling me, I know what he wants. I straddle him, settling my hands on his shoulders. Our eyes meet, electricity crackling between us that sends a shiver down my spine. His palms slide up my thighs to my hips, positioning me the way he wants—sitting directly on his dick. He's not hard, but I don't think he'll stay that way for long.

"You like this, don't you? Women on top?"

"I like *you* on top of me, Emily."

My breathing accelerates, words coming out on a whisper. "You do?"

"I get to see you." His gaze moves down my body and slowly back up before his eyes meet mine again. "All of you. Every. Gorgeous. Inch."

"Venom...."

"Let me see you, Em."

Gripping the hem of my shirt, I pull it up and off, not breaking our stare. He reaches up, gently sliding the straps of my bra down my shoulders before unhooking it in the back. I allow him to remove it, watching his eyes drop to my breasts. His tongue darts out, slowly curling over his bottom lip. It disappears, teeth sinking into his lip. He's looking at me as if he wants to devour me.

And I want to do the same.

"My list," I blurt out. "I know what's next."

"What is it, darlin'?"

101

"You. I want… I want to taste you."

Grabbing my ass, he swings his feet over the side of the bed and stands, taking me with him. He sets me down, immediately losing his hoodie and the shirt beneath it. My heart hammers against my rib cage when he reaches for his belt and jeans. I want to do something, anything, but I'm stuck to the spot, watching flawlessness being slowly revealed. I have no idea why he wants me, someone on the opposite end of the perfection spectrum, but he does. And I intend to take full advantage.

I lay my palms on his pecs, lightly trailing them down. Getting the chance to finally be up close and personal, I take in his tattoos. The logo from the back of his cut is in the middle of his chest, the words "Army Strong" printed over his heart in the famous font. Across his stomach are more words: "It is more fun to reign in Hell than to serve in Heaven." My fingertips brush his nipples, making his head fall back with a groan. I capitalize on that, stepping forward to use my tongue instead. I lick at both nipples, gently pulling on the rings with my teeth.

"Emily…."

He tugs on my hair tie, releasing my hair from its confines so it tumbles down my back. I don't stop, moving down and sliding my tongue up his abs. Before I get to my knees, he grabs my wrist and pulls me up.

"We do this my way, Emily."

He kneels before me instead, relieving me of my leggings. When he finds I'm not wearing panties, he grunts his approval. On his way back up, his fingers glide over my skin—my calves, the backs of my knees, my inner thighs—before ghosting over my mound. My entire body shivers, eyes close, a moan coming from somewhere deep inside me. He continues up my sides, then to my breasts, pinching both nipples. My eyes snap open, meeting his.

"Your body is a playground, Emily. Time to have some fun."

He leaves me and I instinctively turn to watch him. A black metal box is retrieved from his closet and placed at the foot of the bed. The TV is switched off.

"I made a stop on my way back from Atlanta yesterday," he states, unlocking the box and flipping the lid open. "Got us a few toys."

I take a peek, noting how everything is neatly compartmentalized. I've used toys before, but I'm certain those experiences will pale in comparison to this one. Venom removes three items, freeing them of their wrapping. I squirm, my body unable to contain the sensations running through it as he moves toward me.

"Don't worry. They're all new and I already cleaned them." I nod, my voice missing in action. "Are you wet, Emily?" Another nod. I've *been* wet. "Check for me. I want to see."

I slide my fingers between my lips, swallowing hard as I nod again to confirm I am. He takes my hand, inspecting my fingers before placing them at my lips. Without prompting, I take my wet digits into my mouth, sucking my juices from them. He removes them, stare hungry as he focuses on my lips. That's when I realize he hasn't kissed me yet. Leaning in, he presses his lips to mine, tongue sliding between them.

"Mmm," he moans. "My two favorite flavors."

My knees wobble.

Kneeling before me once more, he helps me with the first toy—a purple butterfly stimulator. I step into the straps, impatiently waiting for him to fit it in place.

"How did you know purple is my favorite color?"

"I didn't." He grins up at me. "But thanks for the info."

He rises and I notice a shift in his demeanor. He seems taller, more... compelling. Dominant. Hotter. The next toy appears, quickly and efficiently affixed to my nipples.

"How do they feel?" he asks, pulling gently on the chain connecting them.

"Okay."

He tightens them.

I whimper as a bolt of sensation races down my stomach, zapping my clit. *Holy fuck*! While I fight to contain the feelings flowing through me, he moves around me, fingers gliding on my stomach, to my side, and finally down my spine. Tremors rock my body.

"Hair." Gathering my hair in a fist, I lift it out of his way so he can clasp a collar around my neck. The jangle of a chain sounds before he says, "Hands."

103

I drop them to my sides, my thoughts racing when he cuffs one, then the other behind my back. A slight tug reveals that the cuffs are attached to each other, the chain linking them to the collar. *Ooh, lawd. What have I gotten myself into?* I have no idea but I'm itching to find out.

Venom stands before me once more, meeting my eyes. The sun itself couldn't produce the heat in his gaze. Fascinated, I stare into the flames, knowing they will consume me but not caring. I savor them as they lick at my body, trying to inch closer. The man is a raging wildfire I'd gladly dive head-first into.

"On your knees, Emily."

CHAPTER 10
Emily

I drop to the plush carpet, wondering how many other women have been in this spot. Is that why it's so soft? For our comfort? My brain stops working when he kicks off his jeans and boxers. He grabs his now-hard dick, enclosing it in a tight fist. I shift my position, my pussy beginning to thrum, nipples starting to ache. It's a good ache, if there is such a thing. Venom slides his free hand into my hair, pushing my head back so I'm looking up at his face.

"Eyes up here, Emily." I nod, licking my lips because his tip is mere inches from my mouth. "Now… be a good girl and open up."

Because I *am* a good girl, I follow his instruction, parting my lips wide enough for him to fit. Instead of giving me what I want, he trails the tip of his dick on my bottom lip before moving to the top. To hurry things along, I slide my tongue along the underside. He hisses but pulls away.

"This is my show, Emily." *Shit. That sounded like a reprimand.* "You don't follow my rules, you don't come."

His voice is rough and authoritative, but in no way scary. It commands respect.

Subservience.

"Sorry."

I shift my position, then open my mouth again, eyes trained on his as he guides himself inside. Slowly, with immense patience, he taps the back of my throat.

"I'm going to fuck your mouth, Emily. Just relax and go with it. You can suck, you can lick, but don't fight me for control. Nod if you want to continue."

I nod. Of course I nod. After all, this is what I asked for… what I want. Venom grips both sides of my head, holding it in place as he begins to move. He's gentle at first, giving me the freedom to lick, to taste. Fuck me if Venom's dick isn't one of the best things to hit my tongue. If I'm his favorite flavor, then he's definitely mine.

105

I watch his face, and I can tell he's having a hard time keeping himself in check.

He likes it!

James drummed it into my head that I wasn't good at this, so I stopped. Plus, he wasn't reciprocating, so I figured I might as well accept that oral wasn't going to be a part of our sex life. *Fuck James. He can kiss my fat ass.*

I suck on Venom's dick like a lollipop until he begins to moan. He reaches over to the bed, picking up a narrow, silver object. That's when my butterfly starts to vibrate. It startles me, sending my head forward and jamming Venom's dick to the back of my throat once more.

"Fuck!" he growls.

His movements change, and so does the speed on my stimulator. That fucking my mouth thing? Definitely happening now. I moan and whimper, my hips rocking back and forth even as I try to remain upright. I want to grab his powerful thighs, sink my nails into his flesh so he can know what he's doing to me. I want to inflict pain because everything he's doing to my body hurts so good. But the look in his eyes holds me captive. Even if I weren't cuffed, my hands would have stayed put. Whatever he's doing to me, he's feeling the effects, too. Having me like this is what he gets off on, so I keep my head up and let him use me for his pleasure.

Our pleasure.

He was right. Submitting to him was the best decision I ever made. And now that decision is leading me toward an extinction-level orgasm. I moan around him, which seems to multiply his pleasure. Just as my orgasm hits, he leans in and tugs at the chain on my nipple clamps, ripping them off.

Ho-ly shit!

I don't know if the action propelled me into another orgasm or if it made the current one more intense, but I'm on a roller coaster of ecstasy right now. The burn from my nipples, the vibration on my clit, Venom relentlessly thrusting into my mouth—the combination is heavenly.

"Emily!"

RENASCENCE

A spurt of warm liquid hits the back of my throat before he pulls out of my mouth. I swallow, watching him stroke himself until he comes all over my breasts. I collapse on the floor, twitching and out of breath. The vibration stops. Venom kneels over me, removing the stimulator and cuffs before picking me up. He takes me to the bathroom, gently and thoroughly cleaning my breasts and then tucking me into bed. My lids droop, but before sleep pulls me under, I have one lucid thought.

I'm definitely doing that again.

Venom

I whistle as I make Emily's breakfast. Fuck, the mouth on that woman. I can't believe how hard I came. Having her beautiful green eyes staring up at me as she took everything I gave her made her even more gorgeous. Seeing her on her knees, trusting me to make her feel good... I can't describe the feeling. I've had women submit to me before, but it was nothing compared to last night.

To Emily.

I saw it the day we met. I knew there was a spark between us. I'm just glad she finally realized it, too.

"Good morning."

I turn to find her entering the kitchen, wearing one of my T-shirts with the club logo. I've never seen anything any fucking sexier.

"Good morning, gorgeous."

Her head dips, discomfort at the compliment evident. The woman has no idea how desirable she is.

"I hope you don't mind. Am I even allowed to wear it?" She points to the shirt.

"Of course, darlin'. Hungry?"

"Famished," she answers, taking a seat at the table.

The bread pops up from the toaster and I add it to her plate of bacon and eggs. "How do you feel?" I ask as I place it before her.

"Good. Better." A blush stains her cheeks as she digs into her eggs.

"Your nipples?"

"A little sore but okay."

107

"Think you'll be ready for me tonight?"

"Maybe."

"What's it been, like two and a half years?" I take the chair across from her.

"Yeah, about."

"And James is the only one you've been with?"

"No. I was seeing someone in college before he and I hooked up."

She's quiet, pushing her eggs around the plate. I can recognize the reticence. I feel the same way when I have to talk about my family, so I change the subject.

"What was your major in college?"

"Elementary Education, specializing in English."

"One of those women who loves kids, huh?"

"Don't you?" She glances up at me.

"Sure. I just don't see myself having any."

"Me neither. I figured by my age I'd already have a few but"—she raises a shoulder in a shrug—"life."

"I hear ya. Did you sleep well?"

"Great. You'll have to let *me* make you breakfast one morning."

"Deal. You can do that tomorrow."

"Okay." She looks up at me, a smile tugging at her lips as she tucks some blonde strands behind her ear.

I know I'm staring, but I can't get over how beautiful Emily is. I could easily spend the entire day in bed with her working on that list.

"Got any plans today?"

"I'll be at the pet shop helping Uncle Jeff with inventory."

"I'll pick you up later and we can head to the gym to figure out that plan for you if you still want to do it."

"Sure. What will you need from me?"

"We'll need to talk about your goals, take measurements and such. Let me know if you have any allergies or medical conditions we need to take into consideration."

"I can do that."

"Cool. Eat up and I'll drop you off."

"Yes, sir."

I know she's only joking, but after last night? The word gets my dick hard. I'd love to go a few more rounds with her, but I've got shit to do and so does she. Hopefully I can hold out until tonight. What I hope for most is that she won't be sore anymore. I can't wait to get back inside that sweet pussy of hers.

After breakfast, I resist the urge to join her in the shower, choosing instead to check on my babies. I feed them, then grab a quick shower before Emily and I head out.

"Venom?"

"Yeah, darlin'?" I glance over at her in the passenger seat of the Jeep.

"How many... um.... What else is in that box?"

"You mean the toy chest?" I smirk.

"Yes."

"Don't worry, Em. You'll find out soon enough."

"How soon?"

This time I laugh. I've created a monster, and fuck if it doesn't turn me on. "Depending on how you feel, what do you say we test out a few more tonight?"

"I'd like that."

"You got it, babe."

A few quiet minutes go by before she breaks the silence. "Venom?"

"Hmm?"

"The day we met... what you said to me in Millie's.... Would you really have taken me home?"

"You mean if I would've fucked you? Of course."

"But you didn't know me."

"So? I wanted your body, not your hand in marriage."

"You do that a lot? Sleep with random women?"

"Why not?" I shrug. "It's consensual sex between two adults."

"And that's all it takes? 'Wanna get out of here?'"

"No. Most of the time I say please." I turn my head to give her a smile. "And sometimes the women approach me."

She fights back her amusement. "Is that so?"

"Yeah. Have you seen me?"

She loses the battle, throwing her head back as she laughs. "Aww... aren't you precious?"

109

I join in the laughter, knowing whenever a southern woman says that to you, you're anything *but* precious.

I pull into her driveway at the same time Jeff is about to climb into his truck. I help Emily out of the Jeep, approaching the older man as she jogs inside.

"Just give me a few minutes to change real quick, Uncle Jeff!" she throws over her shoulder.

"Morning, Jeff." I shake his hand. "How's it going?"

"Morning, son. I was going to ask you the same question." He jerks his head toward the house.

"Good. Emily's an amazing woman."

"I know. She needs a strong man right now. A man who will be sensitive to her needs… won't take her for granted."

"Don't worry. I'll take care of her."

"I'm sure you will. Thank you for what you did with the divorce papers."

"My pleasure. After some of the things Emily told me, it was hard not fucking him up, maybe breaking a few bones. Or all of them."

Jeff chuckles, combing his fingers through his white hair. "Wouldn't have bothered me none."

"Glad to hear that."

I wanted to do a lot more than that, but I highly doubt Em's uncle would condone murder.

We stand around for a bit discussing his tax returns before Emily comes rushing out of the house, halting our conversation.

"I'm ready!"

"See you around, Venom." Jeff shakes my hand again, folding his slender frame into the truck.

I kiss Emily's forehead, then open the truck door for her. "See you later, Em."

"Yeah… later."

She gives me a sunny smile that will be haunting my thoughts for the rest of the day. "Later" can't come soon enough.

I dig my phone out of my pocket, calling Kurt as I hop into the Jeep.

"Morning, boss."

"Hey, Kurt. How's it going?"

"Good. What's up?"

"I need you to fit Emily into one of the trainers' schedules today. Just a prelim session."

"Sure. I'll see who has an opening."

"Check with Rianne. I think Emily would be more comfortable with a woman."

"Got it."

"Thanks, Kurt."

"No problem. Stepping up your game there?"

"A little," I answer. Kurt's my employee, and although we're friendly, we're not friends. We don't talk about my personal life. I guess he wants to see what his chances are. He *did* hit on Emily before. "I'll see you later, Kurt."

"Yes, Mr. Hughes."

I hang up, confident he got the message in my tone of voice—stay away from Emily.

With all the work I have to do, I head back home. I tried to get some done last night, but knowing Emily was in my bed, my concentration was shit. I only ended up waking her up every couple of hours so I could play with her. I can't get enough of her right now. Before, I thought her lack of experience would be a problem, but now I see it as one of her best qualities. She's willing to learn, to let me teach her. There's nothing better than a woman I can mold to be whatever I want. In fact, it's getting me aroused just thinking about it. I adjust my dick, walking through the house to my office. Grabbing Jeff's records, I power up my computer and get to work.

It isn't until early afternoon that my growling stomach forces me to take a break. As I wander to the kitchen, I check my phone and find a message from Kurt.

Kurt: Rianne is free at 3.

Before I reply, I check with Emily.

Venom: My trainer can see you at 3. That good for you?
Emily: Yeah. Pick me up?
Venom: Be there in an hour.

After confirming with Kurt, I throw together a sandwich, grab a bottle of water, and hop back in the Jeep. When I arrive at the pet store, Emily's out front waiting for me. It's a little chilly today,

111

and she has her hands shoved in the pockets of her hoodie. I reach across and open her door, waving her inside.

"What are you doing out in the cold?"

"I just came out. Didn't want to make you wait."

"Waitin' on you is not a problem, darlin'." Her head drops, and even though her hood is obscuring her face, I know she's blushing. "Besides, don't want you getting sick. I'm just getting started with you."

"Fiend." She giggles, pushing her hood back.

"For a certain gorgeous, green-eyed blonde."

"That's good, because I think you may be making a fiend of said green-eyed blonde."

"You forgot 'gorgeous,'" I tell her. I know it was intentional, but I won't hassle her too much. Hopefully if I tell her often enough, she'll eventually start to believe that she's absolutely beautiful, and not just to me.

She doesn't reply, only looking out the window at the passing scenery. I park in the gym's lot, helping Emily out of the Jeep by giving her my hand. Pulling her to my side, I wrap my arm around her to warm her up.

"Hey, Emily!" Kurt greets her when we walk through the front doors. "I'd almost forgotten what you look like in the daytime."

"I know. I should probably get some sun. With my vampire hours, I'm beginning to look like one."

I see the smile she gives him, but it doesn't affect me. Kurt couldn't take this woman from me even if I was giving her away. It's conceited, but it's the truth. I'm phonics and Emily is hooked on me.

"Rianne ready for her?" I interrupt them.

"Yes, sir. She's in the main room."

Placing my hand at the small of Emily's back, I nudge her along. Rianne is waiting in a corner by herself, so I take us in that direction.

"Rianne."

"Hey, boss man." She looks up, a bright smile accompanying her cheerful greeting. Turning her head to Emily, she continues, "You must be Emily. Nice to meet you. I'm Rianne."

"Nice to meet you, too."

While the two women shake hands, I stand back and observe them. Physically, Rianne is practically Emily's opposite. She's a brunette, shorter, and not an ounce of fat on her body. Where Emily has two heavenly pillows on her chest, Rianne's tits are virtually nonexistent. The envy in Emily's eyes makes me wonder if pairing them up was a good idea.

"Okay, why don't we get started? First thing, Emily, do you have any medical conditions?"

"No."

"Good." Rianne jots down her answer on a paper attached to a clipboard. "And what are your short and long-term goals health-wise?"

"Well, ideally I'd like to lose twenty pounds. Long term, I need something in place that helps me maintain."

Rianne continues with her questions, Emily growing more uncomfortable with each one. She keeps glancing my way, so I believe I'm the problem. I excuse myself, holing up in my office until they finish. I keep busy, perusing the gym's records. After checking the security cameras and seeing that the women are still at it, I perform a cursory inspection of the place. I've been lucky with the employees I have; they take good care of the business and are trustworthy. I don't spend much time here other than to work out, so I depend on them. They haven't let me down yet. I'm "observing" the pole dancing class when Emily approaches.

"Figured I'd find you here." She smiles, shoving her hands in her pockets as she stands next to me.

"Who, me?" I turn to her with mock innocence. "Just checking on my customers. Helps for them to see the boss every now and then."

"Uh-huh. And it just happens to be the half-naked ones swinging on a stripper pole."

"Yup." I throw my arm around her shoulders and move toward the door. "Especially the half-naked ones."

She laughs, the sound like music to my ears. Emily deserves laughter, happiness, peace... love. I may not be able to give her all those things, but I'll try my damnedest on the ones I can.

"What did Rianne say?" I ask.

She sighs. "Basically the same thing you did, that my BMI is normal. She's going to work with me on a meal plan and exercise regimen."

"Hate to say it… no wait, I don't." I turn to her with a triumphant grin. "Told you so."

"Yeah, yeah."

"Darlin'…." I stop, gripping her shoulders and turning her to face me. "I'd never lie to you, so trust and believe when I say you're perfect. And I'm pretty damn certain I'm not the only one who thinks so."

"You're sweet for saying that, but…." Her eyes drop to the floor. "I'm not."

"You *are*, and fuck James for making you think you're not. No matter what size you are, you. Are. Gorgeous."

I catch the tears welling in her eyes before she throws herself in my arms.

"I wish I'd met someone like you instead of him."

"I'm here now, Em. I made some pretty bold claims, but I can't wipe the last ten years from your memory. Let's just make some better memories, yeah?"

"Yeah." She nods against my chest. "I'd like that."

"Come on, let's go."

As I drive out of the parking lot, I try to think of a way to cheer her up. Sex would definitely work, but I want to do something else. Something selfless that makes her happy. There's only one other thing I can think of that gets all women's panties in a twist—shopping. I head out of town and toward the nearest mall.

"Where are we going?" Emily asks.

"It's a surprise. I believe you'll like it."

"I'd rather go back to your place."

I chuckle at her timid words. "You need to get fucked, Em?"

"When you say it like that it sounds… dirty."

"It *is* dirty. The way I do it, anyway."

"All I know is you make me feel like I've been doing it wrong all my life."

"You have. I bet you wish you'd visited your uncle sooner, huh?"

"Fuck yeah!"

She finally cracks a smile. Reaching over, I squeeze her thigh. "You know, for a school teacher, you have a filthy mouth."

"It's kind of my guilty pleasure. I try my best not to do it in public, so when I'm alone, I let it all go."

"Like that day in the pet shop?"

"*Yeah*," she draws out the word. "You weren't supposed to hear that."

"I'm glad I did."

I slide my hand up her thigh, giving it another squeeze. She shifts in her seat, her body telling me she wants more.

"Is your pussy getting wet, Emily?"

"Um… maybe? You could check."

"Don't tempt me, naughty girl. We're almost there."

"Almost where?"

"Here," I announce as I turn into the parking lot.

"The mall? What are we doing here?"

"A little of what you women call retail therapy. I figured it would cheer you up."

"That's sweet of you, Venom, but I'm not really a retail therapy kinda woman. I prefer to just curl up with a good book."

Well, that's not the reaction I was expecting.

"Besides, I told you what I want to do."

"Okay, consider this one for me," I offer as I park. "I'll like watching you model all the sexy shit I'm going to buy you."

"You don't need to spend money on me."

"Really?" I ask, incredulous. "That's what you got out of what I said?"

I hop out of the Jeep and stomp around to the passenger side, ripping the door open. She watches me, eyes wide in surprise and a bit of fear. I unbuckle the seat belt, grabbing her left knee to swing her around to face me. Her hands fly to my shoulders, lips parting with a gasp when I wedge myself between her legs.

"We're going to go into every store I say, and you're going to try on whatever I pick out until you get me so fucking worked up I'll imagine all the things I'm going to do to you. Then when we get home, I'm going to do every single one. You got that?"

Her head bobs up and down, thighs pressing into my hips.

115

"Good." I give her a smile meant to soften the harshness of my tone. "Now let's go."

CHAPTER 11
Venom

Two hours.

Two fucking hours of watching Emily parade around in shit that would be features in every man's wet dreams. We did tight, short, low-cut, lace, you name it. The lingerie store? My personal favorite. With the commission she'll be getting, the sales girl will be wearing that smile we left her with for a while. The bags are packed on the back seat, and I can't wait to get home so I can rip one of those lacy things from Emily's body. I've been hard since the first store, so it's taking all my willpower not to pull over and drag her onto my lap. I took her to dinner, hoping it would distract me enough to cool down, but no dice.

"You're crazy, you know that?"

"What?" I turn to her, wondering what I missed while I was lost in thought.

"I said you're crazy. I can't believe you bought all that stuff."

"You better believe you'll be wearing every single item. Starting tonight."

"Oh, yeah?"

"Oh, yeah. I know just the one, too."

I can picture it now... green to match her eyes, lace on top, some sheer mesh shit on the bottom, the stringy scrap of material they call panties. She'd tried on the top over her bra so I didn't get the full effect of it, but she still looked amazing.

"Which one is that?"

"You'll see. Just make sure you're ready with the next thing on your list."

"I'm ready. I know what I want next."

"Oh?" I raise a brow. "What is it?"

"I want you to tie me up." Her words come out on a hurried breath.

Fuck.

I press on the accelerator, never wishing more that I was on my bike.

117

Once we're back in Stony View, I head straight to my place. We unload the bags, Emily kicking off her shoes and throwing her jacket on the couch before going directly to my room. I search the bags for the outfit I want and then join her, finding her sitting on the bed waiting for me. I hand her the bag with a smirk.

"Take a shower and put this on for me."

"Okay."

While she's in the bathroom, I use the time to calm down. No woman has ever made me this excited and I'm not sure how to handle it. This is my domain. Here, I'm the boss. I can't lose control no matter how much Emily makes my blood boil.

I grab the toy chest from the closet, intending to remove some cuffs. However, I decide to let Emily choose the one she wants. This is her first time, and I want her to be as comfortable as possible.

She emerges from the bathroom and I swear there's a heavenly glow behind her.

"Oh, fuck." She moves forward, blinking up at me, trying to gauge my reaction. "You look amazing, darlin'. Sexy as fuck."

She stands before me, chest heaving, eyes locked on mine.

"You like it?" Her voice is soft, words hopeful.

"I fucking love it." I swallow hard, trying to get rid of the lump that's suddenly formed in my throat. I shake it off, remembering where we are—*my* turf. "All the things in this box? I got them for you. I want you to choose the ones you want to use tonight."

Emily stares at the contents of the box like the proverbial kid in the candy store. She probably has no idea what most of the items are, but her excitement and willingness to learn are sexy as hell. She picks one up, brows knitted as she turns to me.

"Are these… anal beads?"

"Yes."

"Oh."

"Have you ever done anal play?"

"No, nothing." She shakes her head.

"Then you're not ready for these yet. Is it something on your list?"

"Maybe we could add that for later?"

I nod, watching her rifle through the box once more. She removes the nipple clamps, placing them on the bed.

"I liked these."

My dick jumps. I like that she likes them. In fact, I love it. Her tits looked amazing with those clamps hanging off her nipples. She may not know it, but Emily likes her sex with a bit of pain, and I'm the man to give it to her.

Next, she sets the blindfold alongside the clamps. My mind starts going crazy with the possibilities of what I can do with those two items. Then she grabs the restraints. It's on.

"I think that's it for tonight," she says.

"Okay."

I put away the box, reaching behind me and pulling off my T-shirt as I approach Emily once more. Sitting on the edge of the bed, I slowly take her in from head to toe. She looks away, still uncomfortable with my appreciation of her body.

"Lose the panties, Emily."

I was planning to rip them off, but I definitely want her to wear this again. With shaking hands, she pushes her underwear down, revealing her marvelous pussy. When I don't move, she attempts to cover herself. One look of warning and her arms drop to her sides. I walk to the end of the bed, flipping the hidden lid on the custom footboard. She watches, eyes widening in increments as I pull out the metal bars, snapping them into place.

"That's... creative."

"I'm a resourceful man."

"I'll say."

With everything in place, I turn to her. "Come here."

At the change in the tone of my voice, she snaps to attention, hurrying over. I attach the restraints to the chains on the side bars before securing her hands and adjusting the length of the chains.

"Okay?"

She nods. I reach for the nipple clamps and blindfold, pushing the lace aside to uncover her breasts. I lick each nipple, bringing them to stiff peaks before attaching the clamps. She hisses but her head falls back, teeth sinking into her bottom lip with a moan.

119

"Emily." Her eyes meet mine. "You understand that if you want me to stop, all you have to do is say so, right?" She nods again. "Words, Emily."

"Yes, I understand."

"Good."

I cover her eyes, then stand back so I can appreciate my handiwork. The sight of her practically has my dick forcing my zipper down. Fuck. I kick off my jeans, then stand as close to her as I can without touching her. She gasps, tipping her face up. I trail my fingertips up her sides, watching a shiver work its way through her body.

"You have no idea how fucking hot you look right now... how many nasty things I want to do to you."

"Please," she whimpers.

I think I need to add a playroom to the house. I'm craving a three-sixty degree view of Emily right now. As sexy as the lingerie is, I need her naked. I don't think she'll be wearing this thing again after all. I press my lips to hers, distracting her as I curl my fingers into the neckline and giving it a yank. It rips down the middle, drawing a startled gasp from her. I work on the straps next, the flimsy material falling to the floor. My fingertips ghost over her breasts, then up her stomach, her body trembling before me. Gripping her hips, I pull her forward so my hard dick presses into her stomach.

"Venom, please...."

I gently tug on the clamp chain, leaning forward to suck on the fleshy tops of her breasts. Her hips press into mine while she moans. With a grin, I admire the marks I left before moving down to my knees, dropping gentle kisses on her stomach.

"Spread your legs." I watch them open, licking my lips at the evidence of her arousal on her inner thighs. "You're fucking dripping for me, Emily."

She whimpers, the chains rattling as she pulls on them. I slide two fingers between her lips, sucking her juices from them. I can't remember the last time a woman's taste made me want to eat her pussy every fucking night, but Emily? Shit. She makes my mouth water. I lean in, letting my warm breath caress her pussy. Her hips go wild, begging me to move things along. Instead of giving her my tongue, I kiss her thighs.

"Jesus, Venom. You're killing me."

Her thighs quiver under my tongue as I lick at the juices trickling down. I drop soft kisses on her hips, her mound, everywhere except where I really want to, where she's dying for me to. I slip a finger inside her, watching her face as I glide it in and out. She clenches around it, but there are no signs of pain. She groans in frustration when I stop. I grab a condom from the nightstand, smiling at her restlessness. She can't keep still, head moving around to try and pinpoint my location. I kick off my boxers, roll the condom on, and stand before Emily once more.

"Venom?"

"I'm here."

"Maybe this blindfold wasn't such a good idea. I want to see you."

"You don't need to see me." I trail my nose along her neck, her body shivering as I whisper against her skin, "Feel me, Emily."

Cradling her face, I place a gentle kiss on her lips. She tries to deepen it but I pull back, smacking her ass. She yelps, offering an apology.

"Sorry. You're in charge."

"That's right. Naughty girls don't get to come, Emily."

"I'll be good, I promise."

I chuckle, pressing the head of my dick to her clit. She groans, spreading her thighs wider. I wrap my arms around them, lifting her off the floor and sliding inside her.

"Venom," she moans.

Her thighs tremble, pussy tightening around me. I don't move, savoring the feeling of her tight, wet, paradise pussy. "Fuck."

We need to talk. I have to feel her bare. I'll take every test she wants me to, but me and Emily skin to skin will happen.

I pull back slowly, sinking into her again. Her moans spur me on and I move faster, pumping into her. Her muscles contract, gripping me with every thrust. I grab the clamp chain between my teeth, tugging on it.

"Fuck, that feels so good. More... more!"

I pull out of her, lifting her as I kneel, placing her legs on my shoulders. Burying my face in her pussy, I suck her clit into my mouth. She cries out, thighs locking around my head, and I moan when her taste hits my tongue. I can't get enough of this woman. Swirling my tongue over her lips, I slip it inside her and growl as she screams. I shift again, wrapping her legs around my hips as I slam into her.

"Venom!"

"Scream as loud as you need to, Emily. No one around to hear you but me, and I love that shit."

"Oh… I think… *God*, I'm coming!"

I sink my fingertips into her ass cheeks, giving her everything I have, every ounce of strength, every inch of my dick. Her pussy clamps down on me. My balls tighten. The moment she starts to spasm, I erupt inside her.

"Venom!" she screams again.

"Fuck!"

I thrust deep, holding my position as we both ride out our orgasms. Once I've come down, I release her hands and lay her on the bed. She's limp, breathing heavily. I slip the clamps off, soothing her nipples with my mouth. She moans but doesn't move. I doubt she can.

Her eyes flutter open when I remove the blindfold.

"Wow."

"Thanks, but that's not even my best, darlin'."

I walk away to the sound of her giggles, disposing of the condom and taking care of the toys. When I return after a shower, Emily is under the covers, already drifting off. I could curl up next to her and sleep, breathe in her scent all night. I could, but I won't.

I can't.

I think I'd like it too much.

RENASCENCE
Emily

Beard burn.

It's a thing.

Ooh, lawd, it's a thing! My thighs and vag lips are sore in a way that hurts but reminds me of Venom's head buried between my legs. I've gone from living without oral to not knowing if I can live without it. It's that good.

He's that good.

It's all I can think about as Rianne takes me through my paces. That and trying to figure out what I'm going to get him for Christmas. I know we're not a couple, but still, it's only a Christmas gift. I don't even care if he gets me anything; I'd say fulfilling a girl's every fantasy is more than enough. Not to mention all the clothes and lingerie he bought me. It included new sets of workout gear, one of which I'm now wearing. I was fine with my T-shirt and leggings, but apparently he prefers the close-fitting sleeveless tank—which, thank God, covers the hickeys he left behind—and capris. He threw a bunch of stats at me and reasons why the material is better, but he doesn't know I heard the comment he whispered under his breath about how great my ass looks in them. For once, I'm inclined to agree. Or maybe it's knowing that's what *he* thinks. The look in his eyes last night when I stepped out of the bathroom… never in my life have I felt that desired, like I was the only woman in the world, the only one who mattered.

My first boyfriend, we were each other's firsts. Nick was always eager, but after the first couple of times, it seemed he was more interested in the act itself than in me. Still, I thought I was in love and willing to work on our relationship. When I finally tried to talk to him about it, he confirmed I was right. Turns out I was practice for the girl he really wanted. He needed to get his virginity and awkwardness out of the way so he wouldn't embarrass himself with her. Needless to say, I was crushed.

Enter James.

We worked together at a fast food restaurant one summer in high school and kept in touch after. When I went off to college, he enrolled in an automotive technician program. After what happened with Nick, I went home for a weekend and James and I ended up meeting for drinks. One thing led to another and we hooked up. I wasn't proud of myself, but at least he wasn't some random guy. We kept seeing each other, stepping things up when I moved back home after graduation. To be honest, I was shocked when he asked me to marry him. We had nothing to build a marriage on, but I figured I could do worse.

We were doing well at first. I had no delusions that he was hopelessly in love with me, and I knew he wasn't Prince Charming, but we were okay. Things began to go downhill after our third year when money became tight. By year five, the verbal abuse began. Year seven, I found out he was cheating. I still don't know why I stayed. I was going through the motions until the threat of losing the house sobered me up. I was on the mortgage, too, and I couldn't risk the damage to my credit. Once I had it sorted out, I concentrated on fixing my life. I left him, even gave him the house. There's no way I could live in there with all the bad memories. Nick may have cracked my shell, but James broke me. Getting away from him was the best decision I ever made.

Coming to Stony View is a close second.

If I hadn't, I wouldn't have met Venom. I probably wouldn't have found out that men like him exist. He's my very own knight on a shiny black mechanical stallion. In this story, Humpty Dumpty is made whole again. He's slowly helping me piece my life back together, and it's not just the sex. He's funny, kind, caring, smart, and amazing in bed. If he was the relationship type, he'd be the perfect boyfriend—a man you can bring home to your parents, but who will tie you up and do soul-stealing things to your body.

I'm seriously going to sit and make that fucking list. Now that I know he's serious, I need to put some thought into it, rank everything by order of importance. After all, I don't know how long this thing is going to last.

"Good job, Emily! You did great today."

Rianne's bubbly voice pulls me out of my head and I flash her a smile. That smile gets brighter when I notice Venom approaching from behind her.

"Thanks, Rianne. You've been awesome."

"Aww, thanks! See you tomorrow."

She waves at us both, practically jogging out of the room. I slide the towel around my neck, using the ends to dry my face.

"Hey, darlin'." Without missing a beat, he leans down and plants a kiss on my lips. I blush, looking around the room to see if anyone noticed. "Ashamed to kiss me in public, Em?"

Horrified he thinks that's what the action meant, I step back. I'm about to protest when I look up to see the smile on his lips.

"Asshole." I smack his chest. "I really thought you were offended."

"But I am. Lucky for you I know how you can make it up to me."

"Let me guess, it involves us being naked."

"Oh, it involves a whole lot more than that. Come home with me and I'll show you."

"You weren't kidding about that frequency thing, were you?"

"You'll quickly learn, Em. I never joke when it comes to fucking."

"Trust me, I have. My body is feeling the effects of my... um... education."

"Good." He takes my hand, leading me out of the room. "Maybe it's time you graduated."

"Graduated?" I stop walking, making him jerk back. *Does that mean... is he ending this?*

"Em? What's wrong?"

"What do you mean?"

"I mean"—he presses against me—"it's time to take you to another level."

Whew.

"What level is that?"

He doesn't answer my question, only asking one of his own. "Want to go to a party?"

"Sure. Where?"

"At the clubhouse. The old ladies are doing a whole Christmas thing."

"But I thought women weren't allowed?" I ask, confused.

"Old ladies are the brothers' women. They're not members, but that doesn't mean they're banned from the premises."

"And I can go there?"

125

"You'll be my guest, so yeah."

"Okay." This is exciting! Other than getting food, we haven't really been "out" together. Plus I get to see a part of his life that I have no clue about. "I'd love to. When is it?"

"Tonight."

"Tonight! That's a little last-minute, don't you think?"

"It's a good thing you have all those outfits to choose from, then." He winks, helping me into my jacket. "You can shower and get ready at my place."

"Okay."

The drive to his house goes by in a flash because my mind is occupied by this party. I haven't been to one in ages. Not to mention this isn't just some party—it's a biker party. I have no idea what to expect, but if the other members are anything like Venom, I know I'm going to enjoy myself. What do I even wear? The only leather I own is a jacket. Isn't that what biker chicks wear?

"You can use my shower. I'll use the other bathroom," Venom says when we walk through the door.

"Okay," I answer, distracted by thinking about my outfit.

By the time I've showered and washed my hair, he's already in the bedroom getting ready. He's also laid out an outfit for me. It's cute, but he picked a skirt. A short one.

"Um… I'm gonna freeze my buns off in that."

His gaze flicks between me and the skirt as if he's contemplating which takes precedence—fashion or comfort.

"It's not that cold. Besides, the party is indoors."

"Venom." I tilt my head to the side, eyes begging him to be reasonable.

"Wear the skirt, bring a pair of jeans. If you get cold, you can change. How about that?"

"Why do you want me to wear it?"

"Easy access, darlin'." He winks, his grin devilish.

"Are you planning a show or something?" I joke.

"Maybe."

I instantly stop what I'm doing, spinning on my heels to stare at him. Laughter erupts from him, head falling back, chest shaking.

126

While he enjoys himself at my expense, a thought begins to take root. *I mean... public sex... that's a fantasy-type thing, right?*

"That intrigues you, doesn't it?" His tone is serious as he moves to stand before me.

"*Maaaybe.*"

"What are we talking here? Full-on sex, or do you just want to come in public?"

"You're serious, aren't you? You'd do it?"

"Wouldn't be the first time." He shrugs. "Something you want to cross off your list?"

"You've done it before?" I ask in a barely audible voice, surprised yet fascinated.

"Why are you whispering?"

"I don't know. With who?"

"Does it matter, Em?"

"I guess not. The second one, then," I answer before I can change my mind. "No one can know, though. I mean, public but no audience."

"You got it, darlin'."

He goes back to getting dressed, like we just decided on having chicken instead of beef for dinner. *O-kay then.*

To keep my mind off what I agreed to, I grab my toiletry bag from my purse, trying to figure out what I'm going to do with my hair. Thankfully I have some makeup with me. Since I've been here every night, my little bag has been my lifesaver.

"You can leave that here, you know."

"What?" I turn to face Venom.

"Your bag. No use in taking it back and forth."

"Are you sure?"

"It's just deodorant and shit, darlin'." He chuckles.

"It's just…. Okay. Thanks."

"No prob."

After putting the final touches on my makeup, I find him watching me from the bathroom door. Our eyes meet in the mirror and his approval shows in his smile.

"You look gorgeous, Em." He saunters over, wrapping his arms around me from behind and dropping a kiss on my neck. "Smell good, too."

127

He's wearing his customary T-shirt and jeans. His eyes seem to have a steely blue hue tonight, which goes perfectly with the long-sleeved blue shirt. His hair is down, beard trimmed, and if we're talking about smelling good, he has that one in the bag.

"Thank you."

"Listen." At his sigh, I turn in his arms, disappointment washing over me because I know he's about to cancel our plans. "There are a few things we need to go over."

"Like what?"

"Like what to expect. The old ladies will be around, so things will be pretty tame, but you might still see some things that could"—my brows knit when his smirk transforms into a chuckle—"offend your delicate sensibilities."

"My sensibilities are not delicate!" I exclaim, pouting.

"Try to keep an open mind. These men and women aren't your regular crowd. Whatever you see or hear doesn't leave the clubhouse. You come to me if you have any issues. Understand?"

"Keep my mouth shut. Got it."

"Right. You need anything, you can talk to one of the women. I'll introduce you when we get there."

"Yes, sir!" I salute him, matching his smile with one of my own. "Anything else?"

"No, darlin'. Come on."

I've never seen the clubhouse before. It's quite secluded and looks like a fortress from the outside with the high gates. When Venom pulls up to them, they open and we enter. We could be in Narnia for all I know, because we drive into a whole new world. Bikes and cars are scattered around, music loud, voices louder. I take in the sights and scents, my senses on overload. There are women wearing much less than me; I wonder how they're standing around like it's the middle of summer. Inside the building is no different. Venom's hand tightens around mine as we weave through the crowd. It's the ultimate man cave with a pool table, video poker, pinball machine, and several flat-screen TVs mounted on the walls.

"Over there." Venom points to the bar. "Those are the old ladies."

There's a group of five women, two of whom look young enough to be my daughters. Definitely nothing "old" about them. They're all wearing cuts like the men, but with different words on the back. The ones I can see read "Property of Reaper," "Property of Einstein," "Property of Motor," and "Property of Crow."

"The Latina with the dark hair, that's Raven, the prez's old lady. You need anything, you talk to her. Ellen's the one with the brown hair. She's the VP's woman and the prez's sister. You can't find me or Raven, you go to her."

"Okay. What does that 'property' stuff mean?"

"The names are their old men."

"So they're property of their boyfriends?" I ask in shock. *What century is this?*

"They're not bought and sold, Emily. It's actually a sign of respect."

Yeah... right. As we approach the women, I paste on a smile. They may be owned by men, but they look pretty happy. I watch them talking and laughing, longing hitting me in the gut. I don't have that—female friends. Hell, I don't have any kind of friends. Once I started my second job, all the women I used to hang out with faded away. I didn't even miss that until now.

"Hey, ladies."

"Venom!" the dark-haired girl, Raven, shouts happily.

I was right. This girl is young. It makes me wonder how old the president is, since she's also heavily pregnant. Her stomach is bare, a bandeau the only thing under her cut.

"Emily, meet Raven, Ellen, Marlowe, Renae, and Chrissy. Everyone, this is Emily."

We exchange pleasantries before they chase Venom off. I silently beg him not to leave, but he winks, takes my jacket, and disappears into the throng.

"So, Emily," Raven says. "I don't know if Venom told you, but I'm Gage's old lady. Ellen is with Dr. E, Marlowe and Renae are with Crow and Motor, and Chrissy is with Charger."

"Yeah, he mentioned that," I reply, not wanting the other women to feel left out.

"How long have you been seeing Venom?" the caramel beauty asks. Chrissy, that's her name.

"Not long. I've only been in town a couple weeks."

"I knew I hadn't seen you around here," one of the older women says. I think she's Marlowe.

"Well, I think we'll be seeing a lot more of you from now on." Ellen winks.

I avert my gaze, cheeks no doubt turning red when I realize what she's alluding to. "Oh, it's not like that. We're just hanging out."

"Emily, *mira*." Raven lays her hand on my shoulder. "One, he brought you to the clubhouse, and two, he put you with *us*."

"What do you mean?"

"You're at the good-good table. We're all old ladies here."

"Oh."

I look around the room, noticing more of those scantily-clad women. They don't seem to be here with anyone specific, bouncing from man to man.

"Those are Hounds," Ellen tries to explain. "They're basically here to take care of the men."

"Oh. I see." She doesn't need to be more specific. I think I know exactly what she means.

The women go quiet for a beat before Marlowe pipes up. I get the feeling she's trying to change the subject.

"I'm going to ask the burning question I'm sure we all want the answer to. Give up the goods, Emily. How's the snake man?"

"Huh?"

"The bedroom," Raven clarifies. "I already know Venom's got a big dick, but does he know how to use it?"

All eyes turn to Raven, especially mine.

"Ugh." She rolls her eyes. "I saw it last year. I was on my way to the kitchen and he was over in that corner"—she jerks her head in the general direction—"getting a blow job from one of the Hounds."

Okay, then. Now I understand what Venom meant about keeping my mouth shut about what I might see. At least it was last year and not last week. I also now know he has no qualms about public sex.

"Well?" Ellen prods.

I'm not really comfortable telling these women about my sex life, but I can't stop the blush from creeping back into my cheeks. They burst out laughing, Raven and Ellen high-fiving each other. That's when I notice Ellen is pregnant, too. The women's laughter is infectious, and I can't help but join in. My nerves vanish. I lean on the bar, thanking Renae when she orders me a drink from the young man behind it. When he turns around, I notice there's no logo on his cut, only the bottom patch with the state. As he hands me my drink, I see the small one on the front that says "Prospect."

"Thanks."

"Name's Tyler, ma'am." He tosses his shoulder-length, dirty blond hair out of his face. "You need anything, let me know."

"Um... okay."

My eyes meet with the pair belonging to the other person behind the bar, a pretty brunette. I assume she's one of the Hounds Ellen told me about.

"Sweet prepubescent Jesus," Raven mumbles, bringing my attention back to her.

I follow her line of vision, mouth falling open at the sight of the two men emerging from the back. They're both shirtless and sweaty, hands wrapped as if they were boxing. The blond is ripped and hard, covered in tattoos. His friend with the dark hair and black-rimmed glasses is not as bulky but still defined, only one visible tat. *Holy shit, they're hot!*

The blond steps between Raven's thighs, dropping a kiss on her lips, then one on her stomach.

"Need some help washing my back, babe," he says with a smirk, rubbing her belly. I breathe an internal sigh of relief that he's not some old geezer.

"Hey, beautiful," the other piece of man-candy greets Ellen before turning to the rest of us. "Ladies."

"This is Emily." Ellen tugs me forward. "She came with Venom."

Both men's eyebrows almost touch their hairlines. They recover quickly, shaking my hand.

"I'm Gage," the blond says, his blue eyes lighting up. "This is Einstein. Glad you're here, Emily. You need anything, or if Venom's being a dick, you let us know."

"I will. Thanks." *I like these two already.*

"I really do need a shower, so I'll see you later, Emily."

"Yeah, later."

Gage and Einstein drag their women behind them, and that's when I see the tattoos on their backs. The bit peeking out from under Raven's cut seems to match her husband's.

"They all do that," Marlowe explains. "Kind of a club thing to get their old ladies tatted on their backs. Those two women are the first to get matching ones, though."

I nod, taking a deep breath and a sip of my drink, settling in. That's so sweet how they're willing to display their love for their women so openly.

I think I'm going to like it here.

"Well, my night just got a lot better."

I turn at the sound of the voice, bumping into a solid wall of man. My eyes widen, slowly panning up until I meet the eyes of the giant in front of me.

"Whoa. You're *huge*." *Shit. Did that come out of my mouth?* He's wearing a cut like Venom's, with "Sergeant at Arms" printed on one of the patches, "Razor" on another. His size, the mohawk, the leather and chains should instill fear in me, but there's a kindness in his hazel eyes that calms me.

He winks, giving me an impish grin. "All over, babe."

"Um… yeah… I… I don't doubt that," I stammer.

"Wanna go back to my room and be certain?"

"I can't do that."

"Why?"

A deep voice booms behind Mr. Sergeant at Arms. "Because she's mine."

CHAPTER 12
Venom

"Damn, who's the blonde?"

"That's Emily," I answer Razor's question without even looking. I know she's the one he's talking about.

"Your Emily?"

"Yeah, my Emily."

"Fuck, brother. Now I see why that trip was necessary."

"Yeah."

I finally turn in her direction, watching her. She's more relaxed now than she was earlier, and I'm glad. I don't know why, but I'm fucking happy she's fitting in.

"I also see why you didn't want to bring her here."

"What, you think one of you assholes can take my place?"

"Hell yeah. I'm Razor, motherfucker. You know what that means?"

"You're tiny and flat?" I chuckle.

"I'm sharp." He pops the "p" and his collar.

"Okay, go ahead." I motion to Emily. "Take a shot."

I trust my brother. He knows I'm joking, and I know he wouldn't try anything. Besides, it might boost Emily's ego if another man shows some interest. I don't know why she thinks I only compliment her because I want to keep fucking her. It couldn't be any further from the truth.

"I will. Get ready to go home alone, brother."

"Good luck."

I watch him saunter over, throwing a grin over his shoulder. When Emily spins to face him, I start making my way over there, too. I'm curious to hear what she'll say. She fumbles over her words at first, but her voice is steady and clear when she tells him she can't go to his room.

"Because she's mine."

The choice of words stuns me, but I find the notion doesn't. Shit.

Razor turns slowly, amusement lighting up every part of him. "Is that so?"

"Yeah, it is." I push past him, claiming the free spot next to Emily. "Isn't that right, darlin'?"

"I came with Venom," she tells Razor, leaning in to my side.

"Then you, dollface, need a drink to cope with that asshole. Marisol!" He motions to the girl behind the bar. "Tequila shots!"

We down the first round and I order a couple more, each one sending Emily closer to me. Her eyes are glassy, and there's a constant smile on her sweet lips. I'm not trying to get her drunk, but I need her loose in order to give her what she wants. Taking her hand, I lead her down the corridor to my room. On the way, we bump into Gage and Raven leaving theirs.

"You guys heading in? I was thinking of making a fire," Prez says.

"Nah. Just need a few minutes."

"Got it."

"Come find me after," Raven tells Emily, giving her a knowing wink before the two walk off.

At my door, Emily runs her fingers over the nameplate as I open it.

"Ven-nom."

"Are you drunk, darlin'?"

"Nope." She wanders inside, dropping down on the bed where I'd thrown her jacket. "Are we here to…?" She lets her words hang in the air.

"No, Em. I do need you to give me your panties, though."

"What? Why?"

"Emily. Panties. Now."

"Jeez." She rolls her eyes in annoyance.

I let it slide because I know it's the alcohol talking. She slips them off, and when she brings them to me, I wrap my arm around her waist, drawing her close while I shove the underwear in my pocket. Emily keeps surprising me at every turn. When I suggested this list, I had no idea she'd want the things she's asked for. I can't wait to hear what the next item is.

Her face is tipped toward mine, lids heavy, lips slightly parted. I need to taste them. I press my lips to hers, loving the way she moans as her arms circle my neck. She opens for me, letting me have my way with her. Her taste, her soft lips, the way her tongue plays with mine… I've never thought much of kissing, but kissing Emily? Amazing.

My hand disappears under her skirt, finding her wet and ready.

"Always ready for me."

She whimpers, hips grinding against my fingers. I remove them, breaking our kiss. "Why'd you stop?" she whines.

"Let's take this show on the road."

I help her into her jacket, then tug her out of the room, heading to the back of the clubhouse. The guys have a huge fire going, people—mostly couples—scattered around. I take Emily a few steps from the door, leaning against the building.

"Cold?" I ask.

"No, I'm good."

We can be easily seen, but no one's paying attention to us. Almost everyone is watching the girl-on-girl show going on next to the flames. I pull Emily's body against mine, her back to me. I can tell she's watching the girls, her head leaning this way and that.

"You like that?" I mumble in her ear.

"It's… kinda hot."

Her ass wiggles, rubbing on my hard dick. "Spread your legs a little wider, Emily."

She obeys, the space she creates allowing me to slip my hand up the back of her skirt and between her thighs. She gasps, glancing around to see if anyone's looking.

"Concentrate on me, Emily. On my fingers, my voice." I push at her entrance, my finger gliding in easily. She moans, muscles tightening. "Is this what you wanted? For me to make you come with all these people a few feet away?" She whimpers in answer. "Are you going to scream my name when you come?"

She lets out a long moan, and I have to tell her to be quiet. I move to her clit, all my fingers now drowning in her wetness. This is seriously turning her on. Her hips begin to roll, head falling back on my chest.

"Fuck, that's so good," she whispers.

I want nothing more than to bury myself inside her right now, but this is for her, not me. The clubhouse door opens, banging against the wall. Emily jumps but I keep her steady, anchoring her to me.

"Shh… don't move." I circle her clit faster, kissing and licking her neck. Her entire body is quivering against me. "I love how you always drip for me, Emily. No other man can get you this wet."

"No…."

She gasps, nails digging into my thigh.

"The girls by the fire… what are they doing?" I ask.

"They're… one's fingering the other."

"Like I'm doing to you?"

"Yes, but… with two fingers."

I insert two fingers into her tight pussy, biting into her shoulder as I pump them in and out.

"Oh… I'm going to come," she squeaks.

I return to her clit, concentrating on the little bud as Emily stiffens in my arms. She struggles to suppress a moan, both hands now gripping my thighs. Making her come is one of the most rewarding things I've ever done and probably ever will do. It's magical.

When she stops shaking, she turns to face me, a satisfied smile in place.

"You're amazing, you know that?"

"I've been told a time or two," I reply with a smirk.

"Good, because I know what I want to do next."

"What's that?"

"A girl."

I'm shocked into silence. I have no idea how to reply, because I certainly never expected this. *It has to be the tequila talking, right? Does she really want a threesome?*

"Emily—"

"Hey, you two! If you're done fucking, the food's ready!"

Humiliated doesn't even begin to describe how I feel. I bury my face in Venom's chest, wishing I could hide here forever. *Someone saw us!* Not to mention what I asked for. I'm not into girls, never thought of them in that way. Ever. I've never even watched lesbian porn. One little live show and now I want to star in one?

"Fuck off, asshole!" Venom booms, the vibrations of his voice thumping in his chest. "It's okay, Em. Don't worry, he didn't see anything."

"How do you know?"

"He's just trying to get back at me for something. Come on, let's go inside."

I follow dejectedly, keeping my head down. If he wasn't holding my hand, I'd probably bump into everyone and everything. We duck into a bathroom, and he allows me to clean up and put my underwear on.

Back in the bar area, an older man and woman are serving the food. The man looks a lot like Gage. I don't need anyone to tell me they're related.

"That's Chopper and Nita," Venom says. "Gage's father and aunt." He motions to another older woman exiting the kitchen. "That's Millie. She's with Chopper."

"Oh, I've seen her before. She owns the diner."

"That's right."

"Drink?" a voice asks from behind me. I don't want to turn around because it's the same voice from outside.

Fuck. I just want to crawl into a dark, dank hole.

"I'm sorry. I really didn't mean to embarrass you. I promise I didn't see anything." I finally face him, taking the beer he offers. "I'm Tek."

"Emily."

Tek tosses his long black hair out of his face, revealing brown eyes lined with black pencil. The kid has enough metal in his face to keep TSA occupied for a week—piercings in his ears, nose, brow, and lower lip. He's cute, though.

"You're lucky you apologized, motherfucker. Saved me the trouble of ending you."

Tek gives Venom his attention. "Dream on, snake boy. Maybe *I'll* end *you*, then Emily and I can run off together."

Oh, my.

"Dream on, nerd."

This strange interaction is busted up by Chopper and his sister, who offer us each a loaded plate.

"Which one of these idiots are you with, darlin'?" he asks.

"Um…." I look to Venom, unsure how to answer. If I do, I'm practically calling him an idiot, too.

"She's with me."

"And how did a motherfucker like you land a beauty like this?" a newcomer with a scar on his cheek asks. The Latino man next to him with the greasy hair looks me up and down with a lascivious grin, eyes resting on my breasts. I shift uncomfortably, covering them with my jacket.

"Every time I see Marlowe, I wonder the same thing about you, fucker." Venom turns to the ogler. "And *you*. Eyes north, asshole."

I observe the men, realizing what I'm in the middle of is their brotherly camaraderie. It's sweet. Strange, but sweet. Venom introduces the men as Crow and Rico. They continue to joke around through the entire meal, making the time fly by. When Raven taps my shoulder to tell me she's leaving, I notice there aren't many people left hanging around.

"Let me have your number," she says. "We'll do lunch tomorrow."

"Sure."

After we exchange numbers, Gage wraps his arm around her. "Let's get you home, baby doll. You must be tired."

She tips her head up, a loving smile in place. A pang of jealousy rips through me. The way he looks at her? That's the way I've always wanted a man to look at me—like I'm his world. I don't even know these people, but I can see the love they share. The same thing goes for Ellen and her beau. They surface from the back where the rooms are, Einstein carrying a sleeping little boy. His free hand is gripping Ellen's as they stride toward us, the picture of a perfectly happy family.

"We're heading out," Einstein announces. "See you all tomorrow."

"Bye." I wave to the two couples.

"It was nice meeting you, Emily," both men say at the same time.

"You, too. Thanks for having me."

"Anytime," Gage assures me, his impossibly blue eyes twinkling.

Before they're through the door, Venom wraps his arm around my waist, sliding it down to my hip. "Ready to go?"

"If you are," I answer.

"Come on, darlin'."

In the safety of the Jeep, I ask a question that's been on my mind all night.

"How old is your president's wife? She seems young."

"She should. She's nineteen."

"How long have they been married?"

"Couple months."

"Wow. They look very much in love."

"They are. That man would do anything for Raven."

Must be nice.

I lay my forehead on the window, thinking back to when I was nineteen. I was in college. Nick and I had just started dating. It was before he wrecked me. Before... everything. How I wish I could go back to that time.

Filled with thoughts of a young and carefree me, it takes Venom opening my door to jar me back to reality. I hurry inside, the cold night wind whipping against my bare legs. I'm about to dive under the covers when Venom hands me a negligée.

"Wear this one, darlin'."

I change into the black silk nightie, sliding under the warm blanket while ogling him as he undresses.

"You know what I just realized?"

"What?" he asks.

"When we're having sex, you don't do that."

"Do what?" His brows knit in confusion.

"Call me darlin' or even Em. It's always Emily. Why?"

"Well." He perches on the side of the bed. "The day I met you, you said that's what you prefer. I figure if I'm going to ask for your submission, the least I can do is use your proper name."

"I don't mind. In fact, I like when you call me darlin'."

"Good to know, darlin'." He winks, heading for the door.

Making good use of my liquid courage, I continue, "Know what else I noticed? You're never in bed when I wake up." He stops in his tracks, dropping his head. "When you wake me up during the night, it's like you never stayed… like you leave the moment I fall asleep."

He retraces his steps, standing over me and forcing me to look up at him. I don't know why, but tears well in my eyes.

"It's not about you, Em. I've been working in my office."

"Working?"

"The next couple of months are going to be extra busy for me. Your uncle is not the only one I do accounting for. I'm just trying to get a head start."

I hear what he's saying, and a part of my mind understands. The other part, the part that's dominating right now, is only focused on one thing.

"I just want to be held. I know it's not a part of the deal, but… James—"

"Don't say that name," he growls. "Especially not in here."

"I'm sorry. I just…." I wipe at my tears, not knowing what to say. I need to stop. I can't mess up what I have going with Venom. I *can't*.

"Move over, darlin'." He sighs, occupying the spot I vacated. "Come here."

I practically dive into his arms, laying my head on his chest. His arms surround me, giving me a sense of safety I haven't felt in a long time. My tears disappear, his warmth and even breathing lulling me to sleep. With the rhythmic beat of his heart at my ear, I drift off to dreamland.

***

I crack one eye open against the sun streaming in through the windows. Venom is the next thing I see. I'm not in his arms, but at least he's here. He's sitting up and working, papers scattered on his side of the bed.

"Good morning."

"Good morning, darlin'."

140

RENASCENCE

He doesn't look up from his work, so I drag myself out of bed and to the bathroom. There was no sex last night. I don't know if he was giving me what I asked for or if I fucked things up. No emotions. That was the deal. I not only asked for cuddles, I cried. I fucking cried.

Shit, I'm such a... woman.

Shaking my head, I grab a robe and make my way to the kitchen. *Breakfast. That should take my mind off things.* I gather some eggs and veggies for omelets, along with bacon. There are some blueberries in the fridge, so I grab those also.

Muffins. That's it. I'll make him some blueberry muffins with a streusel topping. I haven't baked in a while, and as I work on the batter, I must say, it feels good. It feels *great*. By the time I slide the tray into the oven, I'm humming a tune as I work. Venom walks in when I'm adding the vegetables to the eggs.

"Mmm... smells good in here."

"Thanks." I keep my eyes on the pan, nerves jittery as I wait for him to speak again. I only hope when he does, it's not to chase me off.

"Lose the robe, Em."

I can't stop my smile. There's my answer. He's not pissed at me.

Like the good girl I am, I slide it off and toss it aside. He's brought his work with him, so I leave him be, concentrating on his breakfast. When I start plating, he issues another order.

"Lose the nightgown, too."

My hands falter, but I regain my composure enough to finish. Taking a deep breath, I pull the nightie off, sending it to join the robe. I pick up both plates, slowly making my way to the table. Venom's gaze is sliding up and down my body, the heat sending a shiver up my spine. His crotch draws my attention, the tented sweatpants a clear indication that he likes what he sees.

Me.

Go figure. I don't think I'll ever get over how much he wants me. My body. The one I've thought flawed for so long, that I've been killing myself to improve. Yet Venom comes along and thinks it's perfect. Even if I don't believe it, he does, and I believe in him.

I take my seat, shifting in discomfort when his eyes settle on my breasts.

141

"We should talk," he announces.

"About?"

"Last night."

Gulp. "I'm sorry—"

"Emily," he stops me. "I meant the next item on your list."

I breathe a sigh of relief. "Oh."

"You had a few drinks in you. I just want to make sure you want to go ahead."

"You mean... you can arrange it?"

"Of course. I intend to keep my promise, darlin'. You have a preference?"

"Preference?"

"The girl. Blonde, brunette, redhead... tall, short, skinny, thick... tattoos?"

I blink and keep blinking because I can't believe the topic of our conversation. It's like he's ordering me a pizza and wants to know what toppings I like.

"Do you even like girls?"

"Um... I don't know. I guess I was just caught up in the moment."

"Is that why your nipples are hard right now?" he asks, lips curled in a playful grin.

Pouting, I cover them with my hands. "They're hard because I'm naked and you're staring."

"So you don't want to do it?"

"Would... would you be there?"

"Trust and believe, Em. There's no way I'd miss that!" He chuckles.

"How would it go, exactly?"

"That's up to you. You don't have to reciprocate if you don't want to. It can be you and her, or the three of us. Me touching her is also up to you."

"Oh. Um... can I think about it?"

"Sure. Like I said, your fantasies, Emily."

The oven timer goes off and I almost jump a mile. Lord, if my parents only knew what was happening right now. Me, sitting naked at the breakfast table, talking about a threesome... with another girl! Shit.

I remove the muffins, taking two to Venom, along with some butter.

"Aren't you having any?" he asks.

"I made them for you."

"So?" He breaks one in half, slathers butter on it, and takes a big bite. "You made this from scratch?"

"Yeah."

"It's amazing, Em. I didn't know you could bake like this."

"Thanks." I blush, clearing the table and washing up. "It's been a while since I've done it, but now that I have more self-control when it comes to food, I think I'll start again."

"You should. Especially for me. Bring me another, will you?"

Pleased as punch, I take it to him. As I'm about to turn away, he grabs my wrist and tugs me onto his lap. He breaks off a piece, placing it at my lips. I shouldn't, but what the hell? It's just one piece. He pops it into my open mouth, finger resting on my lip as I chew. I swallow, sucking the streusel from his finger. He moans, lips wrapping around my nipple.

"Venom." His name comes out on a gasp.

"Turn around."

I straddle his lap, fingers diving into his hair when he begins to worship my breasts. Every inch of each one is subjected to his special brand of torture. Hands knead, tongue glides, lips suck, teeth bite, beard bristles. Jesus. My eyes close, head falling back as I grind on his erection. Christ, one night without him and I'm fiending like a coke addict.

"Fuck, Em." He buries his face in the valley of my breasts. "We need to talk about something else."

Huh? "Talk? Now?"

"Yes, now." He raises his head, grabs my hips, and pulls me closer. "I want you raw, Emily. Are you on the pill?"

"Depo... the shot," I answer, breathless at the desperation in his stare and voice. "I'm due for another soon, though."

"Einstein can sort you out."

"Einstein?" My head tilts to the side, brows drawn together.

"He's a doctor. A legit gynecologist."

"Oh."

143

"Say yes, Em. I'll do whatever test you want me to, but I need to feel you. I'll go get them done *today*."

I wrap my arms around his neck, eyes wandering his handsome face. I need this. Him. With nothing between us.

"We'll go together."

"Yeah?" His brows shoot up in hope.

"Yes. I want to feel you, too."

His fingers tangle in my hair, lips crashing into mine. His kisses have always been passionate, but there's something different about this one. I can't pinpoint the reason; it's sweeter, yet still bold and all-consuming. I didn't think it could be better, but it is.

So, so much better.

"Get dressed, darlin'," he mumbles against my lips. "My dick wants to go skinny-dipping."

Sexual trance broken, I laugh, head thrown back. With a smack on my ass, he rises, setting me on my feet. I retrieve my clothes from the floor, hurrying back to the bedroom. I dig through the mass of clothes and underwear he bought me, picking something to wear. After my shower, I find him dressed and waiting for me.

"Was I in there that long?"

"Women." He shakes his head, letting out a good-natured scoff.

With a roll of my eyes, I reach into my bag for the lotion. "*Men*."

He watches me as I dress but doesn't say anything. No impatient words or gestures… nothing.

"I'm ready," I tell him, grabbing my purse.

"Okay, darlin'."

Again, no comments about how long I took to get ready. This is a new experience for me. James was—no. *Get thee behind me, Satan. Not today.*

On the drive to the clinic, I receive a text from Raven.

Raven: Lunch at 1?

"Raven wants to have lunch at one. You think we'll be done by then?"

He takes a deep breath, looking out the window before he answers. "Probably."

Emily: I'd love to. Where?

Raven: My place. Venom knows where.

Emily: Ok. See you then!

"Can you drop me off at her house after, please?"

"No prob."

His manner doesn't match his words. I sense hesitation and I know why. He doesn't want me getting close to his family. I rub at my chest, trying to ease the sudden pain in my heart.

"Never mind. I'll tell her I can't make it." I lower my head, staring at my hands.

"Why?"

"I just don't feel like it."

"Emily, don't lie to me," he says in his "I'm the boss" tone.

"It's not a part of the deal. I already overstepped last night." I keep my eyes down.

"I can't tell you who to be friends with, and I sure as hell have no say over what Raven does."

"I don't want you to think I'm trying to worm my way into your life."

"I don't think that." He sighs, shaking his head as he pulls over. I still can't look at him. "Look at me, Emily."

Fuck.

I slowly turn to face him. He's conflicted and I don't blame him. This isn't what he signed up for.

"This... *relationship* thing... I don't know how to do it. I didn't exactly have a positive example to learn from."

I sit back, absorbing his words. Am I finally getting some meaningful conversation?

"My parents were always busy with one thing or another. I saw them separately more than I did together. When they were in the same place, all they did was argue. Mostly over me. I joined the Army right out of high school, then got shipped off to Afghanistan. I haven't seen them since then."

"Since you were eighteen?"

"Yeah."

"Wow."

"I vowed I'd never go through that. I'd rather keep women at a distance than try and fail. People will only end up getting hurt."

"I'm sorry, Venom. I didn't mean to bring up bad memories."

"Things have been good for me these last couple of years. Before I came to Stony View, I was working at some accounting firm in

145

Atlanta. I loved my job, but I still felt like something was missing. Then one day, I met Gage and Chopper in a diner. I asked them about their bikes because I was thinking about getting one. We ended up talking about the MC and they invited me down to check it out. I stayed, prospected for a year, and the rest is history. They gave me something I didn't have with my own blood—a real family."

"I can see that."

"I'm sorry, Em. I'm being a dick. Go. Have lunch with Raven. Hang out with the women as much as you want. Maybe they can be for you what the guys are for me. After what you've been through, you deserve to have some people in your corner."

"Are you sure?"

"Positive, darlin'."

"Okay. Thank you."

"Just don't rat me out to the prez." He gives me a smile and a conspiratorial wink. "I know what he told you last night."

"Oh, yeah." I return his smile. "He did say to tell him if you were being a dick. I bet I could get you into a lot of trouble, mister."

"But you won't." He glances behind him, pulling back onto the road.

"What makes you so sure?"

"All the future orgasms I'm going to give you."

"Hmm… you make a compelling argument, Mr. Hughes."

"I do. Now let's go see a man about some tests."

CHAPTER 13
Venom

I needed to think.

I don't know why I came to the clubhouse to do it. Maybe it's because I'm most comfortable here, around my brothers. The fuckers don't know the meaning of personal space, though. Short of going to my room, I won't get a moment's peace. Razor, Crow, and Rico are around the pool table, rowdy as fuck. Each of the Hounds has tried on separate occasions to either suck or fuck me. Funny thing is, it's all put things in perspective for me.

I like having Emily around.

I like having her in my bed, her scent on my pillows.

I like having her in my kitchen, cooking for me.

I definitely like fucking her.

And fuck if I didn't like holding her as she slept last night.

She may not think so now, but she's going to want more. Women are emotional creatures. Even the hardest ones eventually yearn for companionship. To settle down. I can't give her that. I know I should break things off before it's too late, but I can't do that either. I want her too much.

She bought the whole story about my parents, and while that's part of it, it's not the real reason I don't want an old lady. Men like us rarely get a happily ever after. How can I be with someone like Emily, someone good and sweet, knowing she'd be in danger by just being with me? Look what happened with Raven and Ellen. I can't put her through that.

I won't.

I puff on my cigar, contemplating what I'm going to do. Fuck. Why didn't I stay away from her? I wouldn't be in this predicament right now.

The clubhouse door opens and I glance up to see Gage and Einstein walking in. They stop briefly at the pool table, Einstein leaving the others and joining me on the couch.

"You okay, man?"

"Yeah. Just thinking."

147

"About Emily?"

I turn in his direction with a raised brow. He's famous around here for his "talks," but it's been a while since he had one with me.

"You brought her here, brother. I know that's a big step for you. What's going on?"

"I don't know. Things are good. We have… an arrangement. I just think she's heading in a direction I don't want to go in."

"Do you like her? Other than the sex?"

"Yeah."

"Then what's the issue?" he asks.

"I don't want her getting hurt, or worse, because of me."

"I see. It's about what happened to the girls."

I nod, relieved he understands.

"Here's what I think. Emily needs to make that decision for herself. Don't push her away because you think she can't handle the life. Raven and Ellen are still here, and they're happy. I'm happy. Look at Gage." He jerks his head in his friend's direction. "Have you ever seen him happier?"

"No."

"She seems smart, although I can't figure out why she chose you—" I punch him on the arm before he can continue. "Hey!" he protests.

"She *is* smart."

"Then give her the facts so she can make an *informed* decision."

I lean back on the couch, taking a drag of my cigar and mulling over his words. He could be right. Do I let Emily decide, or do I make the choice for her? Regardless of what I do, can I take the chance? If I let her go, I could regret it for the rest of my life. If I don't, can I protect her?

"What are you two females whispering about?" Gage asks, grabbing a chair and turning it backward to straddle it.

"Let me ask you something. If you'd somehow known what was going to happen to Raven, would you have left her alone if it meant saving her from it?"

"Whoa. That's a tough one." He runs his fingers through his hair. "I would've done anything I could to prevent it, but I can't see a life without her in it. Emily?"

"Yeah. What if—?"

148

"What if you let her go and die a miserable old man?" Einstein says. "What if you hold on to her and you both live a happy and fulfilling life? There's no time or room for what-ifs, Venom."

"E's right. She's already fitting in. We left her at the house laughing up a storm with Raven, Ellen, and Chrissy."

"She's had a fucked-up life so far. I couldn't forgive myself if I made it worse."

"I don't know what to tell you, brother. You and your girl need to work it out. Together."

"Yeah." I sigh, knowing Gage is right.

"Listen, I know what will cheer you up." He reaches into his cut, pulling out some tickets and waving them at me. "Tickets to see K.O. Jackson fighting Romero 'The Fist' tomorrow night!"

"Seriously? I thought it was sold out."

"Had a guy who owed me a favor. I got enough for everyone. Bring your lady."

"I don't know if that's her thing."

"Just bring her, asshole. Besides, I doubt Raven will let me hear the end of it if you don't."

"Fine. We'll be there."

"Good. Now let's break up this little circle jerk. I think I feel my balls shriveling up."

I laugh, Einstein joining in. I guess this is why I came here. I still have no idea what I'm going to do about Emily, but at least I feel better.

With a flick of my wrist, I motion to Marisol for another drink, watching her hips swing—with surprising disinterest—as she brings it over. *Hmm... come to think of it, she may be perfect for what I need.*

"Hey, Marisol. I have a proposition for you."

Emily

"Hey, Mom."

I stick a finger in my ear, moving away from the music in the clubhouse so I can hear her clearly.

"Hey, honey. How's Stony View? Ready to come home?"

"It's good, actually. I like it here."

"You sound different."

"What do you mean?" I ask.

"You sound... happy." There's a brief silence before she shrieks, "Emily Ann! What's his name?"

I take a deep breath, having no inclination to lie. "His name is—" I stop myself, knowing the moment I say "Venom," this conversation goes in a different direction. "Liam."

"Liam. Strong name. Is he handsome?"

"Very."

"What does he do?"

"He owns the gym I go to here, but he's also an accountant."

"Is that where you met him? At the gym?"

"At the pet shop. He does Uncle Jeff's accounting."

"Well, if he's raised your spirits, I like him already. Where are you? It's a little noisy."

"I'm...." *In a MC clubhouse, where Liam, aka Venom, is a member. There are half-naked women walking around, and I'm pretty sure someone is smoking weed.* "Hanging out with some girls I met. They're Liam's friends' girlfriends."

"That's great, honey. I'm glad you're making friends. See, I told you some time away would do you good."

"You were right as always, mother mine," I say, a big smile in place.

"That's why you should listen to me more, daughter mine."

"I will. Where's Daddy?"

"Working late. I'll have to put his dinner in the oven."

Mom goes off on one of her "homemaker" tangents, all thoughts of me and Liam vanished. Belinda Pierce has always been a stay-at-home mom while Frank was the provider. It always baffled the two of them that I worked. They thought once I got married I would have become Suzie Homemaker and pushed out a couple

150

kids while James brought home the bacon. They were even more confused when I took the second job. They didn't know the whole story until I left James. They would have wanted to help, and I couldn't allow that.

"What did *you* do today?" she asks.

"Today was great, Mom! I had lunch with the girls, and then we spent most of the afternoon wrapping gifts they're planning on giving out to the neighborhood kids for Christmas. After that we went shopping."

Two of Venom's brothers, Charger and Booker, went with us. I thought it weird that they sort of have bodyguards, but I guess their men are just overprotective. Booker's huge, so I can see how he'd scare people off, but I think his red hair and freckles are cute. Charger is smaller, shorter, and more of a pretty boy. I could see he takes his job seriously because his brown eyes were always keen, constantly scanning the surroundings. With his dark hair and tattoos, it's obvious why Chrissy's drawn to him.

On our shopping trip, the women convinced me to buy the most scandalous dress. Raven said she could live vicariously through me since she won't be able to wear anything like that for a while. Marlowe and Renae weren't there, but I was told they don't hang around the club or other old ladies much. Too bad since they're closer to my age.

I like the women I hung out with today, though. They're all younger than me, but the entire time we were together, it didn't matter. I didn't have that with the women I used to be friends with. Looking back at them now, they weren't my friends at all. They disappeared when I needed them most.

"Sounds wonderful, dear. The kids will be thrilled, I'm sure. What about you? Do you need money, Emily?"

"I'm fine, Mom. Uncle Jeff won't let me pay for anything, so I haven't really spent any of my own money yet."

"And Liam?"

"Mom, I just met him."

"Yes, but he's not making you pay half your dinner bill or some silliness like that, is he? I seriously don't understand men these days."

"No, Mom. He pays the bill."

"Good. You deserve a man who will take care of you."

"He does… and it's not about money. He's everything James isn't. He makes me feel… well, he makes me *feel*. I never thought I'd be able to let anyone in again. I don't know where this is going, but at least I know I'm capable of moving on."

"Oh, honey… I'm so happy for you. I'm sure your father will be, too. We might want to meet this man of yours."

"Mom, it's way too early for that."

"Just think about it. Talk to Liam. If he agrees, you'll know he's serious about you."

"Okay, Mom." I know he's not serious, so that conversation is a nonstarter. "I will."

"Good."

"I gotta go, Mom. I'll call you tomorrow."

"You're coming home for Christmas, right?"

"I'm not sure, but I'll let you know."

"All right, dear. Tomorrow."

"Bye, Mom."

I hang up, searching the room for the women. The clubhouse door opens and in walks Venom. Grinning like an idiot, I start making my way to him. However, I stop in my tracks when he leans against the door, allowing a brunette to walk through. I've seen her before. She was behind the bar the first night I was here, but she's also what Ellen called a "Hound." According to Raven, these are the kind of women who give blow jobs right in this room where anyone can see. *Is that what they were doing? Did he fuck her?* My gaze slides over her body, inadequacy bubbling inside me. Her flat stomach and firm boobs have me looking down at my little pouch, almost hidden from view by my gigantic breasts. Not to mention the god-awful stretch marks.

Shit.

Fuck!

He promised there wouldn't be anyone else while we were together. We went and did motherfucking STD tests this morning! Do those girls even count, though? I mean, that's what they're here for.

"Hey, darlin'."

I look up into his smiling face, not knowing what to say. I'm so conflicted. Disappointed. In both of us. Him for going behind my back, and me for not expecting he would.

"What's wrong, Emily?"

My eyes flick to the woman, Venom turning his head to follow my gaze. He cradles my face with both hands, tilting it up.

"Look at me."

I can't. I close my eyes instead, willing myself to hold back the tears threatening to make an appearance.

"I said look. At. Me." My lids flutter open, meeting his stormy gray eyes. "There's nothing between me and Marisol."

"So you didn't fuck her?" I ask, my tone cynical.

"I have, but not since I've been fucking you."

"Really?" Cynicism turns to hope.

"Really. I was hoping she'd be our third, but I'm not so sure now."

"Our third?"

"For your list, Emily. I took her to get some tests done… to ease your mind."

"Oh. You mean…?"

"For your threesome." He smirks, knowing my anger is dissipating.

"You asked her?"

"Yeah."

"And she said yes?"

I observe her, wondering why she'd agree to have sex with *me*. She's gorgeous. Or is she just willing to put up with me in order to get to Venom?

"Yeah. She likes you."

"She likes me?" My brows shoot up in disbelief.

"Emily." His hands drop to my shoulders. "You're hot. To both men and women. In case you didn't notice, most of my brothers hit on you last night."

"I figured they were just messing with you.'

"No, they weren't. Even Tek unglued his nose from his computer screen for you."

"Oh." I sigh, realizing I once again allowed my insecurities to create issues where there aren't any. "I'm sorry."

153

"Don't apologize, darlin'. It's okay."

"It's not. I'm sorry. Sorry for being...." I shrug. "Me."

"This isn't you. I'm sure the real you will show herself soon."

"I hope so."

"Come on. I'll introduce you to Marisol."

The woman smiles at me as we approach her. I avert my gaze, horrified at how this feels like an interview... for a sex partner.

"Emily, Marisol. Marisol, meet Emily."

"Hi, Emily. Venom's told me a little about you, about what you want."

Jesus. I hope she can't tell how mortified I am. "And... you're okay with that?"

"More than okay. I saw you the other night and thought you were cute. I was a little surprised, but definitely up for it."

"You've done this before?"

"Yeah, I've been with girls. I've had threesomes, too... another girl, two guys." She gives me a devilish smile. "Two girls."

"Information overload, Marisol," Venom cuts in, chuckling. "Don't scare her off."

"Well, you know where I stand, sweetie. Let me know."

She walks off, swinging her hips. My eyes are glued to her retreating back, wondering if I could go through with this. At least she's pretty. Prettier than me. A better body. What if we get to the bedroom and Venom sees that next to her, I don't stack up? I'm really going to have to weigh my options on this one.

Venom takes my hand, leading me to the other side of the room. He drops down on the couch, settling me on his lap. "Did you have fun today?"

"I did. I hung out with Raven, Chrissy, and Ellen. They're awesome."

"Good. Listen, a bunch of us are going to a MMA match tomorrow. Wanna go? The girls will be there."

"I'd love to," I answer, not needing time to think. I've only seen those fights on TV, but I'm not really interested in that. I get to be with Venom and that's all that matters.

He squeezes my thigh, his palm sliding impossibly close to my pussy. I gasp, eyes going wide as he leans closer, voice low and husky.

"I didn't get to taste your sweet pussy last night, Em. That's not happening tonight."

"What's happening?" I whisper.

"I'm going to take you home, tie you to my bed, and bury my face between your thighs."

I shift, curling my arms around his shoulders. "Then what?"

"Then…." His fingers make circles on my thigh. Even through my jeans I can feel the heat of his touch. "I'm going to fuck you until you can't move."

"Like every other night?" I smirk.

"Exactly."

"Maybe we should go. Now."

He grips my thigh, fingers pressing into my flesh. "You need to get fucked, Em?"

"Yes," I answer, unable to breathe. "By you."

His hold tightens, but I barely feel it. The sexual tension between us is tangible; I swear anyone could reach out and touch it. My heart is hammering in my chest, palms sweaty with anticipation.

"Say your goodbyes, Em. Make it quick."

I slide off his lap, heading back to where the ladies are by the bar.

"We know, you're leaving." Ellen giggles.

"How do you know?"

"Are you kidding? We saw that eye-fuck fest over there," Raven says. "You two are *hot*."

I blush, throwing a helpless glance over my shoulder at Venom.

"Don't worry. You'll get over that embarrassment soon enough. These men aren't exactly shy," Chrissy chimes in.

"You're lucky he hasn't tossed you over his shoulder yet."

When Ellen speaks, Raven high-fives her. "Been there."

They all laugh, putting me at ease. "I gotta go, but thanks for today. I'll see you all tomorrow at the fight."

"Bye, Emily," they chorus, wiggling their fingers, moaning, and making kissing sounds.

I grab my shopping bag from the bar, hurrying back to Venom before I die of humiliation. We leave the clubhouse, making it to his house in record time. Just like Ellen said, he throws me over his shoulder, slapping my ass on his way to the door.

"Ow!"

"I told you to be quick."

"I was!" I protest.

"Not quick enough."

The door is kicked closed behind us. Striding with purpose to the bedroom, he tosses me on the bed, pinning my arms above my head. His lips descend, crushing mine in a bruising kiss. Moaning, I open to let him in. Our tongues tangle, his taste of beer, cigar, and mint heightening my senses. His lips move down, my back arching from the bearded kisses on my neck. One hand secures my wrists while the other undoes the button on my jeans.

"Wait...."

"Why?" He groans, pressing his crotch to mine.

"Shower... first," I get out between pants, thoughts of what he said he wanted to do to me running through my mind.

"Seriously?" He stares down at me in disbelief. "I need you now, Emily."

"I promise I won't be long."

"Fine," he gives in, rolling to the bed.

I hurry to the bathroom, leaving him staring up at the ceiling. I keep my promise, out in only a few minutes. The room is empty. I throw on one of his T-shirts, foregoing the sexy lingerie since I'll be naked in the next couple of seconds. He's not in the living room or kitchen, so I try his office next. Standing in the doorway, I watch him. He's punching away on a calculator, checking his results against something on his computer screen. When he finally notices me, he closes the laptop and rises to his feet. I step inside, once again looking over the certificates on his wall. I'm no less impressed than the first time I was in here.

"All this... it's amazing. You must really love what you do."

He shrugs. "I've always had a thing for numbers. Figured I'd put it to good use."

"So your dream was to spend your life with numbers? Formulas and such?"

"My dream was to properly manage money."

His demeanor changes, the way it always does when it comes to discussing anything remotely personal. He's shutting down. Since his discomfort is evident, I won't push.

"That's cool." Approaching him, I wrap one arm and then the other around his neck. "But how about we work on an equation of our own?"

"Yeah? Like what?" His hands slide around my waist and down to cup my ass.

"Like...." I trail a finger down his neck. "We subtract some clothes...."

"Ah...." He picks me up, hooking my legs around his hips. "And I divide your thighs?"

"That's right. Then you add... your dick inside me."

He slowly makes his way to the bedroom, a smirk on his lips as he adds, "Then I multiply my thrusts."

"Definitely." I nod for emphasis. "Lots of multiplication."

I can't believe the conversation we're having. I've never spoken to anyone like this in my entire life. He's the first man I've even flirted with in years. It's not just the topic either. I never use profanity in front of anyone. Ever. Not even the man I was married to. With Venom... everything is different. Better.

"And what's going to be the result?" he asks.

"Oh, I think we both know what the result is. Just make sure you show your work."

He lets out a feral growl, tossing me on the bed yet again.

Playtime is over.

***

"Are you sure this is okay?" I ask, indicating my outfit again.

"Darlin', it's a fight. What you're wearing is fine. You look great."

"I wasn't fishing for a compliment. I've never been to one of these things before."

I slide my palms down the front of my jeans before fixing my sweater and scarf in front of the mirror. Behind me, Venom shrugs into a leather jacket, covering up the gun strapped to his shoulder. Of course he looks good. He always does.

"No cut?"

"Event like this, don't know who we'll run into, so the prez thought it best we don't fly our colors."

"I don't understand."

"Police and regular people like you see a cut and see trouble. There could also be unfriendlies."

"I still don't understand." I sit on the bed, waiting for him to explain.

"You don't know anything about MCs, do you?"

"No. You haven't exactly told me anything about yours either."

"Nothing at all? Not even from that show that was on TV?"

"I didn't have time for TV. Two jobs, remember?"

"Emily, not all clubs are exactly on the up and up. Legally."

"You mean… they're criminals?"

"Yes."

He stares me down, practically willing me to ask the question on the tip of my tongue. "The Dealers?"

"It's complicated."

"What does that mean?"

He takes a deep breath, occupying the spot next to me. "I told you about the businesses we own, but that's not all we do."

"What else?" I wait with bated breath.

"That's club business. Can't tell you, darlin'."

"But it's not legal?"

"Not exactly."

"Do you kill people?"

"I fought in a war, Emily. Killed lots of people."

"I mean your club."

"Let's go or we're gonna be late."

"Venom—"

"Emily, look. Even if you were my old lady, there are things I wouldn't be able to tell you. Anything to do with the club is off-limits."

"I see."

I drop the argument because I've been effectively put in my place. I'm not his old lady. Our agreement does not extend beyond the bedroom. I don't know why I have to keep reminding myself. Besides, in a way, he *did* answer my question. These men do way more than "ride together, talk about bikes and stuff." The stuff they're into makes them leave their cuts behind to avoid attention from police.

Christ. I'm sleeping with a criminal.

"You ready?"

"Um... yeah."

He lets me lead the way, opening my door so I can climb into the Jeep. We're meeting the others at the clubhouse, then taking one vehicle to the venue, so I use the travel time to gather my thoughts. Does this newfound knowledge affect the way I see Venom? My feelings toward him? I don't think so. We're not in a relationship. I'm just the woman he's currently fucking. It's not like we're getting married. Soon, we'll both move on and all this won't even matter.

Move on.

Why does the thought fill me with dread? Criminal or not, I've only been treated like a queen by this man, and that is how he'll be judged, not by what I think he's done.

"You have any questions about me, you can ask them, Em. I just can't tell you anything confidential about the MC."

"Okay."

Despite his offer, I don't speak for the rest of the drive. When we join the others, the girls sense my mood and keep conversation with me to a minimum. I'm grateful because I don't know where to go from here.

The fight is being staged in Atlanta, and when we arrive, I realize it's not too far from my parents' house. Maybe I should spend the night there instead of the hotel we're supposed to stay in. A night at home and a talk with my mother—minus the criminal part—should help me make a decision.

When we enter the venue, they separate the men from the women, forming two lines. A man searches the males while a woman does the same to us. Venom has his gun, so I watch carefully to see what will happen. Gage leads his brothers, shaking the guard's hand when it's his turn to be searched. The man shoves his hand in his pocket, pats Gage's body a few times, then lets him pass. He does the same to the other Dealers.

He was paid off.

Wow.

At this point, I'm not interested in the fight.

159

"Are you okay?" Raven asks when we find our seats. She's on my right, Ellen on my left.

"Yeah. Just have a lot on my mind."

"What did Venom do?" She raises a skeptical brow.

"Nothing, I promise."

"Okay, but if you wanna talk, I'm here." She squeezes my fingers.

"I appreciate that."

Thankfully the introduction of the fighters interrupts our conversation.

"Guys, look! It's him!" Ellen squeals, pointing to a man walking to the cage.

A big, blond, muscled and tattooed chunk of hotness.

"Which one is he?" I ask.

"That's K.O. Jackson," Ellen explains. "I wouldn't get comfortable if I were you. His fights don't usually last long."

Sure enough, K.O. knocks out his opponent after playing with him for a few minutes. I can't believe we drove all this way for that. At least he was hot and we got to see a little man-candy. We hustle out of the venue, meeting up in the parking lot. Gage does a quick head count, and then we start making our way to the van.

That's when I spot him. I wasn't sure at first, but a closer look confirms it.

James.

There's a woman on his arm. A platinum blonde in a pink jumpsuit, looking like a bottle of Pepto-Bismol. She's not the one he got pregnant. Only God knows what he's doing now that I'm not in the picture. As if he feels me looking, he turns in my direction, our eyes locking. Subconsciously, I move closer to Venom, grabbing his arm. James quickly drops his gaze, hurrying away. *Why am I having this kind of reaction to James?* I should be flipping him off and moving along.

"What is it?" Venom stops moving, obviously following my gaze because his body tenses. His arm curls around my shoulder, pulling me to his side. "Come on, Em. Forget him."

I hang on tightly to Venom, putting one foot before the other. We don't get far before we have to stop again, a group of men blocking our path. One moves forward to stand before Gage, looking very

160

much like the Italian mobsters you see in movies. Venom steps in front of me, shielding me with his body. Charger, Booker, Motor, and Tek spring into action, taking me, Raven, Ellen, and Chrissy aside. Razor and Einstein flank Gage, Venom, Crow, and Rico, backing them up. Everyone moved so fast, my head is spinning.

"What's going on?" I ask.

"Just be quiet," Raven answers in a hushed voice.

"But—"

"A little piece of advice: trust your man. Whatever happens, let him handle the situation. Always."

At her words, I quiet down, watching everything unfold.

"Well, well. The Reaper himself. What are you doing in these parts?" the man in front asks Gage.

"You may know my name, but you obviously have no fucking clue who I am. You got ten seconds to get the fuck out of my way."

Uh-oh.

"Oh, I know exactly who you are. Thing is I ain't scared of you." He looks to the other men, briefly settling on Venom before returning to Gage.

"Then you're a stupid motherfucker."

The men stare each other down for a few seconds before Gage proclaims, "Time's up."

"Is there a problem here, fellas?" a deep voice thunders behind us.

I turn to see the giant from the cage match approaching. He stands between the two groups of men, glancing from one to the other.

"No problem, just a minor obstruction," Gage replies.

The other men back away slowly, the leader issuing a warning. "This ain't over, Dealer."

A chill runs down my spine at his words. Not the good kind. I guess this is what Venom meant by "unfriendlies."

A gorgeous woman runs up to the fighter, and he throws his arm around her.

"You guys okay?"

"Thanks for the assist," Gage says, shaking the man's hand.

"No problem."

The men gather around K.O., offering congratulations on the fight. I pull Venom aside, letting him in on the plan that I've now decided on.

"Listen, my parents live a few minutes away. I was thinking I'd stay with them tonight."

His expression is blank as he asks, "Are you sure?"

"Yeah. I'll just get a cab or something."

"No need. We'll drop you off."

Knowing better than to argue, I nod. "I'll call you in the morning."

"Sure thing, darlin'."

We head to the van, and as I climb in, the hairs on the back of my neck stand up. I turn my head to look behind me, thinking it's James again. The face I see has a hard stare and a cold, calculating grin.

And it's not James.

CHAPTER 14
Venom

I'm convinced Emily has put a spell on me with her unicorn pussy.

I haven't heard from her in days, yet here I am, wrapping her Christmas gifts. She never did call me after the fight. I figured she needed some time, so I gave it to her. She's not back from Atlanta either. Jeff told me. Maybe this is for the best. Einstein said I should allow her to make a choice, and I am. If that little bit of information causes her to run, she has no business being around me or my club. She's better off going back to her school teacher life, finding a man who has a reliable nine-to-five and doesn't inject snake venom into a man to get what he wants.

I place the wrapped boxes in my closet, unsure if I'll get the opportunity to give them to her. It's Christmas Day, my family is in the bar enjoying it and each other, and here I am holed up with a bottle of whiskey and a cigar. An unwelcome knock at the door makes me groan. These Hounds don't give up. This is the third time today Marisol has "checked" on me.

"Go away!"

"Venom," comes a soft, tentative voice. One that's definitely not unwelcome. "It's me."

I throw the door open, wondering if I'm hearing things. The woman standing on the other side makes me wonder if I'm seeing things also.

"Emily?"

"Hi." She gives me a weak smile. "Can I come in?"

"Yeah, sure."

I close the door behind us, sitting on the bed and watching her expectantly.

"I'm sorry I haven't called. I've just been... thinking."

"Didn't think I'd see you again."

"Honestly, I almost didn't come."

"Why did you?"

"You." She rubs her palms on the side of her jeans in a nervous manner, sitting next to me. "Like I said, I've been thinking."

"And?"

"And I've been muddying the waters of our agreement. I've never had a relationship like this one, and sometimes I forget. It's not my place to question your actions and lifestyle choices, or ask you to cuddle, or anything you don't want to do. I'm sorry."

"What are you saying?" I ask, wanting to hear the words.

"I'm saying I want to continue our arrangement. If you want to, that is," she quickly adds. "I can't promise I won't mess up, but I'll try to do better."

"Are you sure you want to do this?"

"Yes. I know you won't hurt me, but I'd rather not be in a position like the one you put me in the other night."

"That was on me and I'm sorry. I guess I was muddying the waters, too. I won't try to involve you in club stuff anymore."

"I like it here, at the clubhouse. I don't mind it, but just not... out. Not where the 'unfriendlies' are," she says, complete with air quotes.

"You got it, darlin'."

She closes her eyes, a sense of calm overcoming her.

"I love it when you call me that."

"Well, darlin', why don't you come over here and give me a kiss, darlin'?"

She giggles, straddling my lap without instruction, gently pressing her lips to mine. It's at this moment, the point of contact, that I realize how much I really missed this. Her.

My hands glide up her thighs, grabbing her ass and squeezing. Fuck, her body feels so good against me, in my hands, on top of me.

"Need to fuck you, Emily," I groan.

She moans, mumbling against my lips, "Can't."

"Why the fuck not?"

She pulls back, putting space between our lips. I hate space. I hate space between *us*.

"Chopper told me to tell you that dinner is ready."

"Fuck Chopper, and fuck dinner. I'm getting inside you now. No condom."

"What?"

"Got the test results back."

"Where are they?" she asks eagerly, hopping off my lap.

Fuck. Me.

Growling in frustration, I retrieve them from the drawer on the nightstand, handing her all three envelopes. She looks them over quite thoroughly before handing them back with a grin.

"I saw my doctor while I was in ATL. Got my shot," she teases, backing away toward the door.

"Fuck, Emily. Get your ass back here." I grab my hard dick, adjusting it to ease the ache.

"Dinner. Everyone's waiting for us."

I free my dick from my jeans, stroking it as I approach her. Her eyes drop to my crotch, tongue sliding over her lower lip.

"Do I look like I care?" She backs into the wall, pressing her thighs together. "You want this, Emily. You want me to fuck you against that wall, hammer into you to make up for the time you were away."

"Venom...."

"Did you dream about me?" I cage her in with my arms, planting my palms on either side of her. "Did you wake up wet and horny? Did you come in your sleep?"

"Um... maybe once."

"Once?" I unbutton her jeans, lazily tracing a line across her stomach. Her eyes close, body trembling.

Undoing the top buttons on her shirt, I push the sides apart, tugging one cup of her bra down to release a breast. Her luscious flesh pops out, pink nipple hard and jutting out. Reaching for me. I tease it gently with my index finger, smiling in triumph at her moan.

"Okay... maybe more than once."

I lean forward, leisurely licking her nipple. Her fingers curl in my hair, pulling hard when I suck on it. Getting her jeans out of the way, I wrangle them down her hips with swift jerks.

"Venom...." She whimpers, holding me tight to her breast. "Fuck, I missed you."

I slide my tongue over her sternum and up her neck, stepping to the side so my dick rests on her thigh. I dip my hand into her panties to slowly circle her clit. She's wet, the crotch of her panties soaked through. Her hips roll against my fingers, head falling back on the wall. I want her crazy for me. So crazy she'll beg me to fuck her.

"Need you to come, darlin'," I whisper against her ear.

"I want to, but not now," she says on a series of whimpers.

"What's wrong with now?"

"If you behave… we can add our third tonight."

I pull back, still stroking her lips as I ask, "Tonight?"

"Merry… Oh!" She shivers. "Christmas."

"Your fantasy, darlin', so I think that's my line."

She grips my dick, fisting it as she holds my stare. "She can touch you, you can touch her, but this?" She squeezes my dick, making me groan. "This is mine."

"Fuck, Emily."

Her boldness grows with each passing day. I can't believe this is the same woman who wouldn't even meet my eyes when I gave her a compliment.

"Deal?"

"Deal," I agree, slowly and deliberately sucking her sweet juices from my fingers while she watches in awe.

Flustered, Emily begins fixing her clothes, and I reluctantly tuck my dick back in my jeans. Oh, she's going to pay for this later. Right after I punish her for disappearing and depriving me of her vise-grip pussy.

We head to the bar, and I wonder if anyone can see I'm walking funny. Neglected hard-ons are no joke. I set Emily up in a spot close to the other old ladies, telling her to stay put while I grab us something to eat. The bar top has been converted into a makeshift buffet table, covered end to end with food. Chopper and Nita went all out this year. I spot Marisol, pulling her aside to make sure she doesn't make any plans with another brother tonight.

"Hey, we're a go for tonight."

Her blue eyes light up. "Awesome. Been a while since I had a ménage."

"Listen, tonight is about Emily. You concentrate on her, make her feel good."

"What about you?"

I glance back at Emily, whose anxious gaze is trained on us. "She thinks she wants that, but I don't think she's ready. Let's just focus on her."

"Got it."

I load up two plates before making my way through the crowd back to Emily. She takes hers, balancing it on her lap as she turns to me.

"What did she say?"

"It's all good, darlin'. She's looking forward to it."

"Really?"

"Really, Em. Stop worrying."

"Okay."

She starts eating, but we're interrupted not long after by Nita. She hands us some drinks, stopping to talk to Emily.

"Hi. Didn't get a chance to talk to you the other night. I'm Nita, Gage and Ellen's aunt."

"Emily. Nice to meet you, Nita."

"This one treating you okay?" She jerks her chin in my direction, placing both hands on her generous hips. She may be Gage's blood, but she treats all of us like family. She's kind of our de facto den mother.

"Yes, better than okay."

"Good. You need anything, you let me know, honey."

"I will. Thanks." As she walks away, Emily adds, "She seems nice."

"She is. Eat up."

"Anxious much?" She grins, poking me in the side.

"What do you think? It's been days, Emily. *Days.*"

"Oh, bless your heart. To have to go days without sex. You must be scarred for life," she mocks me.

"I hope you're enjoying sitting down. You won't be doing much of it after tonight."

I can almost hear the gulp as she swallows. She opens her mouth to speak, but before she can, Raven leans over and interrupts.

"Hey, Emily. Wanna go shopping with me for baby stuff? Chrissy's heading back to school soon and Ellen's really busy with work. I'd take Gage, but he'd buy four of everything we don't need."

"Of course. I'd love to."

"Thanks!"

For the next two hours, I'm subjected to more holiday shit. Mingling, nog drinking, and gift exchanges. Usually I'm all for it, but right now I only want to take Emily back to my room. Having her by my side is the only thing keeping me sane. Strange, since she's the reason I'm losing my mind in the first place.

"Who wants dessert?" Nita shouts, answered by whistles and hollers. "This year, we have Millie's apple pie, and this gorgeous gingerbread cookie cake Venom's lady, Emily, made for us."

Emily blushes, burying her face in my chest. Nita's right. The cake is beautiful, decorated with little gingerbread men on the side. There are also a few on top that look like they're playing in the snow. Judging by her muffins, I bet it's delicious. Of course, I make sure I get the first piece. And I was right. Fucking delicious. She declines a slice, saying she's already broken her diet with dinner.

"This is incredible, darlin'. Taste, presentation... all top-notch."

"Thanks," she replies in a timid voice.

The sheer innocence this woman exudes is baffling to me. How can someone so sweet drive me so fucking nuts in the bedroom? *I need her now. Fuck this shit.* I grab her hand and head for my room, motioning for Marisol to follow. Both women watch me lock the door, standing by the bed and awaiting instruction.

I fucking love my life.

Placing a chair at the foot of the bed, I light up a cigar and sit for the show. Taking a puff, I blow the smoke toward Emily and Marisol.

"Clothes. Off."

RENASCENCE
Emily

At Venom's command, Marisol's clothes begin falling off. I watch, transfixed as her body is revealed. *What am I doing?* I look to Venom, whose eyes are focused on me and not the woman getting naked next to me. The message is clear—I'm the one who matters. This is what I asked for, and I can end it all with one word.

But I don't want to.

As if he sees the change in me, he nods to Marisol. The woman moves closer, gently touching my shoulder. I turn to her, searching her face for any reluctance but not finding any.

"Are you sure you want to do this?" I ask.

"No doubt." She gives me a reassuring smile, deft fingers quickly undoing the buttons on my shirt. I take a deep breath, holding it as she pushes the garment down my arms. My jeans and bra are next to go, piled on top of my shirt on the floor.

"Emily." Venom's voice startles me. "Come to me."

I stand before him, pulse racing while I endure his hungry gaze, his threat prevalent in my mind. However, I'm not scared. He won't hurt me. I want him to spank me. I want everything he can give me.

He tugs me onto his lap, maneuvering me onto my stomach with lightning speed. I gasp, nervous anticipation thrumming through my entire body. I turn my head, seeking Marisol, and find her now completely naked, sitting at the foot of the bed, legs spread. Venom and I have full view of her. Her pink lips are parted, chest heaving as she watches us. Venom's palm caresses my ass, squeezing each cheek in turn.

"Naughty girl, did you think you could keep all this away from me?" he asks.

"I… I wasn't—"

His palm crashes down on my ass, cutting off my words. *Why did I have to wear a thong today?* My eyes snap closed, a yelp coming from my lips. He curls his fingers in the waist of my panties, roughly tugging them down. Instead of pulling them off, there's a rip and then they're gone. Both hands knead my cheeks, spreading them before there's a slap just above my thigh. I moan, biting my lip when he delivers another. The sound of a different moan reminds me of Marisol's presence. I glance in her direction, shocked to find her touching herself as she watches us. She likes this, likes to see me being punished. Christ, she's getting off on it.

"See that?" Venom asks, caressing yet again. "Marisol's pussy is wet from watching me spank your ass. She loves to see how red it's getting... my palm printed on the cheeks."

I squirm on his lap, my clit beginning to throb. Wrapping an arm around my waist, he raises me up while slightly parting my thighs. His free hand strokes me, sliding up and down my pussy from clit to entrance.

"Oh, God...."

He grunts, smacking both cheeks in quick succession before dipping a finger inside me.

"Yes!"

I'm lowered back to his lap, his left hand landing stinging slaps while the right gives immense pleasure, thumb rubbing my clit, middle finger gliding in and out of my soaked pussy. Just as I'm about to come, he withdraws his attentions. I groan, body protesting when he sets me upright.

"On your knees in the middle of the bed."

Marisol moves, too, kneeling in front of me. Venom leans back in his chair, puffing on his cigar. The other woman's fingers glide up my arms, sending tingly sensations through me.

"Relax, Emily," she whispers before placing a gentle kiss on my lips.

I remain frozen to the spot as her soft lips move over mine. Her fingers trail over my breasts and around my nipples, pinching them. The action spurs me into motion and I return her kiss, tentatively touching my tongue to hers. She moans—fucking *moans*! I made her feel good. Me! With a burst of courage, I move closer, placing my hand on her hips. Her soft skin, gentle actions, flowery scent, fruity taste—so different from what I'm used to, yet still so arousing. Her fingers leave my nipple, moving to my clit. My hips jerk toward her, slowly grinding on her hand.

"I want to taste you," she continues in the same soft voice.

She gently positions me on my back, parting my legs and settling between them. The nerves hit me. I try to pull away but meet

RENASCENCE

Venom's eyes in the process. His shirt is gone, his jeans open, dick resting against his stomach. Our gazes lock and he wraps his fingers around it, stroking up and down as he watches. It's enough to distract me until there's a gentle swipe on my clit.

"Oh!"

Rising, Venom stubs out his cigar, kicks off his jeans and boxers, and makes his way toward us. He sits on the edge of the bed, leaning over. Marisol's tongue moves down, pushing at my entrance while Venom's takes its place on my clit. I cry out, head thrown back, hand fisting in his hair. It's too much. I don't know how much more I can handle. Venom and Marisol, both tongues moving to their own beat. My muscles begin to clench. Venom's tongue disappears, his body appearing behind me, hard dick pressing into my back. He props me up on his thighs, his big hands cupping my breasts, fingers tweaking my nipples. Marisol inserts two fingers inside me, pumping them in and out while her tongue flicks on my clit.

"Oh, fuck...." I writhe on the bed, my new elevated position showing me that she's fingering herself with her free hand.

"She tastes good, Venom."

"Oh, I know," he says, hand gliding down my stomach, replacing Marisol's tongue. He gently rubs my clit, smacking it, then immediately plunging a finger inside me.

"Venom," I groan, needing more than a finger.

He moves back to my breasts, Marisol resuming her position. My head thrashes from side to side when she sucks on my clit, moaning around it. Venom covers my mouth with his, tongue forcefully tasting as his fingers continue to torture my breasts. He pulls on my nipples, twisting them painfully, but oh so good. My moans begin to mix with Marisol's until I'm unsure which are mine and which are hers. I clench around her fingers, nails digging into Venom's arms.

"Fuck!" I scream, stars dancing behind my lids as I explode, legs quivering.

My hips rise off the bed but Marisol grips my thighs, licking me until I stop shaking. After one final kiss on my clit, I watch in awe as she rises, gets dressed, then walks out the door, blowing me a kiss.

171

"Oh, my God, that was… there are no words."

"Glad you enjoyed it, darlin'."

"Enjoyed is an understatement. When the two of you were… *Jesus.*" I roll over onto my stomach, Venom's still-hard dick now in my face. "Oh."

"Yeah, 'oh.'"

With a smile, I climb on top of him. He likes me this way, and I want to see his face when he slides inside me for the first time without a condom. I curl my fingers around him, rubbing the head between my lips before sinking down on him. My thighs quiver, nails pressing into his shoulders. *God, he feels good.* His eyes close and his lips part, head falling back against the headboard.

"Holy… fucking… shit," he mumbles. His fingers dig into my hips, keeping me in place. "Fuck, Emily." I'm mesmerized by his reaction, unable to move. "Thank fuck you came already because I'm not going to last long."

He shifts, hips pinning me to the bed as he thrusts deep. I grab the sheets, back arching. He starts to move, fast, deep, hard thrusts, as if he's still trying to punish me.

"This is my pussy, Emily. *Mine.*"

"Yes, yours."

"Don't you fucking make me wait so long again."

"I won't. Fuck me, Venom."

Reacting to the urgency in my voice, he moves to his knees and grabs my hips, raising them off the bed to meet his thrusts.

"Fuck, you're so tight… so wet. My fucking pussy!"

"Yes!" I scream, his words pushing me to fulfillment as much as his dick. My muscles tighten, gripping him.

He practically roars, going deep, hips stilling, dick pulsing inside me. I join him, pussy clenching wildly.

"Venom!"

My hips fall back to the bed, Venom collapsing on top me. Both out of breath, we lie there, silent until our breathing calms.

"I swear I could stay like this for the rest of my life and be a happy man."

My pussy jumps.

He groans, lifting his head to look at me.

"Give me five minutes and then we're definitely fucking doing that again."

CHAPTER 15
Venom

No way.

Not fucking happening. In my gym? This fucker better say a prayer to whatever god he serves.

I've been waiting for Emily to finish her session with Rianne. I'm gone for five minutes and return to find some fucker all up on her. She's smiling, laughing with this asshole who's blatantly flirting with her. He's been inching closer and closer to her these last couple weeks, but today he's crossed the line. Emily looks amazing, so I can't say I blame him, but she's mine.

It's time he got that memo.

Despite wanting to break his face, I can't take my eyes off Emily as I approach them. The baggy T-shirts are a thing of the past, now replaced by sports bras. Her arms and legs are toned, stomach flatter than before. She's lost a few pounds, but more inches. It's given her a boost of confidence, but I like to think I've helped her in that department also. To me, that's what's made her more appealing, not the weight she's lost. She's becoming the woman I always knew she could be: strong, poised, independent. It's sexy as fuck. After our Christmas Day romp, we've been hot and heavy. There hasn't been a night when she wasn't in my bed, even the entire week when I couldn't be inside her. That certainly didn't stop me from doing other things to her body, though. It's strange, but the more I fuck her, the more I want to. I can't seem to get enough of her, and it's the same for her. The woman loves to fuck as much as I do. There's nothing more I could ask for.

Except for her baking.

I've been hitting the gym extra hard to work off the calories she's pumping me up with, but it's worth it. She blesses that kitchen and miracles happen. She's even been working with Ellen and her party planning business. Everything she's baked for those events has gotten rave reviews. When she's not fattening up the town, she subs at the high school. I have to say she's fitting into this town pretty well, and is making a good life for herself.

"Hey, darlin', you ready to go?"

I throw an arm over her shoulder, pulling her close while my gaze dares the man to try anything with her. He swallows hard, taking a step back, and then scurrying away like a mouse.

"Yeah, let me just grab a shower."

"I'll wait for you at the juice bar."

I watch her walk away, wondering if she thinks she's getting off that easily. Not by a long shot. Like I've been doing almost every day for the last six weeks, I grab her a drink and wait. She returns with a bright smile, the same one she's been giving me all that time. It's no less beautiful than the first time I saw it. In fact, it gets better every time.

"Ready?"

"Yes, sir!"

I throw her bag over my shoulder, letting her walk ahead of me so I can ogle her ass. I've grabbed it, squeezed it, massaged it, smacked it, flipped it, rubbed it down, and there are still so many more things I want to do to it. She hasn't mentioned anal again, but it's a conversation I definitely want to revisit. It's not even about the sex; I want to claim every inch of Emily's body. I wasn't her first, not even her second, but I *am* the best. This is uncharted territory for her, and I want to Neil Armstrong that shit.

"How was school today?" I ask on our drive to my place.

"Good. I have papers to grade tonight, Liam."

I know that was a warning for me that she won't be able to indulge in one of our all-night fuck fests. The fact that she used my real name means she's serious. No worries. I wasn't planning on giving her my dick tonight after what she did. I might be petty, but I don't play when it comes to her.

"Hint taken, Miss Pierce."

"I'll make you an extra special breakfast tomorrow to make up for it."

"Uh-huh. You will."

"You sound weird. Are you okay?"

"I'm fine. I should be asking you that question."

"Me? What did *I* do?" she asks.

"What were you and that dude laughing about?"

"You mean Carter? He just told me a joke."

"He was flirting with you."

"He was not. You think every man who talks to me wants to get in my pants."

"They do."

"Wait." She turns in her seat, and I glance over to catch the amusement on her face. I clench the steering wheel, knowing what's coming next. "Are you jealous, Mr. Hughes?"

"Of course not. Being jealous would indicate I actually think that asshole could take you away from me. News flash, I don't."

"Oh, you're so confident of that?"

"Are you saying you think he can make you come as hard as I do?"

"I don't think of him like that!" she protests. "You're just being silly."

"Is that so?" I pull into the driveway, shutting off the ignition, not looking at her as I speak. "When we get in that house, go straight to the bedroom and take off your clothes."

As usual, she doesn't argue. Why would she? She knows what I can deliver. While she makes her way to the bedroom, I head to the kitchen and grab a beer from the fridge, slowly drinking, imagining her squirming with anticipation. Taking the bottle with me, I check on my babies. I pause before Benny's terrarium, remembering the last time I got to use the boa constrictor. I was helping Gage with a situation but didn't enjoy it any less. I can still see the way the man's eyes bulged as Benny coiled around his neck. It was beautiful.

"Sweet Jesus!"

I spin to find a horrified and naked Emily at the door. She's frozen to the spot, eyes darting around the room. Fuck.

"I told you to wait in the bedroom," I growl, gripping her wrist and tugging her to me. She's shaking, her fear cutting through me. I wrap my arms around her, her body rigid in my embrace. "It's okay, darlin'. They can't get out. Trust me."

"You said you had one, not an army!"

"Emily." I lift my head, not pulling my body away from hers. She looks up from where her face was buried in my chest. "Do you trust me?"

"Of course."

176

I turn her around, keeping her pressed against me. She shivers when she comes face-to-face with Benny.

"This is Benny. He's a boa constrictor and he's seven feet long." She gulps. Leaning forward, I place my lips at her ear. "Relax, Emily. I would never let anything or anyone hurt you. I take care of what's mine."

"And... I'm yours?" Her voice trembles.

"That sounded strangely like a question. Want to try again?"

"I'm yours."

She lets out a long, shaky breath, her body beginning to relax. I slide my palms to her stomach, gently rubbing my bearded cheek against her smooth one.

"That's right. And because you are *mine*, you don't flirt with other men."

"I wasn't—"

"You don't entertain flirtatious conversations with other men."

"I'm sorry." She whimpers, pushing her ass back against me.

I cup her breasts, pinching the taut nipples. "Spread your legs." She complies immediately. Fuck, I love that about her. She knows when it comes to this, I'm her king. I continue to tweak her nipples as I ask, "Are you a naughty girl, Emily?"

"No, I'm a good girl," she blurts out. "I'm *your* good girl."

"Whose tits are these?" I grip them tightly, pushing them together.

She hisses, grinding her sexy ass on my rock-hard dick. "Yours."

Keeping the pressure on one breast, I reach down to her pussy, palm to mound, fingers to lips, and give it a good squeeze. Her hips rock, begging for more. I stroke her clit, hand sliding up from her breast to grip her neck. "Whose pussy?"

"Yours. Yours!"

Her head falls back on my chest, moaning in desperation.

"You remember that next time *Carter* tells you a joke."

I release her, nudging her toward the door. She waits as I lock it, tucking the key in my pocket. Facing her, I keep my expression stern.

"Get dressed and grade your papers. I'll be in my office."

She nods, slowly backing away. I move toward my office, adjusting my dick to ease the discomfort. *This is supposed to be*

her *punishment, right? Yet I'm the one with the blue balls. Fuck.*
Before I can sit around my desk, my phone buzzes in my pocket.
It's a text from Tek.

Tek: Come to the clubhouse. Important.

Venom: On my way.

Shit. What the fuck is going on now?

Emily is at the dining room table with her papers, and I stop
briefly to apprise her of the situation.

"Will you be gone long?" she asks, shifting on the chair.

With a smirk, I grab my still-hard dick. I'm not the only one
suffering. "You hurting, Emily?"

"You know I am."

"Maybe Carter can help you out."

"I don't want Carter."

"I know, darlin'." I take her chin between my fingers, leaning
down to give her a soft kiss. "Be back as soon as I can. Don't even
think about touching your pussy while I'm gone."

"Okay."

I hop on my bike, pointing it toward the clubhouse. Tek's cryptic
message has me intrigued. A part of me hopes there's no drama
going on, while the other, greater part is hoping I might get to kill
an asshole. Maybe a couple.

I walk into the clubhouse and am greeted by Trixie giving Razor
a hummer in the corner. Chuckling, I set out to find Tek. Not too
long ago, that would have been me. Now all I can think about is
getting back home to Emily.

My phone vibrates again, and when I check the message from a
strange number, I stop in my tracks. I can see right away that it was
taken at my gym, but it's the subject of the image that has my
throat locked up.

Emily.

In the shower.

Naked.

CHAPTER 16
Emily

Stupid.

I'm not totally dense. I knew Carter was hitting on me. I also knew Venom was watching. My little stunt even had the desired effect. However, I expected him to take me home, maybe spank me, then fuck me unconscious, not work me up and leave me high and dry.

Well, high and wet.

Fuck, I'm so wet.

Even now, I'm terribly uncomfortable, wishing he would come home and reconsider this punishment. I briefly contemplate going to the bedroom and utilizing the vibrator he gave me as a joke at Christmas—a replica of his magic dick—but I know he'd know, so I strike the thought from my brain. God knows what punishment he would serve up then. As long as it doesn't involve Benny, I'm good.

I tentatively make my way back to the snake room, checking the door. It's locked, and I don't see anywhere they could get out through. In fact, I now notice this door is different from all the others in the house. It looks stronger. A shiver runs down my spine at the thought of what's behind it. What the hell is he doing with all those snakes? How have I been here all this time and not known about this room? *I guess that's what happens when you think with your vagina, Emily.*

I head back to the table, sifting through the papers as disbelief at what my life is like takes hold. A few months ago, I was in a loveless marriage, lonely, depressed, and exhausted from working eighty-plus hours a week. Now my divorce is almost final, and I have a job I love while also getting paid for my passion—baking. My real Christmas gift from Venom, a twenty-four-piece baking set, helps me out a lot. There may not be any hearts and flowers between me and him, but he's made me happier in a few weeks than I've been in years. I have friends, a social life, not to mention I'm kicking ass with my fitness goals. I'm a changed woman.

ALANA SAPPHIRE

I'm high on life, for the first time in my life.

I guess sometimes all you need is a bad boy to be good to you.

Halfway through grading, the message tone sounds from my phone. Thinking it's Venom, I reach for it, almost dropping it in my excitement. It's not him. I don't know who it is, but I'm staring at my face, eyes closed, head tilted back as I wash my hair in the gym's shower. Naked. The phone slips from my hand, clattering to the ground. I raise my trembling fingers to my lips, baffled as to what the hell is going on. *Who took that picture? Why? Oh, God... who else has seen it?* Panic takes over and I begin to pace, having a freak out of epic proportions.

Raven's voice cuts through the fog in my brain, pushing me to action. *Trust your man. Whatever happens, let him handle the situation. Always.* I pick up the discarded phone, dialing Venom's number.

"Em."

"Venom... my phone... a picture," I ramble, unable to form a coherent sentence.

"Emily, listen to me. The prospect is on his way to pick you up. Pack a bag."

"Okay."

"I'll see you in a bit, darlin'."

I hurry to the bedroom, tossing clothes and toiletries in a bag. It doesn't occur to me that I have no idea where I'm going. All that matters is that this is what Venom wants me to do. He'll take care of me. I know he will.

A knock at the door startles me, making me jump a mile. I heave the bag on my shoulder, checking the peephole before opening the door. Tyler is cautious as he accompanies me to a Charger, taking my bag and helping me in.

My thumbnail is chewed down by the time we arrive at the clubhouse. I seek Venom out in the crowd, running into his arms. The moment they wrap around my body, my nerves begin to fade.

"You're okay, Emily. I'm here."

So is everyone else.

A tentative survey of the room reveals all the men and old ladies, even the Hounds. Everyone seems worried. *What's going on with them?*

"Venom, what—?"

"Don't worry, I'll get to the bottom of it."

My brows knit as I stare up at him. I haven't shown him the picture, didn't even string enough words together to tell him what happened. How does he know there's something to get to the bottom of? That's when I realize he didn't ask any questions. When I called, he didn't sound surprised, not even a little curious. He knew I needed to get out of there. He knew....

"You knew."

"I got the picture, too."

He takes my hand, weaving through the crowd and to his room. I perch on the edge of the bed, but I'm back on my feet and pacing after a few seconds.

"What's going on, Liam?"

"I don't know, but we're on it."

"What does that mean?" I halt my pacing, turning to face him.

"Tek's looking into it."

"Tek?" The word is a shriek, my panic returning. "You mean he's seen it? Who else have you shown it to?"

"I didn't show it to him. He found it—" He expels a breath, shaking his head. "—online."

"What?" I exclaim.

Jesus. I rub my forehead, a persistent throbbing developing in my head. *Online. There's a nude of me on the fucking internet. What the fuck is going on?* I wrap my arms around my body, skin crawling at the utter violation. Why would someone do this to me?

There's a knock at the door, followed by a deep voice. "Venom, church."

"Darlin', why don't you lie down? I have to go talk to the guys, but I promise I'll tell you everything I know when I get back."

"What do you know?"

"Not much, but Tek's taken care of the Internet. He's removed all the images he found."

"He has?"

"Yes. Now we just need to find out who did this. I gotta go, Em. Please...."

"Okay. Hurry back."

181

He disappears after a curt nod. Unable to stay locked up, I walk back to the bar, finding Raven and Ellen.

"Hi, ladies."

"Hey, Emily. Come, sit." Ellen waves me forward, making room on the couch between them.

"Crowded tonight," I comment, hoping to mask my anxiety.

"Something's up," Raven says. "Gage has brought everyone in. Don't worry, you're safe here. This place is a fortress. Everything is bulletproof."

"Bulletproof?"

"Yeah. We had some trouble last year and my brother did some upgrades on security. We don't know what's going on, but after church the guys will probably clue us in a bit," Ellen says.

Jesus. These women seem so comfortable talking about "trouble" and bulletproof clubhouses. Is this what my life will be like being with Venom? Will I have to constantly watch my back? I'm not even his girlfriend. If I was, how much danger would I be in? Would "unfriendlies" be a part of our daily life? Did someone target me because of my relationship with Venom? I break down, choking back a sob.

"Emily, what's wrong?" Ellen asks.

"It's me. We're here because of me."

"Why would you say that?" Raven squeezes my hand.

"Someone took a picture of me in the gym's shower."

"Fuck," both women swear simultaneously.

"They sent it to my phone, but apparently copies were all over the Internet before Tek took them down."

"Emily, listen." I turn to Raven, wiping at my tears. "Ellen and I know better than anyone what these men are capable of. If it's an Internet thing, Tek's got you covered. No doubt. The rest of the guys won't rest until they find the culprit."

"And then what?"

Raven glances behind me nervously, no doubt making eye contact with Ellen.

"Then... they'll take care of it."

My heart skips a beat, panic escalating. "You mean...?"

"You better talk to Venom about that part."

"You're talking about murder, aren't you? They'd do that?"

"Dealers take care of their own," Ellen says behind me. "I'm sure Venom would do anything to protect you."

"Except I'm not. I'm not one of you."

"Maybe not officially, but anyone can see how much Venom cares for you," Raven says.

"You don't understand. What we have... it's not going anywhere."

"Let's just wait and see what happens after church," Ellen suggests. "I'm sure Venom wants heads to roll for this."

Yeah. That's what I'm afraid of.

Venom

"What the fuck, Tek?"

All eyes turn to him, waiting for an explanation.

"Well, basically I have a program continuously monitoring the web for mentions of us... anyone associated with the club. I added Emily that first night you brought her here. I got the notification and blasted the site where the image was hosted. It's down, and I haven't found it anywhere else."

"What about the uploader?" Gage asks.

"Easy. He's good, but I'm better. I got a location."

"Good. Let's move." I surge to my feet, ready to crush someone's larynx with my boot.

"Wait," Gage says in his presidential voice. "I know you're running hot right now, but we can't go in blind. Sit."

I bite my tongue to stop myself from saying that if it was Raven, he wouldn't be waiting. The thing is I know he's right. I drop back in my chair, scowling at the table's surface.

"Tek, what are we looking at?"

"Atlanta, boss. Restaurant in Midtown."

"Restaurant?" Gage asks, echoing my confusion. "We know the owner?"

"I don't think so. I haven't found much, but I'm still digging."

"Keep on it, Tek. We need to know everything."

"You got it, boss."

183

"Venom." Prez turns his attention to me. "This thing with Emily. Is it serious?"

"Why?"

"I'll help her regardless, but I need to know how far you're willing to go with this."

"All the way... especially since I know this is somehow my fault. She may not be my old lady, but she doesn't deserve this."

"I hear you, brother. Has she given you anything useful?"

"Nothing. I think she's in shock. Reeling. Fuck, this happened in *my* gym, Prez. What am I supposed to say to her?"

Razor gives my shoulder a reassuring squeeze.

"What? It happened here?" Gage asks, eyes wide in surprise.

"Shit," Einstein curses under his breath, shaking his head.

"Any idea when?" Chopper asks.

"None. I would bet money her asshole ex is behind this. Probably trying to get back at her for what *I* did to him."

"What the fuck did you do?" Gage demands.

"I may have used a needle to get him to sign some divorce papers."

"Shit." Gage jerks his head at Charger. "Charger, get Emily."

A minute later, he returns with her in tow. She looks around nervously, walking in my direction when she spots me. I pull her down on my lap, arms circling her waist.

"Emily." She glances up at Einstein. "We can't possibly understand what you're going through right now, but we need some information, beautiful."

"What... what kind of information?"

"You have any idea who could've done this?"

"No."

"How about when it was taken?"

"It was today."

"How do you know?" I ask.

"Well, I was looking at the picture with Ellen and Raven, and I noticed that the shampoo is a new one I only started using today."

"Great eyes, Emily," Razor commends her.

"Okay, now we got a timeline. Tek—"

"Pulling up the security feed now, boss."

184

"Darlin'." She shifts on my lap, facing me. "You know anyone who owns or works at a restaurant in Midtown?"

"No. No one. Why?"

"Just something Tek found. We don't know what it means yet. You think it could be James?"

"I don't know. I'd like to think not." She leans in close. "Venom, I'm scared," she whispers, bottom lip quivering. I pull her close, wanting to rid her of the feeling.

"It's all going to be okay, Emily. Trust and believe that."

"Okay, boys," Gage commands the room's attention once more. "Here's the deal. Crow and Motor, I want you two to go case out the place while Tek does his thing. When we have more info, we can make a plan." He turns to me, speaking softly. "Go take care of your woman, brother. We got this for now."

With a dip of my head, I stand, lifting Emily in my arms. I take her to my room, laying her on the bed. She observes me, moving over so I can join her once I've discarded my clothes. Placing her head on my chest, she burrows into my side,

"I'm sorry, Em. I can't believe I let this happen."

"It's not your fault."

"Bullshit. It happened under my roof."

I grab my phone, calling Kurt and telling him to shut down the showers. That picture was taken from the next stall and from above. There's going to be some major renovations in there. I can't allow something like this to happen again.

"Venom?"

"Yeah, darlin'?"

"When you find the people responsible, are you going to... to kill them?" Her voice is low, shaking with fear.

"What do you want me to do?"

"I don't know. I didn't think I'd get caught up in this part of your life."

"I'll make it right. You'll see."

"I know you will. How you'll do it is the problem."

"What do you want me to do, Emily? Write a strongly worded letter?" I move away from her, sliding off the bed. She sits up, watching my flailing arms. "They came in to my business, took a nude of my woman, and posted it on the fucking Internet!"

185

"Venom…."

"You wanted to know about my club, so guess what? We don't fuck around. You hit us, we hit back a hundred times harder, driving you into the fucking ground. You have no idea about the things we've done. The things *I've* done."

"Like what?"

"You really wanna know?" I ask, not holding back my anger.

"Yes."

"Benny, the boa? I watched him wrap his body around a man's neck until it broke."

She gasps, fingers covering her lips.

"Your asshole of an ex? Do you really think he signed those papers because I had a *conversation* with him?"

"Liam, what did you do?" she demands.

"Don't fucking call me that! My name is Venom… just like what I injected him with, and then I watched as he squirmed before I gave him the antivenom."

"Jesus."

"Yeah, so what do you think I'm going to do to the fucker who violated you?"

She climbs out of the bed, coming straight for me. She cups my cheeks, pulling my face down to hers and resting her forehead on mine.

"You want to protect me, I get that. Just not at the expense of your soul."

"You don't have to worry about that, Emily. I lost that bitch a long time ago."

"I don't believe that. You have so much goodness inside you." Letting out a humorless chuckle, I break our contact. "You do," she persists. "Look at what you've done for me. I'm nothing like the woman who showed up in Stony View just a measly two months ago. You saw something in me and you didn't stop until you freed it. You freed me. You unlocked the cage I was trapped in and *saved* me."

"I'm no savior."

"You're mine. Aren't you trying to save me right now?"

"This is different. This is revenge."

186

"Call it whatever you want, Liam. Hell, even your name means 'protector.'"

"How do you know that?" I ask, pausing my tirade to turn to her in confusion.

"My mom told me."

"You told your mother about me?"

I think she realizes what she's admitted, because she turns her back to me. Her shoulders droop, head falling forward.

"Don't worry. I haven't filled her head with any promises of a son-in-law."

"Emily, that's not.... Will you look at me?" She doesn't budge, so I spin her around to face me. "One thing at a time. Let's just get through this, all right?"

"Not if you plan on killing anyone."

"Emily—"

"No, Venom. I can't be a party to that. If that's what you and your club do, then I can't be involved with you."

"What are you saying?" I step back, noting that she can't look me in the eyes.

"I'm saying... maybe it's time to move on."

CHAPTER 17
Emily

His face is a blank mask.

I told him I'm ending our arrangement, and he hasn't reacted. There's no surprise, no disappointment. Nothing. If this was a couple weeks ago, I'd think it's because he doesn't care, but I know he does. What he's willing to do for me proves it. A part of me loves that he'd protect me so fiercely, but I can't condone murder.

I also don't think I can be with a man who thinks so little of ending another human being's life.

"Maybe? You either want to or you don't. Which is it, Emily?"

"I don't *want* to. I've never been happier than I've been with you. I just can't…." I shake my head, searching for words.

"Can't what?"

"I don't know this side of you. I want the man whose bed I've been sleeping in every night, not this… this…."

"Monster? Killer?"

"This version of you," I offer instead.

"This is me. No two sides about it, Emily. This is who I've been for a long fucking time. If you can't accept me for who I am, you're better off without me in your life."

"What are you saying?" I ask, heart racing a mile a minute. I don't know why I'm petrified at the thought of losing him when I'm the one who suggested "breaking up" a few minutes ago. Maybe I expected him to protest, to try and convince me to stay, but I should have known better.

"Me? You're the one who wants to leave."

"So that's it? This, you and me… we're done?"

"I'm not going to beg you to stay if that's what you expect," he sneers, inciting my anger.

"No, 'cause why would I expect any kind of emotion from you?"

"That wasn't the deal."

"The deal. It's always about the fucking deal! Grow the hell up, Venom."

188

"Fuck, Emily!" He runs his fingers through his hair in frustration. "Look, your emotions are running high right now. Just try to get some sleep and we'll talk tomorrow."

"Fine. I'll go back to Uncle Jeff's."

"You're not leaving the fucking clubhouse," he growls. "It's safer here."

"So I've heard. Bulletproof walls and all."

I grab my bag from the floor, taking it with me to the bathroom and slamming the door behind me. He better know he's not coming anywhere near me tonight.

Shit. I only hope I can resist him if he does.

The only thing in the bag that can be used for sleepwear is one of Venom's T-shirts. Go figure. However, it does cover more of my body than what he likes me to wear to bed, so I'm thankful. I'm not feeling particularly sexy right now. In fact, I'll see if he has some sweatpants I can borrow. Returning to the room, I find him already in bed, hands behind his head, staring up at the ceiling. He's naked under the sheet; I can see the outline of his dick on his thigh.

"What are you doing?" I ask.

"What does it look like?"

"Do you really expect me to sleep in the same bed with you?"

"My room, my bed. With everyone here, it's not like I can go sleep somewhere else." I cross my arms over my chest, ready to argue. "I ain't sleeping on the floor either. Fuck that shit."

I roll my eyes, holding myself back from stomping my foot like a petulant child.

"I have some clothes in the chest of drawers if you need anything."

"I...."

I can't find any words. How does he know? How can he infuriate me with one sentence, then make me want to kiss him in the very next one? Trying to hold on to my anger, I search the drawers until I find some gray sweatpants. I pull them on, trudging to the other side of the bed, then lie down with my back to him at the very edge, dangerously close to falling off.

"What are you doing all the way over there?"

"In case you didn't notice, I'm mad at you," I reply.

"You need to get fucked, Em?" he asks in that annoyingly sexy voice that's both exasperating and arousing right now. Especially since he's laughing.

"No."

"You sure?"

"Positive," I reply through gritted teeth.

"You could sit on my face."

Images of the first time he made me do that flash in my mind. I was nervous, but the hunger in his eyes as I stared down at him made everything disappear.

"Or you could hang your head over the side of the bed so I can fuck your throat."

I cross my legs under the covers, memories of that very act attacking my brain. God, the way he'd slid into my mouth, gripping my breasts as he went deeper each time. Closing my eyes, I try to block the mental images. I know exactly what he's doing and I won't fall for it. *I will stay mad at him, goddamnit!*

"Or... you can come over here and let me hold you in my arms and comfort you."

There it is, the sentence that begs me to plant my lips on his. I turn to face him, lips trembling, tears brimming in my eyes. His tattooed chest calls to me and I answer, giving in and letting go of my anger. As usual, he knows exactly what I need. I settle against him, breathing in his scent. He strokes my hair, the action calming me even more.

"I'm sorry this happened to you, darlin'. If I could take away your pain, I would. All I want is for you to be happy."

"I know. I'm sorry, too... for snapping at you."

"I don't care about that. Do whatever it is you need to do to feel better."

I wiggle closer, making him shift slightly to his side to better accommodate me. Both hands wrap around me, filling me with the now familiar sense of safety I've only felt in his arms. Regardless of the things he's done and will do, that hasn't changed. He's still my safe place. My sanctuary.

"Raven told me what happened to her. Ellen, too."

"Yeah?"

"I'm not sure if they wanted me to see my situation could be worse, or that you'll sort everything out. That I should trust you the way they trusted Gage and Einstein."

"I'm pretty sure it's the latter. If anyone knows what we're capable of, it's those two women."

"Liam, I think we should talk to the police."

"No, Emily. No cops."

"Why?"

"Because they start digging into you, it leads them to me. Then they start digging into the club, and that's a shit-ton of problems. We'll handle it."

"Okay," I agree, not wanting to cause trouble for him.

"It's late. Try to get some sleep."

I close my eyes, but all I can see is the image of me in the shower. Eventually I fall into a fitful sleep, haunted by dreams of flashing cameras and snakes biting off the heads of men.

Venom

I stare at the computer screen, watching a dark-haired woman look around cautiously before entering the showers with a cell phone in hand. She's definitely the one who took the picture, because no one else went in or out while Emily was in there. I've also never seen her in the gym before. Tek brings up the information he found on her using facial recognition software, but there's not much to go on. At least we have an address.

Gage's phone rings and he puts it on speaker, laying it on the table. "Crow," he says.

"I'm here, Prez."

"What did you find?" I ask, leaning over the table and closer to the phone.

"You'll never guess who rolled in for lunch," Crow answers.

"Who?"

"That asshole from the fight."

"Interesting," Gage says. "You find out anything about him?"

"Yeah. Name's Luigi Vitalli. He owns the place."

191

Tek starts clacking away at his computer and I know we'll have every piece of information about this fucker in a few minutes.

"Stay on him, Crow. We're going to check out the girl on the security footage."

"Got it, Prez."

Gage disconnects the call and turns to me. "How's Emily?"

"Not good. She's scared and confused. Talked about going to the police last night, but I convinced her that wasn't an option."

"Good. Last thing we need is the cops snooping around."

"I know."

"Who's this Vitalli asshole?" Razor asks. "That night at the fight, he knew who we were. How the fuck don't we know him?"

"Tek?" I prod him for an update.

"Luigi Vitalli. Big-time loan shark operating in Atlanta. He also owns a couple other places. Got a laundry list of charges, but nothing's stuck. He's gotten away every time."

"Loan shark? I've never even heard of this asshole. What issue could he have with me?" Gage leans back in his chair, his question directed at no one in particular.

"Think it has something to do with The Pharmacist?" Rico asks.

The fucking Pharmacist. I'm getting tired of hearing that name. We already dealt with that motherfucker, so I doubt this involves him.

"There's something here about his son, Luca, being arrested for murder," Tek adds. "Looks like he was daddy's muscle. Trial's in a couple weeks."

"Where's he being held?" I ask.

"State."

"We know anyone in there?"

"I know a guy, Prez," Booker answers Gage's question. "I can go see him."

"Can we trust him?"

"Yeah. He's my brother."

"How come you never told us you have a brother in State?" Charger asks, turning to Booker.

"It never came up." He shrugs.

"Okay," Gage says. "Pay him a visit, see if he can tell us anything."

"Sure thing, Prez."

"I've got a contact in ATL I can call, see if he has info on the Vitallis," Chopper offers.

"Thanks, Pop. I hate to cut out, but Raven has an appointment with Einstein. Venom, talk to Emily again, see if she's thought of anything since last night. Tek, keep digging. Send Crow a shot of that woman so he can look out for her, too. I doubt she's still around here." Gage turns back to me, eyes empathetic. "If we have nothing concrete by the time I get back, we'll head to Atlanta. Just give us a couple hours, brother. I promise, when we find who's responsible, he's all yours to do your worst."

Oh, that motherfucker's gonna wish he was never born. "Thanks, Prez."

"I'll let E know what's going on when I see him."

I'm the first to leave the table because I need to check on Em. She barely slept last night, tossing and turning. I felt so helpless, being right there and unable to do anything. As much as I love fucking her, sex is not a panacea. I was only joking with her last night to take her mind off the situation. Don't get me wrong, if she wanted me I wouldn't have turned her down, but I figured she needed more.

More.

A word I've been running from all my life. She wanted it and I gave it willingly, no reservations. Is it something I can sustain? Provide on a long-term basis? I have no idea. Right now, I can't think about myself. Emily is all that matters.

Without thinking, I open the bedroom door and step in. Emily is in the middle of changing and she squeals, grabbing a shirt and covering herself up.

"Sorry, darlin', it's just me." I quickly shut the door, making my way over and pulling her into my arms. She's shaking. "Everything's going to be okay, Em."

"How?"

Stepping back, I cradle her face, forcing her to look up at me. "Do you trust me?"

"Of course."

"Then trust and believe I will *make* it okay. What did I tell you last night? Back at the house?"

"That you take care of what's yours."

"And are you mine?"

Her eyes close, head slowly bobbing. "Yes." Her lids flutter open, tears clouding her precious green eyes. "I'm yours, Liam."

My chest tightens with an unfamiliar feeling. This is nothing like when she says the words while I'm inside her. This... this is as if my heart is beating for the first time, like I was dead and her words jumpstarted the cold, black, shriveled-up organ hidden behind my ribcage. It's pumping blood through my body once again, and I feel revived.

Fucking *alive*.

My throat closes up, words refusing to pass my lips. What would I tell her? That I say things in the heat of the moment and can't back them up? That I'm blurring the lines of our relationship but expect her to stick to the terms of our stupid arrangement? And it *is* stupid. How did I think I could be with a woman like Emily and not develop feelings for her, expect her to be happy with the status quo?

I'm a motherfucking asshole of infinite proportions.

"Get dressed. I'll find you some breakfast."

She changes into jeans and another of my T-shirts, leaving the baggy garment untucked and hiding her curves. I lead her to the bar and over to where some of the old ladies are.

"Hey, Emily," Ellen says, waving her over. Her son is sitting on her lap, having eggs and toast. "Gage left. He took Charger and Rico with him. Booker is off somewhere," she informs me with a dismissive wave of her hand.

"Morning, ladies," Emily mumbles, taking the stool next to Ellen.

"I'm not a lady!" Mikey exclaims. All the women laugh, including Emily.

"Of course not, my little man," Ellen says. "Say hello to Emily."

"Hello, Emily!"

"Hi there. What's your name?"

"Michael Hunter Raymond!"

"Oh, that's a cool name." She leans in to stroke the boy's cheek. "He looks so much like you, Ellen."

"So everyone tells me. I think he looks more like Eddie."

"Eddie?" Emily looks from Ellen to me and back.

"Oh, his biological father. He died right before Mikey was born."

"My daddy's in Heaven," Mikey tells Emily. "But I have a new daddy now."

"Yes, Jon—Einstein," Ellen clarifies, "is great with him."

Seeing that she's more relaxed now, I head to the kitchen. As I walk away, I hear Ellen asking Emily to make Mikey's cake for his fifth birthday. By the time I return, Mikey is gone and the women are huddled up, no doubt talking about one of us men. Emily beams up at me as I set the plate before her. The beauty of her smile leaves me frozen, wondering how this angel could think I deserve her.

"Thank you."

"You're welcome, darlin'. Do you want me to stay, or are you okay with the girls?"

"I think I'm good."

"I'll be over there if you need me." I motion with a tilt of my head.

"I always need you," she says, her voice lowered.

Those four words warm me to the soles of my feet. I take her chin between my fingers, dipping my head to drop a gentle kiss on her lips. "Don't say shit like that, Emily. I just might believe it."

I join the men, sitting on the arm of the couch as I eat. My gaze keeps straying back to Emily. She's the magnet to my steel, the Davidson to my Harley.

I'm fucked.

Well and truly fucked.

"You talked to Emily yet?" Razor asks.

"Nah. I don't think she knows anything. Her ex is the only one she's had problems with. After what we did to him, he'd be stupid to mess with her like this."

"So you don't think it's him anymore?"

"I'm not ruling him out, but no."

"Fuck. Our women can't catch a break, huh?"

"And that's exactly why we shouldn't keep any around. It's too dangerous, Razor."

"I hear ya. What are you going to do about her?" He lifts his chin in Emily's direction.

I stare at her, knowing the best thing I could do is cut her loose, but I don't want to. I also don't want it to come down to a situation where I'm forced to, in order to keep her safe. If anything happens to her, I'd never forgive myself.

"I don't know, Razor. I don't know."

"What *do* you know, brother?"

"I know her angels play nice with my demons."

Our eyes meet from across the room, and she excuses herself to come to me. Razor gives up his seat to her. I move to the floor, settling between her legs. Her fingers sift through my hair, nails gently scratching my scalp. I want to purr like a fucking cat, but I keep quiet, laying my head on her thigh instead.

"You okay down there?" Emily asks, chuckling.

I tilt my head back to look up at her, knowing if she weren't going through hell, I'd be in heaven right now. She slides her palm down my cheek and to my neck, keeping me in place as she leans forward, softly pressing her lips to mine. Her hair brushes against my cheeks, the smell of her new coconut shampoo surrounding me.

"You wouldn't happen to have a toy box here, would you?" she whispers.

My dick jumps. "No, but I'll go and fucking get it if that's what you want."

"That's what I want."

I turn to face her, brows drawn together. "Are you sure? I don't want—"

"I'm sure, Liam. I've spent most of my life being scared and ashamed, allowing other people to dictate what I do and how I behave. Other than my family, you're the only one who's been supportive. You care about who I am on the inside, not only how I look. Because of you, I'm learning to love myself. So yes, I'm sure. I want you."

"Fuck, Emily. I... I don't know what to say."

She smiles, thumb caressing my cheek. "Say you'll hop on your bike and get that box."

"I'll hop on my bike and get that box."

"Good boy."

I growl at her words, the role reversal making me hotter than I ever thought it would. If Emily wants me and my toys, that's what she'll get.

"Be ready for when I get back, naughty girl."

"Like you said, I'm always ready for you."

"That you are, darlin'. Wait for me in my room."

Her phone rings and she pulls it from her pocket, giggling at the screen. "It's my mom. Think she knows what we were talking about?"

"I hope the fuck not."

She places the phone at her ear, laughing before she greets her mother. I bolt to my feet, making it to my house and back faster than I've ever made the journey before. Gage and Raven have returned, and they brought Einstein with them.

"Everything okay?" I ask Raven, touching her belly.

"They're perfect," she beams.

"Know what they are?"

"We're gonna wait and be surprised."

"You want to be surprised," Gage cuts in. "I already know they're boys."

Raven rolls her blue eyes before facing her husband to placate him. "Of course, babe. A big hunk of manliness like you could only produce two strong, healthy boys."

"Fuckin' right."

I walk away laughing, eager to be with Emily. Before I can even get to the corridor, Tek fills the entryway, eyes focused on me.

He found something.

Approaching Gage, he whispers something to him that makes him shout, "Chapel!" over the noise in the room.

We quickly make our way there, taking our seats.

"What did you find?" Prez asks the moment his ass hits the chair.

"The link between us and Vitalli."

"Well?" I ask in irritation.

Tek turns his computer around so the monitor faces me. The image on the screen solidifies my decision about Emily. It's at this moment that I know I have to let her go. What happened to her is one hundred percent my fault.

"Who's that?" Razor asks.

197

"The judge in Vitalli's case. I think I should let Venom explain."

The man on the screen has aged since the last time I saw him, but there's no doubt as to his identity.

"Venom?" Prez turns to me. All my brothers' eyes are on me. "Who is he?"

"My father."

CHAPTER 18
Emily

Liam's been gone a long time. I've moved past the anticipation stage and am now just plain restless. I paced, played on my phone, then took a long shower. *Where the hell is he?* I turn the TV on, flipping through the channels, but nothing is appealing to me. My mind is set on one thing, and that man of mine seems to be getting off on making me wait.

Man of mine.

It has a nice ring to it, but is it true? Is he mine? Let's examine the facts: I've been sleeping in his bed since the beginning. He told me he didn't do sleepovers, yet night one, there I was. Next fact: he's been taking care of me, and not just in the bedroom. I've barely spent a dime of my own money since we started seeing each other, no matter how much I protest. Third fact: all the emotional support he gives me. He doesn't play on my insecurities to get what he wants. The very things I hate about myself are the ones he seems to love. He even encourages my baking, eating everything I put before him and telling me I could be a professional. Surely a man wouldn't do that if he wasn't interested in more than sex? Fact number four: he brought me here, introduced me to all his brothers, integrating me into his club, his family. Fact number five: he's willing to do illegal, immoral things for me. I don't even want to think about those things. Fact six, and most important: he said I belong to him, that I'm his and he takes care of what's his. That's not blurring lines, it's erasing them. I thought it was weird how the women wore cuts proclaiming they were some man's property, but I get it now. It's not about being *a* possession but being possessed. Owned. It's about handing over your trust, your heart, your body, your life, to a man who will protect them. I've never had that before, and I finally think I can.

With Liam.

A niggling voice in my head keeps chanting "he's a murderer," but there's something comforting and a bit empowering about knowing someone cares so much for you that they're willing to protect you at the highest level. The heart wants what the heart wants, and mine wants him. Every beat in my chest gets louder, drowning out my thoughts.

Fuck it.

I love him.

I'm in love with Liam "Venom" Hughes.

For years I was buried under the rubble of what was left of my life. Liam saw the potential beneath the broken doors and shattered windows, rebuilding me into what I am today—something better... stronger. He's the reason my heart beats.

As if he can hear it pounding for him, the door opens and he steps inside, box in hand.

"You're back!" I leap off the bed, but before I can go to him, his expression stops me. "What's wrong?"

"Sit, Emily," he says as he sets the box by the foot of the bed.

I watch him cautiously, not liking the tone of his voice. Whatever's coming, I know I won't like it. "You're scaring me, Liam."

"Don't be scared. I just want to explain what's going on."

My heart drops to the bottom of my stomach. "You found him."

"We're still piecing things together, but we know most of it."

"And?"

"The woman who took the picture, she works for a man named Luigi Vitalli."

"I don't know who that is."

"He's the same guy from that night outside the fight."

"I remember him giving me a creepy look that night, but... why would he do this? I don't even know him."

Liam sighs, dropping his head in his hands. "He did it to get to me."

"What? Why?"

He turns to me, the pain in his eyes breaking my heart. "His son Luca is facing murder charges. My father is the judge on the case. We figure he thinks he can use me to get to my father. Hurting you gets to me."

"What are you going to do?"

"We'll take care of him. Hopefully I can do that without having to deal with Mother and Father dearest."

The thought seems to cause him physical pain. Laying my palm on his cheek, I stroke it with my thumb.

"What happened? With you and your parents?"

"We didn't get along, that's all."

"Why?" I push, needing to know what hurts him so deeply.

"My parents acted like they hated each other most of the time. As a kid, I thought they were staying together for me. At times, I even thought they regretted I was born. If I wasn't around, they could separate and be done with each other."

"Liam...."

"They would fight constantly about what to do with me. By the time I was in high school, it was unbearable. My mother wanted to send me to military school so she'd have more time with her socialite friends. My father wanted me to attend the fancy private school he went to."

I keep caressing his cheek, hoping it relaxes him enough to continue.

"He wanted me to be a lawyer like him. When I told him I wanted to go into accounting, he said the only way he'd pay for college was if it was for law. That night, I started researching ways to finance it myself. The Army won, and I enlisted right after graduation. Left and haven't looked back since."

"They never tried to contact you?"

"My mother sent me a letter once when I was in Afghanistan." He lets out a chuckle, void of amusement. "To tell me how I was throwing my life away."

"I'm sorry, Liam. I wish I could make it better."

"I don't need fixing, Emily. I still have some residual feelings toward them, I'll admit, but I accepted my situation a long time ago. I'll never have parents like yours, and I'm good with that."

"You have me," I offer, voice high-pitched with hope. "I may not be much but—"

"You're everything, Emily. You're the fucking moon and the stars, and I don't deserve you."

"I think I'm the one who should be saying that."

"You keep selling yourself short. Any man would be lucky to have you. Never let anyone make you feel less than you are. Not James, and especially not me."

"Liam." I move to my knees, straddling his lap and cradling his face in my hands. "You're the best thing that's ever happened to me, and that's not me selling myself short. If I was good before, you've made me better. I love who I am when I'm with you."

"Emily…."

His eyes are conflicted, opposite emotions battling inside him. I want to make him feel better and there's only one way I know how.

"Make love to me, Liam. I need you."

Grabbing my ass, he shifts so I'm lying on the bed with my legs around his hips.

"You should forget about me, Emily. I'm no good for you."

"Because of one little picture? Kiss me, Liam."

"You'll get hurt."

"I won't."

I pull his head down, pressing my lips to his. He groans, hips pushing me into the bed.

"Fuck, Em. I've never wanted another woman as much as I want you."

"Then show me," I reply, breathless from his lips trailing down my neck.

He reaches under the T-shirt I'm wearing, gently tugging my panties off. After tossing them aside, he removes his cut, then reaches behind him to pull his T-shirt off. My tongue slides over my bottom lip, eyes feasting on his naked, tatted chest. I sit up, hands on his sides as I drop kisses on his stomach, licking the peaks and valleys of his abs, and the V on his hips. His fingers tangle in my hair, guiding me lower. Eyes locked with his, I quickly undo his belt, button, and zipper, freeing his dick and taking him in my mouth. This is the first time he's allowed me any kind of control and I intend to make use of it. With each lick, he grows harder and harder. Gripping him in a tight fist, I stroke him up and down, in sync with my mouth. He moans above me and I echo the sound, the vibrations making him pull on my hair. Using my free hand, I cup his balls, sliding my palm over them.

"Let me see your tits."

I lose the T-shirt, palming both breasts and pushing them together. He watches, mesmerized as I tug on my nipples. Stroking his dick, he leans in, sliding it between my breasts. I let him fuck them, hands on top of mine, controlling the pressure on his dick.

"Fuck, your tits are perfect," he says on a groan.

"I want your mouth on them."

He obliges, hands replacing mine as he sucks a nipple into his mouth, forcing me to lie back. A cycle of nibble, suck, lick ensues, moving from one to the other. Tremors rock my body, pussy clenching with need. Reading my body like a book, he circles my clit before sliding a finger inside me. It glides in and out, his mouth worshipping my breasts.

"Please, Liam...."

He doesn't make me wait any longer, slowly guiding himself home while burying his face in my neck. My back arches, arms and legs wrapping around him.

"Fuck, darlin'...."

"Oh, Liam," I choke out, getting teary eyed.

"What is it?" He raises his head, staring down at me in confusion.

"You called me darlin'."

Not only that, but this is the gentlest he's ever been with me. This is not about him dominating or me submitting. It's just us... Liam and Emily.

"That's because I've lost all control when it comes to you, Em."

Before I can respond, his lips are stealing my breath. He pulls out of me, pushing in with deep strokes, hand gripping my thigh.

"Harder," I pant, scratching at his back. "Fuck me, Liam. I'm all yours." He grunts, picking up the pace, thumb circling my clit. "Yes. Yes! Just like that!"

He takes my nipple between his lips again, and the added stimulation sends pleasure radiating through me.

"Oh, fuck, I'm gonna come!"

He thrusts harder, grunting with effort. The moment I fall apart, clenching around him and screaming his name, he shudders, going deep. When he collapses on top of me, I can't hold back my giggle.

"What's so funny, naughty girl?"

"Just that you went all the way home for the box and we didn't even look at it."

"Do you think we needed it?"

"Nope."

As his dick slides out of me, he smacks my thigh. "Go clean up."

After a quick trip to the bathroom, I curl up next to him on the bed, laying my head on his chest.

"What now?" I whisper.

"Now... now we do what we do. I can't give you details."

"I meant with us."

"What do you want?" he asks after a pause.

You.

I rattle my brain, trying to think of something more eloquent to say. After all, English is my thing. He's the numbers man, yet he never seems to have a shortage of words.

"Um...." I nervously trace a pattern on his chest with my finger. "Wanna come to dinner at my uncle's place this weekend?"

"What's the occasion?"

"No occasion... just—" I take a deep breath for courage. "—my parents will be there."

His body goes taut beneath me. *Shit.*

"You want me to meet your parents?"

"It's no biggie. Just dinner."

"I don't know, Em. Sounds pretty big to me."

He shifts, moving me off his chest and sitting on the edge of the bed, his back to me.

"It's just... we've been spending so much time together, I thought—"

"We talked about this, Emily. In the very beginning, I told you not to expect anything more."

"Liam—"

"What do you want from me?"

The acid in his tone startles me. He's never been like this with me before. I should have kept my mouth shut. *What was I thinking? He's right. I knew the deal going in. Why did I ever think he'd be interested in a real relationship? With me?* As the tears gather behind my lids, I slide out of his bed for what I think is the last time.

"Too much, I guess."

I grab some clothes, blindly shoving limbs into them. I need to get out of here.

"Don't make me out to be the bad guy. You knew what this was."

"Yeah, I did."

"Emily."

I don't answer, only picking up my shoes and bag, heading for the door.

"Emily!"

His voice squeezes the air out of my lungs. Struggling to breathe and trying to fight back my tears, I soldier on. Before I can get there, Liam grabs my elbow, turning me to face him.

"Tell me what you want."

"I want to go home."

"*Tell me what you want.*" He places emphasis on every word.

"Fuck you!" I tug my elbow from his hold, but don't get far before he's blocking my attempt at a getaway. My eyes meet his, anger and confusion warring within me. "You want to know what I want? I want you. That's the number one thing on my stupid list. *You.*"

Taken aback, his eyes widen. My words come rushing out. "I love you but I hate you and I need you but I don't. You say you don't want a relationship but you keep telling me I'm yours and I belong to you. You're hot and cold and up and down and you... *confuse* me. I just...." I shake my head, trying to stave off the sobs. "I just want you to want me," I finish, helplessness taking hold.

"You think I don't?" he demands, voice raised in anger. "You think I don't want—" He stops, reeling back in what he was about to say. He looks at me with what I can only determine to be regret. Whether it's for what we started or what we could have become, I don't know. What I do know is that Liam and I are over. I can't continue with him knowing he'll never want more than this. Not when my heart is invested. I can't bear for it to be broken again. Not by him. There would be no coming back from that pain.

"I've been hurt. I've been degraded and ridiculed until I broke. I met you and you liked me even when I despised myself. You brought me back. You helped me heal. But for what? So you can leave me in more pieces than you found me?"

His gaze falls to the floor, ashamed to meet mine.

"I didn't think I had any love left inside me, but you showed me that I do. Every little bit I can wring out of a heart I know still beats because of you... it's yours."

He finally looks up, face frozen and blank despite my meltdown. Despite the fact that I told him I love him.

"I can't do this, Liam." My hands rise and fall in resignation. "I thought I could, but I can't. It was supposed to be fun. You weren't supposed to make me fall in love with you." He stares at me with that same expression, silence filling the room. "Please… just take me home."

"You can't leave—"

"Don't fucking tell me what I can and can't do. I'm going back to Uncle Jeff's whether you take me or not."

He stares at me for what seems like forever before he gives me a curt nod. He dresses quickly, following me out of the room. I try to hurry through the bar unseen, but Raven spots me.

"Hey, Emily. Where are you going?"

"Home."

She takes one look at me, then gives Liam a disapproving stare. "What did you do to her, *pendejo*?"

"Nothing," I answer. "I just want to go home. I don't belong here."

"Bullshit. I'll get Gage. He'll sort this shit out."

She waddles off, cursing in Spanish, and I use the opportunity to make a dash for the exit. Liam follows, still silent. He doesn't even glance at me while he straps my bag to his bike. As I climb on and wrap my arms around him—both for the last time—I shed the tears I've been holding back.

And not for the last time.

CHAPTER 19
Venom

"What the fuck did you do?" Gage accosts me the second I walk into the clubhouse.

"She wanted to go home." I shrug as if I don't know I just pushed away the best thing in my life.

"Oh, and you just let her go? With everything going on?"

"I put the prospect on her."

"What's wrong with you? Yesterday you were ready to kill someone, and I'm supposed to believe you don't give a shit now?"

"They want *me*, Gage. What happened to her is because they were trying to get to *me*. Well, they did. I'm doing what's best for her. I won't make the mistake of waiting until something worse happens."

"Like I did?"

Shit. My words struck a chord with him. I wasn't even thinking about Raven, but now I've pissed off my president.

"Prez, I didn't mean—"

"We need to get to the warehouse," he cuts me off. "Apparently Crow and Motor are coming back with a package."

He leaves me with my foot in my mouth, rounding up the other men.

"Rico!" he shouts. "Find out where the prospect is and give him a hand." He turns back to me, pointer finger aimed in my direction. "Get your head out of your ass. You either pull it out yourself, or I'll do it for you."

Sighing, I walk back to the courtyard to wait, closing my eyes against the memory of Emily sobbing behind me as I rode her home. Every tear she shed was like a nail to my palm, but a few tears now is better than her getting caught in the crossfire again. The next time might be worse.

After my promise to Jeff, I'm relieved he wasn't home when I dropped her off. I don't know if I'll ever be able to look either of them in the eyes again.

As Rico rides away, he gives me a look. Whether it's disappointment or disgust, I can't really tell. I want to kick his ass for it, but I know I deserve it.

We pile into one of the vans, needing to keep a low profile whenever we go to the warehouse. The men are quiet, but I don't mind. I welcome the silence; it gives me the opportunity to brood without interruption. I should have ended things with Emily a long time ago. Better yet, I shouldn't have started anything in the first place. I knew where it would lead.

I fucking knew.

But I let my dick do the thinking. I wanted her too much to pass up the chance to get inside her, and now she's paying the consequences. Hopefully they'll leave her alone now that I have.

Or have I made it easier for them to get to her?

Fuck my life.

No matter what I do, it seems to be the wrong thing. Not to mention I've pissed off Gage, which by extension means Einstein, too. I know it's just a matter of time before he hears what I said, and he'll also take it personally because of what happened with Ellen. Losing Emily, and both my prez and VP mad at me. How did I fuck things up so royally?

Is it even really my fault? I can't help the family I was born into. This isn't about the club; it's simply a case of who I'm related to.

This time.

That's what I need to keep reminding myself. Eventually something club-related will come up and she'll be in danger again. And again and again. I need to be strong. This is the best thing for Emily. She's better off without me.

Even if it kills me to let her go.

The van door opens, sunlight bursting into the dark cab. I hop out, heading inside when Gage unlocks the warehouse. We bypass all the cars and bikes he has parked inside, going through the hidden door and making our way downstairs to where we know Crow and Motor will be. Sure enough, they're in one of the rooms, eyes glued to a woman sitting in the center. She almost jumps out of her skin when we enter.

"What's this?" Gage asks.

RENASCENCE

"Vitalli made us," Motor answers. "We lost him but grabbed her. She's the one from the video, right?"

"Yeah, that's her," Tek confirms, slowly circling the woman.

"She said anything?" I ask.

"Oh, she's been extremely cooperative," Crow replies, handing a phone to Tek. "This is hers. She said the picture's on there and she only emailed it to Vitalli."

"Please," she begs. "I'll tell you everything I know. Just please let me go."

"Why should I?" Gage steps forward.

"Look, you already know I took the picture, so I won't try to deny it. That's all I did, I swear. Luigi said he'd pay me five grand, so I did it. You know how long it would take me to make that kind of money on my waitress salary?"

"Don't care." I move to Gage's side. He may be the president, but this is my fight.

The woman looks up at me, eyes going wide. "You...."

"What about me?"

"Luigi has something planned. I don't know what it is, but I know it involves you. Your picture was on his desk."

"What else?"

"I heard him and his men talking once. He tried to buy off the judge in Luca's case and he didn't bite. Said he'd have to find another way to get to him."

Son for a son. Unfortunately for Vitalli, this judge doesn't give a fuck about his offspring.

"What are we going to do about her?" Razor asks.

"Keep her here for now," Gage answers. "Get her some food until I decide what to do."

"I'm sorry for what I did," the woman says to me. "I saw you with her. Can you tell her I'm sorry?"

"I think it's a little too late to apologize."

I walk away, the words as much for me as they were for her.

Before I can climb back into the van, Gage pulls me aside, his phone to his ear. "Stay with her. Both of you. I'll send money for expenses." He listens for a while, then replies, "Until I say so."

"What's going on?"

209

"Your girl is heading back to Atlanta. Packed up her uncle's truck and they left a few minutes ago."

"Oh."

"That's all you're gonna say?"

"What do you want me to say? To do?" I ask in frustration.

"Man the fuck up! What happened to Raven, I didn't see it coming. Regardless, I still blame myself for it every fucking day. You have an opportunity I didn't. If you don't do everything in your power to prevent something from happening to her, you'll regret it for the rest of your miserable life. And trust me, you *will* be miserable, because I've seen you with her. My wife? She's the only thing that makes life worth living. You think about that before you push Emily away forever."

He leaves me staring at his boot prints in the dirt, contemplating his words. Somewhere in the recesses of mind, a voice tells me he's right.

If only I could believe it.

Emily

Nervous.

Relieved.

Anxious.

Those are just some of the things I'm feeling as I walk into the courthouse.

Today's the day. Today I'll finally be rid of James Sinclair. Jesus, I'm glad I didn't take his last name. It only makes this so much easier. I can't wait for every trace of this man to be erased from my life.

"Emily?"

I cringe at the voice, turning to the owner with disgust evident on my face. "James."

"Almost didn't recognize you." His eyes move up and down my body, making me cringe harder, if there's such a thing. "You look good."

"I know."

My reply stuns him. I may look different, but I also have a whole new mindset. The broken woman he turned me into is gone. He probably has no idea how to handle the one I've become.

"Guess I can't call you Miss Piggy anymore," he says with a smirk.

"Guess not." I shrug, my indifference turning his smirk into a scowl.

"Where's your biker?" He tries to get under my skin once more, looking around.

This is the one area he can touch on that will affect me, and from the look on his face, he's realized it.

"Get tired of you already?"

"You already know he's not here or else you wouldn't be standing here."

"You know what he did to me, don't you?"

"I only just found out. While I regret how he handled it, I can't say that about the outcome. You should've just signed the damn papers."

"That why he left you? 'Cause you can't handle his lifestyle?"

"If you must know, I ended things with him, just like I did with you."

"I warned him, you know. Told him what a frigid bitch you are."

"Just because you didn't know how to handle me doesn't mean he didn't. FYI, he did."

"Taught you a few things, did he?" He licks his lips. "Maybe you can show them to me when we're done here."

"As if I'd let you touch me again." I scoff. "You're just a memory I'm trying hard to forget."

His blonde from the fight shows up next to him, linking her arm through his and giving me a dirty look. I turn to her with a saccharine smile.

"You know, the rumors are true. I traded up to a *bigger*, better model, and let's just say I'll never go compact again."

I leave them with their mouths hanging open, sauntering toward my lawyer, Johnathan, who just entered the building.

Put that in your pipe and smoke it, bitch.

I was dreading seeing James today, but our little exchange taught me something. Sometimes the only way to move forward is to look back, to deal with the things in your past. I believe he has been effectively dealt with.

We don't have to wait long before our case is called. James and his woman side-eye me the entire time, but I remain focused on the proceedings. I didn't want anything from him. He'd already blown through our joint savings, and since I sold my car, all that was left was the house and everything in it. I let him have it all and didn't even ask for alimony. All I want is to be free. When the judge bangs his gavel, I almost leap for joy. Johnathan turns to me, shaking my hand.

"Well, Miss Pierce, you're a free woman now. What's the first thing on your agenda?"

"I have no idea," I answer. I was looking forward to celebrating with Liam, but that's out of the question. He doesn't want me. "What do you suggest?"

"Drinks?" He raises a hopeful brow, blue eyes meeting mine.

Oh.

James catches my eye, his glare telling me he's heard our conversation. I return my attention to Johnathan, a smile firmly in place.

"Sure. Why not?"

We walk out arm in arm, and he drives us to a nearby bar. While he finds us a table, I run to the ladies' room to check my makeup. As I stare at my reflection, I wonder why I'm even bothering. I'll be crappy company since my mind will be on Liam the entire time. It's too soon.

I have an inkling I'll feel like this for a long time to come. It's only been three days. Three days since I left Stony View, since Liam dropped me off at my uncle's and I watched through the curtains as he rode away. He didn't even hesitate or glance back. My most painful memory of that day is of his retreating back, the sound of his bike slowly fading.

I miss him.

I miss him so much sometimes it's hard to breathe. He hasn't called or even texted to see how I am. I doubt he's even thought of me since I left. It's my own fault for falling in love with him. I should have known better. When someone tells you who they are, believe them.

212

Sighing, I turn on my heels to head back to the bar. The door opens and a man walks in.

"This is the ladies' room, sir."

"I know."

He holds the door open for another man to enter. My purse falls from my fingers, a scream lodged in my throat as the man from the fight walks in. While he approaches me, the other man checks the stalls and then locks the door.

"Hello, Miss Pierce."

"Come near me and I'll scream."

"Calm down. I'm not going to hurt you. I just need a favor."

"Why would I do you any favors after what you did to me?"

"Because if you don't"—he tilts his head to the left—"*then* I'll hurt you."

I swallow hard. "What do you want?"

"Your boyfriend."

"He's not my boyfriend. I mean, we broke up."

"Too bad." He smiles, approaching me. I step back until I collide with the sink. A chilling shiver runs down my spine when he raises his hand, trailing his finger down my cheek. "For him."

"Don't touch me." My words come out weak.

"Do as I say and you'll be fine. Go back to Stony View, find out what he knows and what they're planning to do. That's all."

"Why do you think he'd tell me? They don't tell their women anything about the club, and like I told you, we broke up. There's no reason for him to even talk to me."

Licking his lips, his eyes drop to my breasts. "I'm confident in your persuasive skills, Miss Pierce." He hands me an old phone. "This is a burner. I'll call to check in for info. Your first call will come in twenty-four hours."

When I don't take the phone, he sticks it in my cleavage, backing away. They're gone by the time I blink.

Shit. What am I going to do?

Again, Raven's voice echoes in my head. Liam may not be my man, but he's the only one I can think of calling. I scramble for my purse, dumping the contents on the floor to find my phone. I check the door to make sure the men have left, then dial his number.

He doesn't answer.

After three tries, I give up and call Raven.

"Emily!" she exclaims. "You left and didn't say goodbye."

"I'm sorry. I just...."

"It's okay. I know Venom was being a dick. Are you okay?"

"I was actually hoping to talk to Gage, if that's okay."

There's a pause before she asks, "Are you alone?"

"Yes."

"Hold on, I'll get him."

I tap my fingers nervously on the sink until Gage's voice comes through the speaker. "Emily, are you okay?"

"Yes. Um... I tried calling Liam but he didn't answer. I didn't know what else to do."

"What's wrong?"

I recount what happened, telling him everything Vitalli wants me to do.

"You did the right thing calling me, Emily. Find a table and sit down. I'll call you back in a few minutes."

"Okay. Thanks."

With unsteady hands, I push the door open, making my way back to the bar on even more unsteady legs. Johnathan waves to me from a booth and I hurry over, sliding in opposite him.

"Are you okay? You look a little shaken up."

"I'm fine," I answer, flagging down a waitress. I order a shot of whiskey, periodically glancing around the room.

"Looking for someone?"

"I'm sorry, Johnathan. I'm just... not feeling so hot."

"Would you like me to take you home?"

My phone rings and I immediately answer it, forgetting my manners.

"Hello?"

"Emily. Keep an eye out for Rico and Tyler. They're gonna take care of you, okay?"

"Thanks, Gage."

"No problem. See you soon."

I watch Johnathan's eyes widen, prompting me to seek out what he's looking at. I almost blurt out "Thank God!" when I see Rico and Tyler striding to our table. *How the hell did they get here so fast?*

They both nod to Johnathan, and then Rico motions for me to stand. "Let's go, Emily."

"Emily, you know these men?" Johnathan asks.

"Yes, I do. I'm sorry but I have to go."

"Emily—"

"It's fine, I promise. I have to go."

Rico hustles me out the rear, loading me into the back of a van. I have no idea where I'm going, but anywhere is better than here.

CHAPTER 20
Venom

Emily went on a date.

I'd like to say I'm happy for her, happy she's moved on. She's an amazing woman, so good for the guy.

But I'd also like to break the asshole's face.

Three days. Three days was all it took for her to get over me. I believed her when she told me she loved me. Looks like she quickly realized it wasn't love after all.

I'd be lying if I said I didn't want to answer when she called. What did she want? Permission to date some fuckface I've never even met? I know she's okay. If she wasn't, I'd have heard from Rico or the prospect. Getting Emily out of my system is something best done cold turkey. I couldn't deal otherwise. She's strong—stronger than me it seems, for her to be on a date. I've never given much thought to names and their meanings, but after she told me about mine, I looked hers up. If any of that shit is true, then she'll be fine. Me? I've been keeping busy with renovating the showers at the gym just to keep her off my mind. Hasn't worked for shit.

"Where is he?" Gage's voice echoes through the clubhouse.

The crowd parts, giving him a clear path to me. He stomps over, Einstein in tow.

"Stand up," he growls.

Whatever's coming, I probably deserve it, so I do it without argument. Two seconds later, I'm on the floor, my jaw smarting from my prez planting his fist in it.

"Consider that me keeping my promise. You don't answer your phone anymore?"

Forgetting the pain, I jump to my feet, heart hammering in my ears. The only calls I haven't answered are *hers*. "Is Emily okay?"

"Oh, so now you care?"

"Prez…."

He takes pity on me, answering, "She's fine, and on her way here. You got about two hours to get your shit together, motherfucker. After that, I'm personally helping Emily find another man."

He storms off, mumbling under his breath.

"I guess you've made your decision," Einstein says.

"Yeah."

"And Emily? You find out what she wants?"

"Me." I shake my head, still unable to understand why.

"I wonder why," Einstein voices the words I was thinking.

"Save the sarcasm, Doc. Emily deserves the best. I'm not it."

"Okay. If you really believe that, I'll drop it."

"I do."

He nods, backing away. I head to my room, cleaning it up so Emily can stay there. Gage is right about one thing—I need to do everything I can to protect her. Cutting her loose didn't help. If anything, it made her more susceptible to harm. I only hope she can forgive me.

After getting the room in order, I head to Sweet Treats to get her some of those cannoli. She seemed to love them. Fuck knows I loved licking the cream from her body.

Her body.

Fuck, I miss her in my bed. I can't fuck her out of my system because I can't even look at another woman. All I do is compare them to her.

"Hi, Venom!" the girl behind the counter greets me when I walk in.

"Hey." I don't even know the chick's name, so I just point to what I want. "Let me have six of those."

"Sure thing. You should get your fill before they're gone."

"What do you mean?"

She nods to the window and I glance back to see a "For Sale" sign taped to it. *Huh. Interesting.* I'll mention it to Gage and see if he wants to go into the bakery business.

"Why's it selling?"

"The owner's retiring and moving to Florida."

"Oh. You have a number for the owner?"

She hands me a card along with the box of pastries. I pay her, watching as she scribbles something on the receipt. Her number. I shove it in my pocket, giving her a wink before I leave. I think she's pretty, but I've forgotten what she looks like by the time I walk out of the store. My mind is focused on a single purpose—Emily. I expected her to be at the clubhouse by the time I got back, but instead I find an antsy Gage pacing the bar. He looks up expectantly when I walk in, but once he realizes it's me, he goes back to being worried. I survey the room, noticing everyone there seems tense. Booker is back from visiting his brother, and I wonder if he didn't bring good news.

"You heard from Emily or the guys?" Gage asks.

"No." My heart beats triple time, anxiety going through the roof. "Why?"

"They're not back and not answering their phones. I don't like it. Tek's working on tracking them."

This time, my heart stops beating, falling to the pit of my stomach. Emily. *If something's happened to her, I'll never be able to forgive myself. Hell, I'd gladly switch places with her if it meant keeping her safe. I don't give a fuck what happens to me, but her... not her. Please, God, not Emily.*

"Boss, look at this."

Tek's voice jolts me into motion and I'm by his side before Gage, squinting at his computer screen.

"What is it?" I ask.

"Tracker from the van and the guys' personal trackers are moving, heading this way."

I watch the dots on the monitor, wondering if the guys are really in that van, if Emily is with them... if she's okay. Why didn't I get her a fucking tracker? My head's been so far up my ass, I doubt I can ever remove it. Now Emily could be paying the price for my stupidity. If I get her out of this, I promise I'll make it right.

"Okay, people, look alive," Gage says, loud enough for everyone to hear. "Booker, take the women to the back. Raven's taking a nap. If she wakes up, you make sure she keeps her ass in our room. And tell Einstein to get out here." With the women out of earshot, he continues giving orders. "Razor, I need comms and rifles with scopes and silencers. Don't wanna bring the sheriff around with any noise. Crow, Motor, Charger, you're on the gate when Razor gets back. Tek, put the security feed from the entrance on one of the TVs."

Watching him, I'm reminded of my days in the Army. He's a good leader and I'd follow him into battle any day. I'm just glad he's on my side.

"What should I do?" I ask.

He takes a deep breath. "Be prepared. We don't know what's coming."

He squeezes my shoulder, turning to watch the security feed. Not knowing where Emily is or what's going on is killing me. I swear if Vitalli's laid a hand on her, I'll tear him limb from limb. He has no idea who he's dealing with. His entire family and organization are going down. And Rico and Tyler? What the hell is going on?

"What did Booker say?"

"Little Vitalli has very few friends inside. Just a few men his father pays for protection, including one guard," Gage answers. "If we need to get to him, shouldn't be a problem."

"Oh, we're getting to him. Vitalli started this, but I'm ending it."

"Whatever you want to do, we got your back."

"I have an idea. He's a loan shark, right? My guess is the money is being laundered through the restaurant. We hit him where it hurts—his pocket. That should flush him out."

"I like the way you think." Tek grins, his fingers flying across the keyboard. "All his money won't be sitting in a bank somewhere. Maybe we can ask the girl if she knows about any locations he frequents."

"I can go," Einstein offers, emerging from the back.

"No, we need you here." Gage's eyes flick to me and back to Einstein. "Just in case. Let's wait and see what happens first."

Just in case. Just in case Emily's hurt. Fuck.

Razor returns, the men strapping up and heading out, testing their mics. They're not even through the doors when the van screeches to a halt at the gates. On alert, we all watch the TV. The side door opens and a body is tossed out. Shock and horror don't even come close to describing what I feel when I see the blonde hair and outline of the body. I know that body better than the back of my hand.

"Emily!"

I take off running, drowning out Gage's voice as he tries to stop me. In the courtyard, I hear the van peel out and drive away. I ignore the boots crunching on the concrete behind me, my thoughts on the other side of the gates.

"Open the gates!" I shout.

The automatic gates open slowly, and I squeeze through as soon as there's enough room.

"Emily!"

I drop to my knees, carefully turning her onto her back. Her face is bruised and only God knows where else. My brothers surround me, Einstein kneeling next to me.

"Emily... darlin', can you hear me?"

The lids on her swollen eyes flutter, her chest wheezing with every breath. "Liam...."

"It's me, darlin'. Let's get you inside."

I lift her into my arms, praying for the first time in years as I stand. *God, please let her be okay.* Crow, Motor, and Charger are in place on the perches, rifles poised over the top of the gates. Gage and Razor are scanning the street, Einstein giving me instructions I don't even hear.

"Liam," Emily whispers. "Run."

"Shit. Move!" Gage shouts. The men hustle at the sound of a vehicle speeding toward us. Bullets hitting metal and glass ring out, the return fire from the van echoing throughout the otherwise silent night. So much for keeping things quiet. I get through the gates before the van reaches us, but not before they close. I take a hit. My left calf burns from the shot and I fall to a knee, desperately clinging to Emily. There's a loud crash right before someone tries to take her from my arms, but I grit my teeth and start moving. Gage is shouting orders once more, men running around frantically.

"Get her in a bed," Einstein orders. "I'll get my bag."

I take her to my room, laying her down and sitting next to her on the bed.

"Darlin'... I'm so sorry. This is all my fault."

"No. I shouldn't... I shouldn't have left."

"Did they...?" I take her hand, trying to swallow the lump in my throat. "Did they *touch* you?"

"Not like that."

220

I should be relieved but I'm not. *They're dead. Every last one of them. Starting with the one who put his hands on her. I'm going to throw him in a pit with all my snakes.*

Einstein bustles into the room, Booker in tow.

"Get his boot off and cut away the leg of his jeans. Put some pressure on his wound. We need to stop the bleeding."

"Take care of Emily first," I insist.

"I will. I'll take a look at her while Booker deals with your leg."

Booker gets to work and I watch the doc elevate her head before examining her face and asking about her injuries. She tells him where it hurts, and I swear I feel the pain in every one of those locations on my own body. I flinch when Booker presses a towel to my calf. I lie back, finally feeling the effects of the fucking bullet in my leg.

"I haven't found anything too serious," Einstein says. "Just cuts and bruises. I gave her something for the pain. Let's get this bullet out of you, and then I'll do a more thorough examination."

He grabs a syringe and a bottle, explaining before injecting me, "This is a local. Looks like I need to go digging."

He flips me over and I listen to him and Booker as they work. Just cuts and bruises, he said. *Just.* I don't care if they'd only breathed on her; they'll suffer so much they'll beg for me to send them to Hell to be tormented by the Devil for all eternity. It's the thoughts of all the shit I'm going to do to them that passes the time quickly. I don't know how long Einstein took to patch me up, only coming back to reality when they move me next to Emily. Seconds later, Marisol comes in to clean up my blood.

"Is she okay?" she asks, brows creased with worry.

"She'll be fine," Einstein answers. He leaves the room, returning with a cold compress for Emily's face. She's fallen asleep, groaning when Einstein applies it.

"Rico and Tyler?" I ask, feeling shitty for only thinking of them now.

"They were in the van, too. We got 'em. Banged up but okay."

"Good."

I lie back, closing my eyes, fighting a battle with sleep and losing.

"What are we going to do with them?"

"That's up to Venom," Gage answers Crow's question.

There were four men in the van, and now we have them gagged and tied up in the backyard. We haven't been able to move them yet, so everyone's been warned to stay inside the clubhouse. I'm sitting in front of them, my bandaged leg resting on a chair. Emily is still asleep, Marisol watching over her and changing her compress.

"They give you anything?" I ask Prez.

"Nothing... yet. Haven't really asked properly." The men squirm. They're all in one piece, but that won't last long. "I sent for the girl. If she can't give us anything, I'll do a more thorough interrogation." He smirks, folding his arms over his chest.

When the driver got shot last night, he crashed the van into a pole by our gates. That's when our guys swooped in. Rico and Tyler were tied up in the back, and we still have no idea what was going to happen to them. The van, broken glass, and spent shells were quickly cleaned up, the bent pole the only indication that something happened.

"Where's your boss?" I ask. "He's got to know by now that we have you. I don't hear a cavalry coming."

They all shrug. These situations all start out the same way. They think they'll keep their mouths shut and we'll either give up or just kill them. Me? I'll keep them alive if only to continuously inflict pain. Some people like to think of themselves as walls—solid and unmovable. What they fail to recognize is that people like me are motherfucking wrecking balls.

Gage checks his phone, then jerks his head toward the clubhouse. I follow him inside, favoring my leg. It hurts like a bitch, but there's no way I'm sitting this out. Razor's returned with the girl, leading her to a window that looks out into the backyard.

"You know those men?" Gage asks.

"I've seen them at the restaurant. They work for Mr. Vitalli."

"You know where he does business?"

"The loans? People normally come to the restaurant. I always assumed he had a safe there or something."

"You ever see him moving money around?" I ask.

"Sometimes his men come and go with duffel bags, but I don't know where they go."

"You're doing good," Gage tells her. "You keep talking and you'll be outta here in no time."

"Thank you."

Razor takes her away and Gage turns to me. "How's the leg?"

"It's fine."

"Emily?"

"I'm going to check on her now. What did Tek find?"

"A few accounts. Seems some charities received sizeable anonymous donations last night." He chuckles, shaking his head. "The men who are protecting Junior will also find their commissaries empty."

"Good." I turn to walk away, but his voice stops me.

"You give any thought to contacting your old man?"

"Not really. I don't see why I need to."

"I know your history with them isn't good, but people change."

"Not those two. Didn't need 'em before, sure as fuck don't need 'em now."

"Okay, brother. Your call. Emily's bag was still in the van. Gave it to Marisol."

He backs away and I hobble to my room. Raven and Ellen are lounging on the bed, but Emily is missing.

"Where's Emily?"

"This is your fault. You know that, right?" Raven rolls, unable to sit up until Ellen helps.

I take a deep breath, getting ready for the onslaught.

"If you hadn't pissed her off and let her leave, this wouldn't have happened."

"I know that."

"How are you going to fix it?" Ellen asks.

The bathroom door opens, granting me a reprieve. Out comes Emily, assisted by Marisol. Our eyes meet, hers dropping to the floor as she limps to the bed. After seeing she's comfortable, Marisol leaves, telling her to call if she needs anything. The other women head for the door, motioning for me to go to Emily. Once we're alone, I move to the other side of the bed, snagging the

223

painkillers and a bottle of water from the nightstand. I pop two pills, propping my gimp leg up on the bed as I lean against the headboard.

"What happened?" comes Emily's timid voice.

"Got shot, darlin'."

"My God! Are you okay?"

"I'll be fine. How do you feel?"

"I wasn't shot, Liam." She moves closer to me. "Your condition is more important than mine right now."

"Darlin'." I turn to her and cup her cheek, thumb gently brushing a blue and purple bruise. My blood boils with fury. "I didn't protect you. This happened because of me. How can you even be concerned about me?"

"No. You warned me. I'm the one who ran off half-cocked. Maybe you would've been at the courthouse with me if I hadn't left."

"The courthouse?"

"Yes. My divorce is final. I'm free, Liam."

CHAPTER 21
Emily

"Em…."

Liam stares at me, no words coming from his lips. I climb onto his lap, burying my face in his neck. "*That's* because of you. Thank you."

He wraps his arms around me, causing a sigh to pass my lips. I'm finally back where I'm supposed to be.

"What now?" he poses the question I asked him not long ago.

"That's entirely up to you. You know what I want."

"Still?"

"Still."

"Emily, how can you say that after what those motherfuckers did to you?"

I sit up, meeting his troubled gray eyes. "I don't want to be with those motherfuckers. I want to be with you."

"Yeah, but shit like that? That's what happens when you're with someone like me."

"You're the numbers man, right? What's the probability of things like this happening on a regular basis?"

"Emily…." He shakes his head, expelling a frustrated breath.

"Low, right? What I know for certain is that you make me happy, Liam. Don't you like being with me?"

"There's no question about that, but I can't risk you getting hurt."

My eyes burn with unshed tears. "Can't you see you're the one hurting me?"

I don't understand why he's being like this. His brothers have women, wives. How dangerous can his life be? I move back to the bed, chiding myself. We want different things, and it's time I accept that.

"Emily, this isn't about heartache. I'm trying to keep you alive!"

I don't respond, only turning my back to him as I lie down.

"You said I'm a protector. Well that's what I'm doing—protecting you. Your name means 'striving,' so you'll get

225

through this, Em. You'll move on, and one day I'll just be a memory."

Tears slide down my cheeks, wetting the pillow. Liam is strike three. I should accept that a happily ever after is not in the books for me. I'm destined to be alone.

"I want to know what happened."

"Rico and Tyler picked me up at the bar." I sigh, running through the events in my mind. "Before we even left the parking lot, we were surrounded. They took me to a back room in a restaurant. I didn't see the guys until we were all back in the van."

"Tell me everything," he forces out the words.

"Vitalli said he was disappointed in me for not following instructions. One of the men smacked me around a bit, saying it was my punishment."

"We have the men who grabbed you. Which one put his hands on you?"

"And if I tell you? What are you going to do with him?"

"They hurt you, Emily... used you as bait. Do you really want to know how this is gonna go?"

"No. I want to call the police."

"Em—"

"You've made it abundantly clear that I'm not your woman," I say, force behind my words. "That means you don't get to make decisions like that for me. I'm calling the police."

"That's what you want? To do things legit?"

"Yes."

I turn to him at the sound of numbers being dialed. His phone is on speaker, and after three rings, a woman picks up.

"Hughes residence."

My mouth drops open. Liam takes a deep breath.

"It's me. Liam."

There's a pause before the woman asks, "What do you want?"

Bitch.

"Nothing." Liam grits his teeth.

"Then why have you called after all this time?"

"I need to speak to your husband about a case of his that I've been dragged into for some reason."

"They found you," she says, voice low and filled with surprise. "I didn't think they would."

"Not hard for someone who's looking." His mother doesn't have a comeback, the line remaining silent. "Your husband?" he prods.

There's muttering in the background before his father comes on. "Liam?"

"William."

"What's this about?"

"Vitalli. For some reason, he thinks he can get to you by fucking with me."

"I already told him I can't be bought. When he threatened you, we didn't think much of it because we figured you were somewhere far away."

"Yeah, well, he found me. My girl's face is all busted up."

"Jesus. Will she testify that it was Vitalli?"

"It was his men, but it shouldn't be hard trailing it back to him."

"Good. Go to the nearest police station and file a report. Have them contact ADA Nichols. He's prosecuting."

"Yeah, okay."

"Liam…."

His thumb hovers over the End button. "Yeah?"

"Nothing. Goodbye."

He tosses the phone aside, closing his eyes. It's like the call drained him of all his energy. I lay my hand on his shoulder, sliding it up to stroke the back of his neck.

"Liam, I'm sorry. You didn't have to do that for me."

"I didn't do it for you. Well, not entirely. Maybe I just needed to see if they'd changed. Guess not. At least they're still together. Seems I was the problem after all." He shrugs me off, getting to his feet. "I gotta go talk to the guys."

"Liam."

He stops at the door, hand frozen above the knob. I try to speak, but no words come. What the hell would I say? The silence stretches on until he gives up, opening the door and stepping through it. It closes behind him, the finality of the resounding *click* echoing in my heart.

"She wants to do what?"

"Go to the cops," I repeat, meeting Gage's stare.

I'm already a little pissed that she doesn't trust me enough to handle this, but now I have to tell that to my brothers. They won't say it, but I know it's what they're all thinking.

"And how are we supposed to explain all this?"

"I don't know. That's why I'm bringing it to the table."

"I guess it would be easier to let them do the work for once," Razor weighs in. "This could be the first step toward our legit operation."

"What do we do about Vitalli?" Chopper asks. "My contact gave me two locations where he could be keeping his money."

"Where?" I give him my full attention.

"One right outside of ATL and another not far from here. Of course, there's also his house."

"I have an idea," I announce. "We'd need help, though. Lots of bodies."

Gage nods, not even asking me to explain. "I'll call Jacksonville and SC, see if they can help out."

I reach for a map, spreading it on the table and asking Chopper to mark the three locations.

"We're going to need three teams, hit them all simultaneously. We take the money, torch the place."

"And Vitalli?" Razor raises a brow.

"I want to ram my fist through his throat, but Em wants this done right. Through the 'proper channels,' anyway."

"Best way would be to have the cops find the money," Gage says. "Otherwise all they'd have him on is kidnapping, assault, and trying to bribe a judge."

"There's also the picture. If the girl will testify that he paid her to do it, that is, and if Emily is okay with handing it over to the cops," Tek adds. "It will show he targeted her before the kidnapping. I'm still working on getting into his email, but we can scrap that so the cops can find it. If we're going this route, our plans need to be airtight. So far, Vitalli's been like Teflon when it comes to the law.

228

He tried to access his accounts, too, so he knows that money is gone."

Listening to my brothers makes me realize how half-cocked my plan was. I mean, I only thought about it for a few seconds. It's a good thing I have these men to ground me.

"So we give the cops everything we have? Except for the fuckers from last night. They're mine."

"Shit." Chopper shakes his head. "If this isn't turning over a new leaf, I don't know what is. Cops?"

"It's not how I would do it, but like I said, it's what Em wants."

"Now whose woman's got whose balls?" Gage asks. Einstein snickers.

"She's not my woman." My voice is loud enough for everyone to hear, the words leaving a bitter taste in my mouth.

"Yeah, whatever. So we're agreed we're letting the law handle this?"

"Yeah, but they're getting off too easy. Booker." I turn to him. "Get a message to your brother. See if he can set up a playdate for Junior."

"Sure thing."

"So, fellas, we votin'?" Prez asks.

There are "ayes" around the table, and then Gage turns to me. "There you have it. I'll call Renley. We'll give him everything except the men. They're waiting at the warehouse for you."

"Thanks, Prez."

We leave the chapel and I head right back to my room. Marisol is here, keeping Emily's company as she eats. In normal circumstances, I'd make a joke about her stealing my girl, but she's not really mine, is she?

"Do you want me to stay?" Marisol eyes me briefly before focusing on Emily.

"No, it's fine. Thanks for feeding me."

"No problem."

When she leaves, I perch on the side of the bed, careful not to touch Emily. It's not that I don't want to, but I wouldn't be able to stop if I did.

"We decided to do things your way. Gage is gonna call the sheriff and you can file a report."

"Okay."

"You'll have to leave out the part about me getting shot. Also, we can't exactly explain away why we kept the men here, so your story is that they shoved you out of the van and drove off."

"What's going to happen to them?" she whispers.

"We haven't decided yet. We're going to hand over the girl who took the picture, too."

"She's here?" She looks up at me, eyes wide.

"Not at the clubhouse, no. She said Vitalli paid her to take it."

"Oh." She tries to set her tray aside but I take it from her, placing it on the floor. "Thank you for doing this, Liam. I know it's not what you wanted."

"What *you* want is all that matters."

"Except when it comes to us, right?"

"Emily—"

"I know. It's for my own good."

"You'll realize it soon."

"Liam, I know I have no right to ask this, but can you… can you hold me?"

Without hesitation, I crawl in next to her, curling an arm around her shoulder when she lays her head on my chest. I sigh, wishing I could give her what she really wants.

"It's going to be okay, darlin'."

She sobs, shoulders shaking against me. I haven't shed a tear since I was a kid, but I swear sometimes Emily makes me want to break down. It's killing me that she's hurting because of me. I promised her I'd never hurt her, and what's worse, she trusted me.

"Liam." She straddles me, tears running down her bruised cheeks. I want to turn away but I force myself not to. Having this image in my head will remind me why I need to stay away from her. "I know you don't want a relationship with me and I look like hell right now, but… please. I need you one last time."

She presses her lips to mine, pulling back with a hiss and touching her split lip.

"Em, you're hurt."

She leans forward again and I sink my fingers into her hips. I would have taken everything she's giving if not for divine intervention.

Or at least whatever causes the big bang coming from the bar.

"Stay here."

She moves to the bed, pulling her knees to her chest, eyes wide, chewing on her lip. I hop to the door, cursing Vitalli for not being able to function at a hundred percent. I listen carefully, but I can't make out any of the muffled sounds. Opening the door, I stick my head out.

"Don't move. We have a warrant!"

Fucking hell. Just what we need.

"It's the cops," I tell Emily. "Wait here until I come for you."

"Okay."

I lock the door behind me, heading to the bar to find an all-out standoff. The cops are on one side, our men on the other, blocking them from going any farther.

"Move out of my way, Hunter," Renley growls. "Or don't. I'll throw you in jail for obstruction."

"If you tell me what you're looking for, we can make this process easier. I'm not letting you tear up my clubhouse, Renley."

"It's in the warrant," a man next to Renley says.

"What if I can't read?" Gage jokes, turning the warrant upside down.

"Emily Pierce, or any sign that she's been here," the man says, straightening the jacket of his expensive suit.

"See? How hard was that? Of course Emily is here. She's Venom's woman."

"I highly doubt that."

I step forward, ready to knock the smug look off the motherfucker's face. "What do you want with Emily?"

He looks to me, his expression faltering. I guess my pretty-boy prez didn't seem intimidating enough. Guess he never heard that looks are deceiving.

"Those two"—he points to Rico and the prospect—"took Emily, and she hasn't answered my calls."

"And who are you?"

"Her lawyer."

"Well, Em's lawyer, they didn't kidnap her, if that's what you think."

"I'll judge for myself when I see her. She may have walked out the door with those men but she was scared, no *terrified* of something."

"Renley," Gage steps forward, all business. "I was actually about to call you."

"Is that so?" the sheriff sneers. Our history with him isn't great, and he especially hates Gage.

"Tell your men to back off. Come to my office and let's talk."

"What the fuck do we have to talk about?"

"Emily."

He grits his teeth but nods. While they head to the office, I get Emily from my room.

"What's going on?" she asks.

"Need you to talk to the sheriff, darlin'. Apparently your boyfriend thinks we kidnapped you."

"Boyfriend?" Her brows knit, confusion written on her face.

"Some lawyer prick in a suit."

"Johnathan? He's here?"

"Yeah."

"We were supposed to have drinks, Liam. I hardly think that constitutes a relationship. Then again, you wouldn't know."

"I'm not doing this right now, Emily."

She turns up her nose at the forceful tone of my voice, walking to the door. I take her to the office, knocking before we enter. Renley's eyes almost pop out of his head when he sees Em's face.

"Fucking hell, Hunter! When are you idiots going to learn?"

"Watch it, Renley," Gage warns. "Your badge only gets you so far."

"Look at her! You'd think what happened to Raven would've—"

"My *wife* is none of your business. This had nothing to do with us."

"Yeah," he says, voice rife with disbelief. He approaches Emily carefully, not even glancing in my direction. "Miss Pierce, would you be okay to come down to the station?"

"Can't you talk to her here?" I ask.

"That's fine," Em answers his question as if I hadn't spoken. "Can you give me a ride to my uncle's after?"

Her words knock me back a step.

"Sure. I'll put two guys on the house until we catch this Vitalli asshole."

He places his hand at the small of her back as they head for the door.

"Em...."

She doesn't answer, doesn't look back. Unlike the first time she walked out on me, something tells me this time she's not coming back.

"You okay?" Gage squeezes my shoulder.

"No." There's no reason to lie.

"What do you want to do?"

"The warehouse. Now."

CHAPTER 22
Venom

I stare down at the broken, bloody mess in front of me.

One down, three to go.

I didn't even stop by the house for my snakes or venom… nothing. The rage inside me needs an outlet, and I couldn't ask for a better one than these men's faces. Gage and Crow are the only ones with me. One to monitor, I guess, and the other to clean up. By the time I get done with them, I doubt there will be much for Crow to get rid of. None of them have owned up to hitting Emily yet, but it doesn't matter. They're all dead. Wrapping a bandana around my fist, I move to the next asshole, wishing he was Luigi Vitalli.

"Do what you want to us. You don't mess with Mr. Vitalli and get away with it," he snarls.

"Who, little Mario?" I chuckle at his annoyance at me getting his employer's name wrong. "I think he's used up all his lives, right, fellas?" I turn to my brothers and back, losing the smile. "This is the final level, and he's not getting past this boss."

I plant an uppercut to his chin, bones giving way beneath my fist. His chair topples, falling to the floor with a bang. I step to the next one, who has the common sense to look scared.

"Please, mister," he begs, teeth chattering. "I'm new. I don't even know what's going on."

"You know which one beat up the girl?"

His head turns nervously to the man on his right, who shakes his head in disappointment.

"A-are you going to l-l-let me go?"

"Tell you what? Since you were so cooperative, I'll make it quick."

Pulling out my Beretta, I put a bullet between his eyes. I move over, a maniacal grin in place.

"You." I rub my palms together. "I'm going to have some fun with you."

A phone rings, but I drown out the sound as I trail the barrel of my gun down the man's cheek. *Hmm... which body part should I shoot off first?* I aim it at his dick, but Gage interrupts me, touching my shoulder.

"What?"

"That was the prospect. There's a problem at Jeff's."

"Emily?" My blood pressure instantly goes through the roof.

"Her ex is there."

"I'll be back," I tell the man tied to the chair. "Don't you go nowhere now."

Fucking James. He picked the wrong fucking time to show up. Or maybe the right time.

I'm going to fuck that motherfucker up.

Emily

This day keeps getting worse.

After telling the cops my side of the story a million times, I had to deal with Johnathan. I appreciate his concern, but he didn't have to call the police. With everything that's happened, being rejected by Liam again, plus my ordeal at the police station, all I wanted was to come home, have a hot bath, and curl up in bed. Instead, I arrive to find James being pulled by his collar away from Uncle Jeff's door. Liam looks pissed, but the sight of him still makes my heart jump.

"Stay in the car, ma'am," one of the officers instructs.

With hands poised over their guns, they approach Liam, Gage, Tyler, and Crow. It's obvious that James is drunk, so I have no idea how he got here. He spots me sitting in the cruiser and tries to stagger over to me, but one of the officers stops him.

"Em-Emily!" he shouts. "L-let's talk. I just wanna talk. Come talk to me."

He stutters and slurs his words, beckoning me to him. The longer he waits, the angrier he becomes.

"You *bitch*!"

He lunges in my direction but Liam pulls him back, saying something I don't hear.

"You know what she did?" James asks the officers. "In… in front of my girl, she says I have a little dick. I don't have a little dick. Do you think this is little?" Despite the situation, I burst out laughing when he attempts to show the officers his penis.

"We'll take your word for it, buddy," one of them says, stopping James from whipping it out.

"You," James turns his anger to Liam. "She said you're th-the bigger, better model. Wha-what do *you* have that I don't?"

"I think that's pretty obvious," Liam answers, smirking while grabbing his crotch.

Everyone except James laughs.

"What's so funny?" he asks.

"Come on, let's get you to the station so you can sleep it off."

"My girl's here," he tells the officer. "She can take me home."

I look around, and that's when I see the blonde fuming in the car across the street. If looks could kill, I'd be dead ten times over. I ignore her, turning my attention back to the men. James is led to the car and helped inside, the officers giving them a warning and telling her to drive straight home. When they leave, Liam and his brothers hop on their bikes, riding behind the car. I'm bummed he didn't stay, but I also know I need to put space between us. My two bodyguards lead me to the house, telling me they'll be out front. Uncle Jeff is waiting by the door, arms outstretched.

"Baby girl." I soak up his warmth, finding comfort in his embrace. "I called Belinda. She and Frank will be here in the morning."

"You shouldn't have done that, Uncle Jeff."

"You should've called them yourself. No matter how old you are, you're still their baby."

"I know. I just don't want them to see me like this."

"It's okay, sweetheart. Come on, I'll get you some ice for your face."

Foregoing my bath, I grab a quick shower and crawl into bed with an ice pack. I watch my phone on the bed next to me, praying for it to ring. It finally does, but it's my parents. I cry exhaustion after a few minutes and they hang up. As much as I love them, they're not what I need right now.

It doesn't matter what Liam says. He's already in my heart, and if there's a way to get him out, I don't know of it. I wish he'd even check on me, see how I'm doing. Nothing.

I close my eyes against the tears, willing them back. I refuse to cry over that man. How can he be so smart yet so dense? I got hurt because I *didn't* listen to him, because I wasn't with him. He could have protected me, but I didn't allow him to.

He thinks he's the reason Vitalli got to me. *I'm* the reason. My stupidity is the reason. My need to have more than what I was promised is the reason.

Now what do I have?

Nothing.

Venom

I see red.

It's everywhere.

The walls, the floor, my clothes... my hands. Especially my hands.

I stare down at my bloodstained fingers and palms, sticky with the thick liquid. This is what a man's life is reduced to—a few pints of gooey fluid. I look back to the man in front of me, barely hanging on to this world. Even if I wanted to get some venom into him, he's bleeding so much it probably wouldn't do a thing.

"You get it all out of your system yet?" Crow asks.

"No, but this helped."

"Go clean up, brother. See your girl. I'll take care of this."

My girl. My insides shrink at the thought of Emily. If she saw me now, she'd surely want nothing to do with me. She's the type to do things through cops and courts, not torture. It's just another reason why I should stay away from her. I'll bring her nothing but pain.

I move to the sink in the corner of the room, cleaning up as best I can before heading home. My foot hurts like a bitch, especially after riding my bike, but I try to ignore the ache. I bag up my clothes and shoes to give to Crow for disposal, then stand under the spray of the shower, watching the crimson water spiral down the drain. My anger is renewed, but not at Vitalli and his men. At myself. I fucked things up with Emily. I broke my own rule and made things personal. She shouldn't have been sleeping in my bed every night. I shouldn't have taken an interest in her life. I shouldn't have... fuck. There are too many things I shouldn't have done, and even more I should have. Hindsight is a bitch.

I scrub every inch of my body, drying off and climbing into bed naked. I know sleep won't come. I just wish my bed didn't feel so big and empty.

***

"They got him."

"Thank fuck." A part of me breathes easier at Prez's words.

"Yeah. He didn't expect us to go to the cops. Motherfucker was armed up and planning to hit us when the cops stormed in. He's got a few weapons charges heading his way, too."

"Caught in the act. Let's see him worm his way out of this one," Razor says.

"I hate to say it, but you made the right call, Venom." Chopper nods his approval. "If we'd gone in, who knows what would've happened."

"Guess we should listen to our women more, huh?" Crow chuckles.

"Raven would want a seat at the fucking table," Gage says, making everyone laugh in agreement. "Probably mine. Especially now with pregnancy hormones times two. Shit."

"You just make sure you give her whatever she wants, motherfucker," Chopper warns. "Those are my grandbabies."

"Yeah, yeah, Pop."

"Speaking of family, I wanted to put something to the table." All my brothers focus on me, silly grins on their faces. "It's not what you think. It's about our next legit business."

"What you got?" Prez raises a brow.

"Sweet Treats... it's for sale." I hand him the owner's business card. "It seems to do good business, but the owner's retiring."

"A bakery? Who would we get to run it?"

"Emily," I offer without hesitation.

238

Maybe I just want to keep her around so I can torture myself by seeing her every day, or maybe I want her to achieve her dream. Who knows?

"She definitely knows what she's doing in the kitchen," Motor agrees. "What about the business end?"

"She can do it."

"Fellas?" Gage looks around the table. "I'll check it out, and then we take a vote. I'm liking the idea, though. It's local and zero opportunities for conflict. Could integrate with Ellen's Events, too." Mumbles of agreement sound around the table. "Okay, fuckers, get outta here. We'll deal with the Krueger issue another day."

We file out of the chapel and into the bar. All the women are gathered there, old ladies on one side of the room, Hounds on the other. Nita and Millie enter from the kitchen, setting out food. I make my way over, stomach growling. *When was the last time I ate?*

"I just talked to Emily," Raven says when I sidle up next to her.

"Yeah?"

"Yeah. She's going back to Atlanta with her parents tomorrow. Quit her job and everything."

I pile food on my plate, trying to seem indifferent. "Okay."

"Okay? That's all you're going to say?" she asks, sounding like her husband.

I shrug. "I told y'all it wasn't serious."

"Mm-hmm." She dismisses my answer. "I drew something for you."

She scrolls through her phone until she finds what she needs, turning the screen to me. It's an image of a snake eating its tail, its body curved into a heart. The heart is shaded red, mine and Emily's names inside it in bold, black letters. Mine is on top, the *e* extending down to form the one in hers. Shit. I hate to admit it, but it's badass. I knew she was talented, having designed the tattoos for her and Gage, and Einstein and Ellen, but this? My back itches with the need to get it inked on my skin.

"It's good, but not necessary." I shovel a forkful of food into my mouth.

"Why you—ooh!" She stops, grabbing her belly.

"Raven?" I turn to her, now on alert. "What's wrong?"

Without answering, she takes both my hands, laying my palms on her belly. I want to yank them away, knowing what these hands were involved in last night. However, the movement against them makes me pause.

"Wow." My breathing picks up. "The babies?"

"Yeah. Feel that? They're both moving."

The smile she gives me conveys nothing but happiness. What's even more shocking is that it gets brighter when Gage walks up behind her and she looks up at him over her shoulder.

"Get your hands off my woman," he says good-naturedly.

His hands replace mine, and suddenly I feel as if I'm intruding on a private moment. The unburdened looks in their eyes, the smiles, laughs... the love between them. Gage is living a life I never thought men like us could. They share something so deep; they've persevered and are happier than ever. There's no resentment in Raven's gaze, only love.

My heart contracts, thoughts of Emily bombarding me. I want what they have.

With Emily.

I can see it more clearly than that Jimmy Cliff song. She's mine. Always has been, always will be.

I back away, stomping toward the exit.

"Hey, where you going?" someone shouts.

"To get my woman."

There are hoots and hollers, but a voice rises above the noise. "Wait, you'll need this!"

I turn around, watching Razor jog to the chapel, coming back with a cut. I inspect it, throat closing up at the words on the back—"Property Of Venom."

"How... when...?"

"Don't mind that. Just go get her, brother."

I nod to my best friend, clutching the cut to my chest as I move as fast as I can to my bike.

I'm coming, Emily.

I just hope I'm not too late.

CHAPTER 23
Emily

He's here!

I run to the window, moving the curtain aside to watch him limp up the driveway. Excitement shouldn't be bubbling in my veins, but it is. God, he's a sight for sore thighs. *Eyes. Fuck, I meant* eyes.

He looks up, almost catching me, but I dodge just in time.

"Are you okay?" Mom asks.

"Yeah, fine."

I almost jump out of my skin when the knock comes at the door.

"I'll get it," Dad offers.

I inch closer to the door, trying to hear the conversation.

"What's wrong with you? Who's at the door?"

"Mom, it's Liam," I whisper.

"Oh? Why doesn't Frank invite him in?"

She wanders off, despite my efforts to keep her here with me. Shaking off my hand, she heads for the door.

"Liam! So nice to finally meet you. Why don't you come in?" she says loud enough for the neighbors to hear. I giggle, knowing it's for my benefit. I'm acting like a schoolgirl, but who cares?

"I'd love to, but I can't stay, ma'am. I just need to talk to Emily."

"Okay, I'll get her."

Mom walks into the room fanning herself. "Jeez, Emily. You didn't tell me he was such a handsome young man. And so muscular!"

"Mom, stop perving." I roll my eyes.

"Go, sweetheart. He's waiting."

I take a deep breath, wiping my sweaty palms on my jeans. He could probably hear my heart beating from a mile away, but I can't let him see how his presence is affecting me.

As I approach, Daddy shakes Liam's hand, then offers me a smile before leaving us. Liam cringes at the sight of me, but I know it's because of the bruises. Once upon a time, I would have thought it was my face.

"Hi, Em."

"Venom." I try to act detached. He accepts it, shoving his hands in his pockets. "What can I do for you?"

"I came to apologize. I've been a dick—"

"You were a motherfucking asshole."

"I was a motherfucking asshole, and I'm sorry. I don't expect you to forgive me now, but maybe one day."

"Is that all?" I ask, trying to keep hope out of my voice.

"I also want to do something for you, darlin'."

"And what's that?"

"I made you a promise, and I didn't keep it."

"Which one?" I ask, raising a brow. "The one where you said you'd never hurt me?"

"The one where I said I'd make all your fantasies a reality. Tell me again what you want, Emily."

I take a step forward, chest heaving as I stare up into his gorgeous gray eyes. "How do I know you won't reject me again?"

"Tell me what you want, Em."

"I want you. I want us. I want to be with you, and not for some silly arrangement. I want everything, Liam."

"Then you'll have it… me. I'm yours, Emily."

"Liam!" I throw my arms around his neck, squeezing when he picks me up. "Are you sure this is what you want?"

"I want *you*, Em. Nothing else."

He sets me down but I keep my hands in place, stroking the back of his neck. My heart constricts at the look in his eyes that supports his words, the one I've been searching for my entire life. He wants me and only me. "Take me home, Liam."

Without hesitation, he grabs my hand and leads me to his bike. I climb on, knowing this is only one of many more times to come. Pressing my body to his back, I close my eyes, smiling all the way to his house. He helps me off but stops me before I can head inside.

"Only one way you enter that house, Em."

"How?" I ask, eying him with skepticism.

He reaches into his saddlebag, removing a cut and holding it up for me to see the back.

"Wearing this."

242

I bounce in place, turning around so he can help me into it. Property of Venom. I never thought those words could make me as happy as I am. I guess this means I'm officially his, but I've belonged to him since the day we met.

I face him once more, meeting his eyes. "I'm yours?"

"There's that question again."

"I'm yours," I say on an exhaled breath.

"Mine, Emily. I didn't realize it, but you've been mine since you bitched at me the day we met. You were mine when you let me taste your sweet pussy, and you were damn sure mine when you let me put my dick in you."

I roll my eyes, but he wouldn't be my Liam if he didn't talk like that.

"Em...." He pulls me close, arms sliding around my waist. "I want everything with you, too. You're my forever."

"Oh, Liam." I lean in, pressing a gentle kiss to his lips. "I'll wear it everywhere."

"I'd carry you inside, but...." He points to his leg.

"Come on." I take his hand, leading him directly to the bedroom. He sits on the edge of the bed, gaze sliding up and down my body. "What do you want me to do?" I ask, breathless.

"Whatever you want, darlin'."

"But...." My brows knit, confusion taking over.

"No agreement now, Em. You're my woman, I'm your man. You ask for what you want."

"You... in control."

"Are you sure?"

"Yes," I answer immediately.

"Are you certain you want to put your trust in me?"

The look on his face tells me this is about more than sex, and I know why. He thinks I didn't trust him enough to handle the situation without the police. "I trust you with my life, Liam."

He rises, trailing a finger down my cheek. "My beautiful Emily. You don't know how much I've missed you."

"Show me."

He presses his lips to mine, careful and gentle. I know he's being mindful of my injuries but I need all of him. I open up to him, tugging the tie from his hair to free it. With my fingers roving his scalp, the intensity of his kiss increases. His tongue dominates my mouth, my lips throbbing from his kiss.

This is him owning me. Finally.

This is me being possessed and loving every second of it.

I belong to him.

I moan, pressing my body to his. Breaking away, he takes my hand and I follow him to the bathroom, watching as he fills the tub and adds soap. Slowly, he removes my clothes until I'm standing before him naked. His fingers ghost over my bruises, the light touches sending shivers down my spine.

"Are you in pain?"

"No." I shake my head, not wanting him to hold back.

He cradles my face, lips gently brushing the bruises there. "So sorry, darlin'. This is all my fault."

"Liam, please stop blaming yourself."

He grips my head so I have nowhere to look but at him. "I promise, Em, I won't let anything happen to you again. I'll protect you with everything in me... with my *life*. I'd die before I allow you to get hurt again."

"I know, Liam. I know." I fist my hands in his shirt, desperate for him to believe me.

Closing his eyes, he presses his lips to my forehead, then helps me into the tub. Shedding his own clothes, he joins me, hanging his injured foot over the side.

"Come here, darlin'."

I move to him, eyes closing as he begins to wash my body. He massages my shoulders, soapy hands gliding down to my breasts. I straddle his thigh, sliding back and forth.

"Naughty girl." His voice is thick with arousal. "You missed my dick?"

"Yes. I need you inside me, Liam."

He reaches down, fingers stroking my clit before one slips inside me. I ride it, eyes locked with his. His free hand grabs my ass, spreading my cheeks. The finger inside me is withdrawn, another slowly moving back until it's circling my anus.

"Oh!" I tense, grabbing his shoulders.

"Relax, Em."

I nod, closing my eyes as it slips in. It's a weird feeling, not unpleasant, but also not like when he fingers me. He slides the tip gently in and out, groaning when I move with him.

"Bedroom, Emily. Now."

My eyes snap open, going wide at what I see brewing in his. I don't think I'll be able to move tomorrow, let alone walk. I hop out, grabbing a towel and drying off on my way to the bedroom. He joins me a few minutes later, going straight for the metal bars coming out of the foot of the bed.

"Sit." He points to a spot on the bed. I hurry over, taking my place. "Lie back."

He grabs my ankles, restraining them on the bars and leaving me open to him. Next he moves to the headboard, removing a cuff from under the mattress. With my right hand secured, he walks to the other side to work on my left. Jesus. My heart hammers in my ears, goose bumps taking over my body. Back at the foot of the bed, he pulls me toward him, leaving no slack in my wrist restraints.

"Emily, what do you do if you don't like something?"

"Ask you to stop."

"Good." He leans over me with a devious smirk, palms pressed into the mattress. "Let's begin."

I squirm when he sucks a nipple into his mouth, biting into it, then rubbing his beard against it before sucking again. My other nipple gets the same treatment while he circles my clit with the head of his dick.

"Liam…."

He kisses down my stomach, muttering against my skin, "Gonna eat your pussy now, Em. I swear you got that death-row, last-meal kinda pussy."

My muscles clench, a sharp cry coming from me when he sucks on my clit. His fingertips slide along my inner thighs, then under my ass, lifting it off the bed. His tongue swirls over and between my lips, flicking on my clit. My thighs quiver, toes curling, chains rattling as I try to move my legs. I pull at the cuffs on my wrists, wanting to grab his hair. With everything I've experienced with Liam, nothing we've done prepared me for the sensation of his tongue on my back door.

"Liam!"

He doesn't stop, tongue skimming, pressing. A thumb strokes my clit, trying to distract me. I feel like I shouldn't want this, but God, I don't want him to stop. I groan in disappointment when he disappears. The metal box bounces on the bed next to me. He removes a few items, and then he's between my thighs once more. Cool liquid tickles my anus, a finger dipping inside, slowly moving in and out. I moan, clenching around it.

"Look at me, Em." I force my eyes open, raising my head. "I'm going to put this inside you, so I need you to relax and breathe."

He shows me the small toy, and I know it's not for my pussy. I nod, head dropping back to the bed as I take a deep breath. Slowly, gently, and with immense patience, he begins inserting it. Initially, it hurts. Like a lot. However, he doesn't go too deep.

"Okay?" he asks.

"Yes." I adjust my position, following his earlier instructions. More lube trickles over my lips, sliding down to where he needs it. He removes the plug, giving me a reprieve. My feet are released and I'm flipped to my stomach, positioned on my knees. My fingers curl around the straps on my cuffs, muscles clenching when Liam enters me. I whimper, hips rocking.

"Fuck, Em…."

"Fuck me, Liam. Please…."

More lube.

The plug is gently inserted again, a smack to my ass surprising me. I yelp, pressing back against him. With each push of the butt plug, Liam's palm comes down on my cheek. I moan, missing the pinch of the clamps on my nipples. With the plug fully inserted, he leans forward to tug on my nipples.

"Fuck, yes!" I growl, in awe at how he can read my body.

His hands move to my shoulders, using them as leverage to bury his dick deep inside me. I stop breathing, words stuck in my throat.

"Love fucking my pussy," he says, fingers trailing down my spine. "My old lady has the best pussy in the world."

He grabs my hips, slamming into me.

"Jesus, Liam!"

My thighs tremble, threatening to give out from the pleasure. I can feel the plug rubbing against his dick, no doubt providing added stimulation for him also. I bite into the sheets, a scream coming out muffled. Just when I think he can't make this more intense, he reaches around to my clit, four fingers rubbing and stroking. My muscles begin to contract, one eye squinting at the unicorn orgasm I know is coming.

But then he's gone.

"Fucking hell, Liam! Why the fuck did you stop?" He chuckles, freeing my wrists. "I was *this* close to coming!" I bring my thumb and index finger together to demonstrate.

"I know."

"Asshole."

Something else is removed from the box and then he drags me to the edge of the bed, lining up my mouth with his dick. It now occurs to me that I just gave him a whole lot of sass. What if he decides to punish me? Memories of my last punishment send butterflies flitting in my stomach and I decide that's not such a bad idea. He doesn't seem to have that on his mind, though, and I almost squeal in delight when he attaches the nipple clamps. He slaps both breasts, grinning.

"You love these."

"Yes," I answer, even though it wasn't a question.

"Spread your legs, Em." The moment I do, he smacks my clit. I groan, hips rising off the bed. "Think you'd ever be interested in me using more than my hand?"

"You mean... like a whip?"

"Yes."

That scares me a bit; then again, so did spanking. Now look at me. I know Liam wouldn't hurt me physically, and like he said, anything I don't like, he won't do.

"Maybe."

He smirks, his beautiful face taking the focus away from his hands. When he begins to work a dildo inside me, I clench around it. It starts to vibrate, ripping a moan from me. I realize it's a rabbit when something flicks against my clit.

"Fuck, Liam." I shudder, thighs pressing together before he forces them apart again.

"Open up, darlin'." I part my lips, but he pulls back, concern creasing his brows. "Are you sure you're not in pain?"

247

"Positive."

I take his dick in my mouth, squeezing the base in a fist as I suck him off. He works the vibrator, tugging on the nipple clamps. With all my holes filled, my body is one big conductor of sensation. I moan around his dick, giving in to him because I can't concentrate on anything but what I'm feeling. I grab his thigh when he goes deep, hitting the back of my throat. He holds the position, hand to the back of my head, keeping me in place. Before I can even begin to gag, he pulls out, letting me catch my breath. The vibration in my pussy intensifies.

"Liam!" I cry out, burying my face in his thigh. He tugs on the clamps, pulling until I raise my head. "Fuck!" There's a battle between pain and pleasure going on in my body, and Christ help me but I don't know which one I want to win. They meld so beautifully, creating a love child that someone should definitely name. Plein? Pasure? Fuck, I think he's fucking me senseless. Added to that fact, he seems so much more personal now. Gone are the formal "Emilys," replaced by "Ems" and "darlin's." It's the perfect mix of dominant and loving, hard and soft.

When I'm on the cusp of orgasm again, he pulls out the vibrator.

"Swear to fucking Christ, you do that again, I'm going to castrate you!" I growl.

This time he laughs, grabbing another item from the box. The wand-like toy is pressed to my clit, my legs thrown on his shoulders as he slides inside me.

"Need to be inside you when you come, darlin'."

Oh. Then it hits me. Maybe I should… ask? The thing on my clit starts vibrating, shutting down my cognitive functions. He crosses my ankles on one shoulder, leaning forward so the vibrator is held in place between my thighs and stomach. When he moves, my eyes roll back in my head.

"Fuck, Em…."

"Fuck me, Liam!" I cry out, searching for the words to make him lose control. The first night we made love comes back to me. "You like your pussy, Liam?"

"Fucking love it," he grunts.

"Then fuck me, Liam. Fuck your pussy until I come all over your dick."

That does it. He goes crazy, pumping into me, hitting that spot inside me only he's been able to find. There's no way he'll stop now.

"Please, Liam. Please, may I come?"

"Fuck!"

He spreads my legs wide, arms wrapping around my thighs as he moves faster. The vibrator rolls away but I pick it up, pressing it to my clit.

"Please, please!" I beg, my orgasm just beyond reach. "Please let me come!"

"Come!" he growls.

My world ends. Volcanoes erupt, earthquakes open up the ground below. The sky goes black, sun and moon imploding, stars falling into the gaping nothing below. That's what my orgasm feels like. Total annihilation. I scream so loudly, I've probably woken the dead and there may be a few zombies walking around tomorrow. Liam's name is a litany on my lips.

Dear God, I love this man!

He slowly removes the plug from my ass, turning the vibrator off and setting it aside. I don't even know if he came, and I certainly wouldn't be able to help him right now if he didn't. When he pulls out of me, the liquid running down tells me he did. *Thank fuck.*

"A couple more times with this"—he waves the butt plug at me—"and then it's my dick in your ass, baby."

I scoff, trying to find the energy to laugh. "So romantic."

"That's why you love me."

I don't argue because he's right; his sense of humor is one of the sexiest things about him. I vaguely acknowledge him removing the clamps and cleaning me up, settling me under the covers. Through heavy lids, I watch him take care of the toys and put away the bars on the bed before joining me.

"Wake up, sleepyhead."

"Hmm?" I bury my face in his chest, inhaling his heavenly post-coital scent.

"Still wanna be my old lady?"

"Fuck yes." He chuckles at my admission. "Are you kidding me?"

"Just thought I'd check."

"Still wanna be my old man?"

"You're the only thing in this world worth wanting, Emily."

"Oh, Liam." I somehow find the strength to sit astride him, cradling his face. "I love you."

"I love you, too, darlin'."

As much as I enjoyed our fuck-athon, those five words fill me with more joy than I've ever felt in my life.

"You do?"

"Baby, I'd give up my snakes for you." He smiles, resting his hands on my waist.

"That much, huh?"

"That much. Trust and believe."

I gently press my lips to his, happy tears sliding down my cheeks. I came to Stony View with my eyes closed, depressed and dead inside. All it took was one man with his dirty words and fantasy list to awaken me and show me what I've been missing all these years. His interest and attention invigorated my mind and body.

Like the phoenix from the ashes, I've risen.

Revived.

Renewed.

And utterly, totally in love.

EPILOGUE

Two months later

I watch Emily play with Ellen's kid, Mikey, imagining her with a kid of our own. I've never had the urge to procreate, but Emily's changed a lot about me. Why not this, too?

Einstein and Ellen walk into the clubhouse and the boy runs to them, prompting Em to join me on the couch.

"What do you say?" I nod to the kid. "Think you might want one?"

"I don't know. Maybe. Do you?"

"It would be cool to have a little Emily running around."

"Or a little Venom." She gives me a wistful smile, her green eyes twinkling.

"So that's a yes?"

"It's a maybe."

"Good enough. We can convert the snake room into a nursery." The room now stands empty, all the snakes donated to the zoo once Emily moved in. The only one I have left is Doom, and his terrarium is now in the living room. Strange thing is I don't even miss them. "Or we can begin adding a second floor."

"I said *maybe*."

"Yeah. The kid will already have built-in playmates with the prez and VP's kids."

"You've made up your mind, haven't you?" She tries to fight the amused smile tugging at her lips.

"I heard you, darlin'. You said maybe."

"Mm-hmm."

She leans in to my side, taking my hand and wrapping my arm around her waist. I use the opportunity to stroke the spot on her hip where our tattoo—the one Raven designed—is inked. Tek comes over, kneeling before us.

"Got some news."

"What is it?" I ask.

"Vitalli. Seems he hanged himself in his cell last night. Guards found him this morning."

"Jesus. First the son, now him?" Emily remarks.

The guys we got to jump Junior a couple months ago took things too far. Apparently they'd been after him for a while; we only made it possible for them to get to him. Since Vitalli couldn't pay the guard anymore, he happily took our bribe to look the other way. As for James, he doesn't bother Emily anymore. It could be the restraining order she got against him, or it could be the fact that I broke his arm that day he showed up at Jeff's house. Either way, he's gone silent.

Tek nods to me, then walks off.

"You didn't have anything to do with that, did you, Liam?"

"Vitalli had a lot of enemies, darlin'."

I catch the look she gives me, not missing that I didn't answer her question. She doesn't push the issue, only returning to her position on my chest. There's no way I was letting Vitalli off that easily, and I was definitely not allowing Emily's picture to get passed around because of a court case. We got rid of every copy we could find—digital and physical. Now she won't have to endure a trial.

Gage catches my attention from across the room and I nudge Emily.

"Come on, we gotta go talk to Gage."

I grab a stool, watching Em to see her reaction when she hears the news.

"Emily, we have something we'd like you to consider," Gage says.

"What's that?"

"Sweet Treats. You know the place, right?"

"Yeah, but it's closed now. Why?"

"It's closed because it's changing ownership. To the club."

"You bought it?" She glances between me and Gage.

"Yeah. And we want you to run it."

"What?" Her eyes widen in shock.

"We want you—"

"Shut up!" She covers her mouth, jumping in place. "I mean, I don't mean shut up, I mean… Oh, wow, are you serious?"

"Of course. Everyone here can vouch for your skills. We'll be here to help on the business side."

"I'm… speechless. Thank you, thank you, thank you!" She jumps into Gage's arms before turning to me and peppering my face with kisses. "I know you did this. I don't know how, but thank you, Liam."

"Anything for you, darlin'."

The prospect comes over and pulls Gage aside, whispering something in his ear. Something he doesn't like. I watch his face scrunch up, wondering what the hell could be going on now.

"Liam, let's go to our room so I can thank you properly."

My woman's voice draws my attention to her, and I forget about the prez and any drama that could be brewing. Everything I need is right here in my arms, and I'll be damned if I ever let her go.

The End

INTENTIONALLY LEFT BLANK

ABOUT THE AUTHOR

International bestselling author Alana Sapphire has a great love for writing and music, and always finds a way to combine the two. Her books, though in various subcategories, are all in the Erotic Romance genre. Like a little suspense with your romance? So does Alana! Pick up one of her books and you'll get romance, suspense, drama, and lots of sexy time. With books ranging from MC to paranormal, an Alana story is out there for you. Her characters are like old friends—near and dear to her heart—and she hopes for her readers to enjoy them as much as she does.

I'd love to hear from you!

Website – alanasapphire.com
Facebook – Facebook.com/AlanaSapphire
Twitter – Twitter.com/AlanaSapphire
Instagram – Instagram.com/Alana_Sapphire
Goodreads – Goodreads.com/AlanaSapphire

Made in the USA
Monee, IL
17 July 2020